RIFT WALKER

EMBER & ASH BOOK 1

This is a work of fiction. Any references to historical events, people—living or dead—or places is purely coincidental unless otherwise noted.

Cover design by: MiblArt

Chapter One

The overpass crumbled beneath me, plunging me feet-first into darkness. I scrambled to grab onto something, anything, but the only thing I could find were more falling rocks and rusty rebar. My fingers caught a handful of slimy fur and closed. I used the grip to pivot my body and leapt up onto a furry forearm. The creature's arm was as wide as my body and belonged to the most putrid-smelling monster I'd ever encountered.

Lightning flashed in the darkened sky, briefly illuminating the creature's crooked, bulbous nose, oversize, squinting eyes, and copious white body hair. He stood an impressive fifty feet tall, towering over the decaying overpass and the convoy of armored trucks trapped on one side.

Ugh, a troll. Why'd it have to be a troll?

The troll snarled at the sky and shielded his eyes from the brief flash of light before swatting at his forearm where I perched. I was already gone by the time his giant palm came down, halfway up the troll's arm. The troll grunted and lifted his hand to swat at me again. I made it to the shoulder and slashed at the side of the troll's neck. Sparks flew. Dammit, just my luck. Not only was he a troll, but he was a rock troll. No amount of slashing or stabbing was going to get through his granite skin. Time to move to plan B.

I narrowly avoided getting smashed by the troll's meaty palm by sliding down his shoulder blade. The troll roared and spun, swatting at his back while I used handfuls of back hair to climb down. When the troll finally realized he couldn't reach me with its hands, his tail whipped up and snapped at me. I let go to keep from getting smashed. Wind rushed by, burning my face as I fell, arms flailing.

I hit the ground and rolled. A burning pain surged in my shoulder where I struck concrete. I didn't have time for pain. The troll lifted its foot. The air chilled as the giant foot hovered over me, bathing me in shadow. I rolled to one side, and the ground shook as the troll's foot came down inches from me.

A rope dangled over the side of the broken overpass. I pushed myself up and ran for it, ignoring the worsening pain in my shoulder. The troll spun and roared at the same moment as I grabbed the rope and yelled, "Pull!"

The rope slid steadily upwards, but not fast enough. I gripped a section of the swinging rope above my head, grunted, and pulled myself up.

The troll swatted at the edge of the broken road. Someone above screamed. The rope stopped moving. All I could do was pull myself up the rest of the way. Agony burned in my shoulder, worsening with every inch. Blood raced down my back from the deep gash, and tired muscles screamed. My lungs burned with the need to catch my breath. The ground trembled as the troll rampaged. Guns fired and flares burned to life, painting the smoky ground blood red. Dammit, I'd told them not to light the flares except as a last resort.

With one last pained grunt, I pulled myself up and over the edge onto the road where the convoy waited. Three armored trucks sat abandoned, their drivers in the road, shooting flares and fumbling to nock arrows with shaky hands. They fired, and enchanted arrows struck the troll, creating a shower of sparks.

The troll swept his hand along the line of drivers and their escorts, knocking one of them to their deaths far below.

"Stop shooting, you idiots! You're just pissing it off!" I waved them back from the edge, but they were too panicked to listen. I doubled over for a second to catch my breath with a huff before standing straight and limping toward the rear truck. "Guess if you want something done right, you've got to do it yourself."

I hopped up onto the side of the truck and

fought to pull myself up onto the roof. A huge cloth tarp covered the back of the truck. I cut the ropes holding it down and jerked the cloth away to reveal a huge, circular light mounted atop it. Three car batteries powered the light, but they were disconnected to keep them from overloading, which meant I had to attach the cables before it'd be of any use to me. I wiped sweat from my forehead and rushed to attach the clamps in the correct order while people shouted behind me.

One more... Blue sparks erupted as the metal teeth of the clamp latched onto the battery terminal. I lifted an arm to shield my eyes. The giant spotlight blinked to life, casting a brilliant white column of light into the night.

I stood and slid behind the spotlight, scanning the darkness for the troll. I gritted my teeth and gripped the handholds, swinging the light around to shine directly on the troll.

The troll roared and dropped the broken man he'd been holding onto to put both hands in front of its face.

"Smile, asshole." I pulled the lever.

The spotlight strobed.

The troll bellowed and swung wildly until his movements slowed. White powder coated the tips of the troll's fingertips, quickly spreading over its skin and freezing the troll in place. Inch by inch, the strobing light turned the marauding fifty-foot troll to stone. Less than a minute passed before the murderous beast was only a stone statue, fingers just inches from the front car in the convoy.

I let out a relieved sigh and bent to unclamp the battery cable before the light drained the batteries completely.

The convoy leader was waiting for me when I climbed down off the back of the truck. His nostrils flared. "About time. We lost two good men, no thanks to you."

I glared at his haggard, blood stained, and bearded face. He was a dwarf, a short and stalwart people prone to quick tempers and rash decisions. Namely, challenging me while I still had my sword bared.

"That's a funny way to say thanks." I touched the wound on my shoulder and pulled my hand away bearing a thin line of blood. It felt a lot worse than it probably was.

The convoy leader followed me as I limped toward the middle vehicle. "I'm filing a petition to deduct their hazard pay from the escrow."

I spun around. "The hell you are! It's not my fault you didn't listen when I told you not to fire arrows and flares, and it's not my fault we ran into that thing. I told you not to take this route!"

"It cut an entire day off the journey!"

"And it cost you two people." I stepped up to stand face to face with him.

His face hardened, but he was breaking inside. They always did. For whatever reason, they always thought they could renegotiate my fees. Maybe it was because I was a lone woman; maybe it was because I charged the same as a three-man team. Then again, I'd just done the work of three men. Why shouldn't I be paid like it? If he filed his petition, I wouldn't get paid at all until after a thorough investigation by some bureaucrat, and I couldn't afford that.

I folded my arms. "I did my part, so I'm taking full pay. Unless you want to take it up with the bounty office when we get to Atlanta. Maybe next time you'll listen to me when I say we should avoid overpasses after dark." I turned my back.

He spat loudly on the concrete. "Poacher."

"You don't like it? Hire a guild next time." I grabbed the passenger door to the second truck and yanked it open. The driver was already inside, waiting for the convoy to move.

It took him a minute, but the convoy leader eventually realized I wasn't open to further negotiations. He spat again and stomped to the front truck. With one foot inside, he made a sweeping circular gesture. The trucks purred to life and the armored convoy made a u-turn.

It was another twenty minutes before we found our way to the desolate ground below the freeway, headed south through the edge of No-man's-land. Convoy wheels rolled over the skeletal remains of pre-Cataclysm yards and overgrown cul-de-sacs. The rotten carcasses of houses that hadn't been built to withstand waves of magic and mutated monsters cast sharp shadows over the land. Above, a waxing half-moon hid behind silver clouds and their constant threat of rain. Humidity stuck to everything like a damp blanket.

Some things never changed.

No one alive remembered a time when those houses, yards, and cul-de-sacs formed the suburbs of Atlanta, or when the land had been a place called Georgia. The Cataclysm was ancient history for me, taught in my elementary lessons along with the extinction of the dinosaurs. I'd grown up learning about the founding of the twelve kingdoms, how they had all grown from being lone city-states, each of which had once been a part of the larger United States. It had seemed so impossible that a single legislative body governed both Pacifica and Appalachia.

The one thing every generation could agree on was that southern humidity was a beast all its own, and the Kingdom of Atlanta was famous for its sticky nights.

I spent the last part of our journey using the truck's mirror to bandage my shoulder wound as best I could. Proper treatment would have to wait until I completed the job. I could've done a better job if I were willing to strip off my shirt in the truck cab, but I knew better than to do it with anyone watching. If anyone found out the truth about me, I'd be as dead as the troll I'd just killed.

It was roughly eleven o'clock when the first lights of Atlanta reflected off the cloud cover, and another thirty minutes before we saw the city walls. They jutted a hundred and twenty feet into the air in a massive octagonal shape, with anti-aerial beast cannons on the battlements. Spotlights on swivels swept the ground in front of the city for threats so the two million souls within could sleep soundly.

As soon as we were within range, the radio on the dash buzzed to life as the convoy head called into the city to announce our arrival. "Kingdom Control, this is postal convoy echo-zeta-Charlie en route. ETA twelve minutes. Requesting permission to enter. Over."

There was a brief pause before the radio crackled back to life and a female voice said, "Convoy echo-zeta-Charlie, please transmit FOF code. Over."

"Roger that, Kingdom Control. Code is two-one-seven-four November-foxtrot-India. I say again, code is two-one-seven-four November-foxtrot-India. Over."

"Confirming code. You are cleared for entry, convoy echo-zeta-Charlie. Please proceed immediately to gate four and onto decon. Thank you for your service and welcome to the Kingdom of Atlanta."

Massive gates cracked open like a hungry mouth, spilling light into the night. Our convoy crawled into the opening and into the outer city, a wide space with several stables, stalls, and smaller outbuildings. Potholes jostled the truck roughly back and forth. Anyone who might have fallen asleep immediately woke.

During the day, the place would've been crawling with lines of traders checking in their goods and waiting for permits, or to be cleared by decontamination. There were still a few people standing about after dark, but definitely not the crowds I would've expected in the daytime. There was something to be said for coming into the city late rather than at the height of the day.

Road weary men and women looked up from their lantern-lit tables or the shadowy corner stalls where they bent over dice games with cigarettes hanging from their lips. Dark eyes locked onto me as I climbed down from the convoy to retrieve my bag. I glared back until every one of them turned away.

The convoy leader busied himself dealing with the bureaucrats, their forms, and procedures while I went to collect my equipment from the back of the truck. Several dock workers had already started unloading crates marked with red postal service stamps. I bypassed them to grab my black duffel bag. The weight of their eyes followed me all the way to a door. A small wooden sign hung over the door, announcing it was the Kingdom Jobs Office. I pushed the door open, and a string of jingle bells announced my arrival in the darkened office.

The smell of fresh wood polish tickled my nose as I looked around. It was a small office with only a few folding chairs as seating. A few feet ahead, the night shift jobs secretary waited behind a wall of impact-resistant glass. She was a tiny lady with sharp features. Her hair had been pulled back into a harsh bun, her face frozen in a bored stare.

"Welcome to the Kingdom of Atlanta Jobs Office," she said, sounding as bored as she looked. She lifted a clipboard from a hook on the wall next to her, licked her finger, and thumbed through the first few pages. "You're with the mail convoy?"

"Name's Ember Dixon," I said, leaning on the counter. I dropped my bag on the floor by my feet while I waited.

Her eyes flicked up to my face for a moment before dropping back to the page with a snort. "You're early."

"Not by choice." I shrugged.

Her pen scribbled across the page. "That covers the name. What guild?"

"None."

She eyed me again. Her nose twitched, probably from all the effort that kept her from spitting "poacher" like a curse. Then she turned back to her sheet and wrote my answer. "Anything to declare?"

"I killed a bridge troll about an hour north-west of here. Other than that, it was a pretty uneventful ride." *Would've been even less eventful if the convoy leader would've listened to me.* I rolled my shoulder and winced.

"Injuries?" She didn't look up.

"Nothing serious."

She finished filling out the form and slid it through the tiny slot. "Please sign here, initial here, here, and here." While I signed and initialed the half dozen forms, she opened the lockbox and started counting bills onto the table, her face sour.

I didn't care how she felt about paying a poacher. Money was money to me, and a job was a job. I hadn't traveled all over the eastern half of the continent to make friends. I did it to make enough money to buy what I needed to live. Still, it would've been nice to get a thank you occasionally. It'd never happened, not so long as everyone got hung up on the poacher thing. While I could mitigate the whole thing by joining a guild, doing so would require me to submit to a physical, one that I would never pass.

I slid the clipboard back to her, and she passed my money to me, careful not to touch me. I thanked her and tucked the money safely away in my money clip, which I attached to a chain, and slid into my pocket. Pickpockets were an epidemic in cities.

Outside, the air felt even more oppressive than before. The convoy leader was still going through his paperwork with the locals, and I didn't want to be around when he finished. Last thing I needed was to get yelled at some more for his mistakes. The only way into the city proper from the outer city was to pass through decontamination. Not only would that take forever, but I could never clear decontamination. Not without setting off a city-wide alarm.

I slid into the shadows at the edge of the outer city yard and worked my way along a wooden fence until I found a loose board. A couple of well-timed strikes and the board moved easily to the side, providing a space just wide enough for me to slip through.

More shops and closed food stands lined the street on the other side. Their lights were dimmed or darkened, signs flipped to closed. Aside from a few stragglers and some feral cats, the streets were empty. I took two steps before the sky opened and rain fell. Just my luck. At least I couldn't complain about the humidity anymore.

I put a hand over my shoulder and limped through the street while raindrops ran through my hair, down my nose, and sank into my bones. The main streets would provide more cover via their awnings, but I stuck to the back alleys. It wasn't just practical; it was a necessity to find what I needed.

My feet and shoulder ached from the long walk. Water seeped into my clothes. Even as the rain intensified, I kept going. There was no other choice but to move.

Atlanta's broken midtown skyline rose in the distance, the jagged upper floors of long-abandoned skyscrapers dark reminders of a world that once built up instead of down. The sky was safer then, home only to birds and planes. Now, the old Westin Hotel on Peachtree looked like something had taken a bite out of it. Massive claw marks scarred the exterior, and the building sat lopsided. The other buildings were just more of the same, protruding from the ground like old headstones in a forgotten graveyard.

I turned away from midtown and stayed to the eastern side of the city, ducking into low-running alleys and through narrow arches. Iron gates blocked off some paths, but there was always a way forward for someone who knew how to look.

I paused next to a cracked wall of concrete and crumbling brick. Stamped into a single brick at the corner was the image of a serpent eating its own tail. The head faced the alley, pointing the way. I ran my fingers over the rough surface of the image and followed the way it indicated.

The further I went into the sleeping city, the more awake it became. People sat on broken garden walls, smoke drifting up from small, sparkling rolls of paper pinched between their fingers. Cigarettes laced with low-quality potions. It wouldn't be enough to give them powers, but for an hour or two they'd feel like they could see further, move faster, and understand deeper.

I passed through a thick cloud of the smoke on my way down a pair of smooth, stone steps and waved it away. At the bottom of the stairs stood a wooden door with a Caduceus painted on it. Anyone not in the know would think it a strange symbol, the two warring serpents coiled around Mercury's winged staff. Then they'd pass on by, none the wiser. That was, if they found the place at all. I'd only found it the first time by following the tiny ouroboros carvings placed on inconspicuous surfaces around town. Like the hobo signs of old, these symbols were hard to spot if you weren't looking for them, and even more difficult to decipher. Only the initiated understood their meaning.

I gave the door three solid raps, and it opened on its own.

Walking into the shop beyond was like stepping back in time and strolling into a medieval alchemist's shop. Strange contraptions sat on wooden tables. A metallic model of the solar system spun on its own, powered by nothing but gravity. Wooden shelves lined the walls, each filled to the brim with glass jars. Some of them were no bigger than a shot glass and contained brightly colored liquids. Others were large enough to contain the pickled heart of a yeti, or the testes of an ogre. Dragon scales that had long ago lost their luster hung on the wall. Snake skins draped from hooks next to two-headed blowfish. Dusty tomes with titles in Latin, Greek, and Arabic occupied a shelf close to the counter where small aquariums housed live frogs, scorpions, and insects. A gray cat with bright yellow eyes hopped onto the counter and licked its paw, paying no mind to me.

"I'll be right with you, dear," called a woman from the back.

I leaned forward to glimpse the back room where three massive iron cauldrons steamed under a red light.

The beaded curtains moved aside, and a heavyset woman came out of the back, pushing a bandana up her forehead. Her cheeks were flushed almost enough to hide her freckles. "Oh, my! Aren't you a sight? Guess I was right about the rain. Mistress Marigold, at your service!" She wiped her hands on her apron before extending one across the counter to me.

"I'm just here to buy a few potions."

Her face fell. I couldn't tell if it was because I didn't want to shake hands, or my announcement. "Oh. Well, you've come to the right place. What kind do you need, honey? I've got a whole bunch. Love potion? No, you look more a fighter than a lover. How about a strength potion? I'm experimenting with this new cherry flavoring. It's very popular in the Lakelands!"

"No, thanks." I counted out several bills

and placed them on the counter. "I just need an antigen potion."

The last of her enthusiasm faded, replaced by sympathy. "Oh, well that's... I... One second. I think I have some of that around here." She turned her back and flipped through some keys before selecting one and unlocking a cabinet behind the counter. "Here it is!" The shopkeeper gingerly lifted a small box of a dozen vials, each full of a charcoal black liquid. She glanced at me, giving me a good look up and down. "I'm sorry to say it's quite expensive, the ingredients being so rare and all."

I counted out a few more bills. "How many can I get with this?"

She took the money, counted it, and plucked two vials from the box, carefully placing them on the counter. Half of my pay for two vials of life-sustaining antigen. It was enough to keep me going for a week, maybe ten days. No more.

I sighed and took the vials. "Thank you."

"Wait!" she called as I turned away. The apothecary scanned the shelves behind her before grabbing a larger draught of ice blue liquid. She rushed out from behind the counter to press it into my hand. "For the pain."

"Oh, I can't afford..."

"It's on the house, dear." She closed my fingers around it, pity widening her eyes. "It's the least I can do."

I stared down at the bottle in my hand,

shame burning in my heart. “Thank you,” was all I could mumble before stumbling back out into the rain.

Chapter Two

With my sword at my side, I walked the streets of Atlanta in the rain, arms crossed and shoulder aching.

Somehow, I found myself in the old stadium district. The ancient, round sports complex still stood, used now as a practicing ground for guild fighters. Most of the entrances had been sealed. The few that hadn't boasted thick iron chains and padlocks only guild leaders could unlock.

I passed the stadium, navigating broken sidewalks to where an old newspaper stand stood, still open, despite the weather and the hour. I bought a copy and tucked it safely under my arm before slipping into a residential neighborhood.

Hidden among the square-stacked apartment buildings stood a tiny liquor shack with a flickering neon sign out front advertising beer and pool inside. The bars on the windows matched the same smoky dark steel holding up the billboards near the stadium. The front door to the bar was one of those rolling corrugated metal doors, the kind they put on shipping and receiving doors. It was up, revealing some industrious person had installed a set of batwing doors. The slow, ambling rhythm of a guitar playing the blues drifted out the open door.

I pushed through the batwing doors and stopped just inside. Rain dripped from my hair and clothes to pool in a dark circle on the poured cement floor. There wasn't much inside, just a couple of chairs, overturned barrels to serve as tables, and a ratty old pool table shoved, unused, into one corner. The bar itself got points for ingenuity, though. Someone had stacked a bunch of railroad timbers and driven big thirteen-inch railroad spikes into the corners to keep them together. Someone had rigged old railroad crossing signs up behind the bar to blink, providing most of the light for the tiny bar.

A couple of guys at the bar twisted in their seats to look at me. The guy on the right with the cowboy hat wouldn't be any trouble. He turned away as fast as he looked at me and tucked right back into his drink. He saw a girl with a sword and decided he didn't want to ruin his buzz. Skinny on the left must've been hard up for entertainment, though, because he elbowed the guy in the cowboy hat next to him and nodded to me.

I made a point not to look at either of them

as I found an empty seat on the far side of the bar. "Just a beer," I said to the bartender.

He grunted and pressed a dusty glass under a tap. The beer he put in front of me was flat, but I hadn't ordered it expecting much. As long as it hid the taste of the antigen, it'd be worth the price. I checked to make sure no one was watching and dumped one of the black potions into the beer. It bubbled and hissed.

Bottoms up, I thought, and gulped down the whole thing before signaling for a refill.

"I swear that's what he said he saw," said someone loudly off to my right.

"Come on," chided the guy in the cowboy hat. "Everybody knows that once you fall into a rift, there's no coming back."

"What reason would he have to lie to me? His information's always been good. I'm telling you, Dex. If Trillium says the guy walked straight out of a rift, then that's what happened."

"Trillium is an Institute sellout, Lucas."

"Doesn't mean he's lying."

"No," replied the cowboy, "just that he's not even loyal to the people who pay him. How much did you pay to hear his bullshit story? Too much, I'd wager."

The story piqued my interest, and I tuned into the conversation without turning my head.

The man telling the story wore torn, mud stained clothing and drank with a shaky hand. A fresh burn scar marked his cheek. A small group of people had gathered around him to listen.

"Maybe he just got really close," the cowboy suggested.

The scarred man shook his head and stared off into the distance, gripping his cup. "If my informant says he came out of the rift, then he's sure of it."

"Or at least he believes he's sure," said the second man.

The scarred man shrugged and reached across the bar to refill his drink. "All I know is the guy is trouble, and you're a moron if you're thinking of signing up with him. You'll get yourself killed, Dex. People don't walk out of rifts like they're fucking doorways. It just doesn't happen."

A ghost story, I thought, staring down into my beer. *No one comes back from the other side of a rift. I should know better than anyone.*

My fingers curled around the handle of the mug while the scene from five years ago replayed in my head. The loud whooshing sound of the open rift drowned out my cries as I screamed for Ash not to go. But it was too late. He was dead, and the only thing I had to show for our hunt gone wrong was a bleeding gash on my stomach. My hand went instinctively to where the cut had been.

The band ended their song, and I snapped back to the present. Chairs scooted across the concrete floor and shadows pressed in closer to me from behind. I ignored it. The bartender had put my second glass in front of me and I aimed to enjoy it.

"I don't know you," said the asshole behind me. "Are you one of those Iron Company freaks?"

"Nah," said someone else. "No way one of Ike's people would be stupid enough to come in here. They know better. She's a poacher."

"Well?" asked the first voice. "*Are* you a poacher?"

I moved to pick up my drink.

Skinny's hand slammed down on my wrist. Beer sloshed out onto the bar, turning it a deeper shade of gray. "I asked you a question, girl."

I scowled at the spilled drink and met Skinny's yellowing brown eyes. He had a thin face, all angles and no meat, but no jawline. He'd tried to make up for it by growing in some patchy facial hair. It made him look more like the fifth grader who got held back a couple times than anything threatening.

Poachers were the lowest of the low as far as the guilds were concerned. Freelance mercs who rolled into a town, took all the high paying work, and moved on as soon as they lined their pockets. Every guild everywhere hated their guts, but everyone secretly wanted to be one. There was steady cash in guild work, but it wasn't always lucrative after everything was divided equally. Everyone knew freelancing was where the money was, and no one could deny there was an appeal to the travel.

Except they forgot about the lonely nights, the three on one fights, and the way everyone everywhere spat on you just for trying to survive. If the option had been open to me, I would've joined a guild and put roots down years ago. It's like the old saying: the grass is always greener in someone else's yard.

I jerked my arm away from Skinny. "What I am is thirsty. All I want to do is have a few drinks. Warm up. Dry off a bit. I didn't come here to fight. Let me finish my drink and I'll move on. Until then, I'm a paying customer, just like everybody else."

"You listen here, you—"

The cowboy who'd been sitting beside Skinny at the bar suddenly stepped in, pulling Skinny away by the shoulder. "I think the lady said she just wants a drink, Kenny."

"Fuck you," Kenny said, and took a swing at the other man. It connected with his jaw, which was apparently a mistake. All the guys who'd previously had Skinny's back when he was harassing me took a step back. Skinny's eyes widened, processing what he'd done.

The man ran a thumb along his lower lip. "Now, I know you're drunk, Kenny. Otherwise, you'd never've taken that shot at me. So, I'm gonna let you off easy." His hand clamped down on Kenny's shoulder and he gave him a gut punch so solid I heard him deflate like a balloon.

Kenney went down, falling back into the crowd he'd counted on for back-up. They must not've liked Kenney that much because they let him fall straight to the floor.

"Sorry about Kenny. He's really not a bad guy when he's sober." The cowboy extended a hand.

I ignored it and worked on finishing my drink.

After a long beat, he lowered his hand and cleared his throat. "I'm Dex Cavalieres."

"Ember Dixon."

He waited for me to say more, but I stayed silent. When he realized I wouldn't respond, he didn't take the hint, either. He just kept going. "I run the Marauder's Guild here in Atlanta. You've heard of it?"

"Nope." I shoved my glass to the other side of the bar, hoping for another refill. The bartender ignored me. Just my luck I'd wander into a guild bar. I waved for him to bring me the tab instead, but he continued acting like he hadn't seen me. *Guess I'm not going to get to settle the bill until I give this creep the time of day.*

"We're not as big as the Iron Company, or as well funded… yet. But there's something to be said for a smaller, local crew. We can take jobs they'd pass on, go places they won't," Dex continued.

I put on my best regretful smile and turned

on the barstool to face him. "Look, you can save the sales pitch for someone else. I'm not looking for a guild to join."

He crossed his arms. "Oh, so you *are* a poacher?"

I ground my teeth a moment before I realized I was doing it and forced myself to relax. "I'm not here to take jobs from any of the guilds. I just brought a mail convoy in from Baltimore."

"Plenty of guilds in Baltimore to escort the mail," Kenny chimed in. He gripped his stomach and climbed back onto his stool.

I narrowed my eyes at him. "Guess they were all busy."

Dex sighed. "Look, do you want to get out of here? Talk somewhere a little quieter?"

I gave him another, more lingering glance. It wasn't often anyone tried to flirt with me. Of course there were the looks, the whistles, the whispering. It's something you just get used to when you're a woman working alone with a lot of men on long trips. People get lonely. But from a guild leader? To someone like Dex, I should've been as attractive as dog food.

I smiled. "You're either desperate, or stupid."

He shrugged and leaned on the bar next to me. "Or I choose not to judge people without getting to know them first. I'm sure you have your reasons for not being in a guild. I'd love to hear them."

"Would you now?"

"Bet you've seen some interesting things, been to interesting places." He folded his arms on the bar and gestured for the bartender to refill my drink. "Me, I don't get out of Atlanta much. It'd be nice to hear about some other place a bit, hear from a fresh voice. And I could listen to you talk all night."

I restrained a laugh. "I'm not much of a storyteller."

"Aw, come on. Just look at you. You've got enough road dust on you, and that sword's worn. You've seen things, been places. What's the biggest thing you've ever killed?"

I shrugged and pulled my refilled glass closer. "I just dealt with a nasty bridge troll on the way here. It's probably the biggest, but not the most difficult thing. Worst one was a rogue vampire." I noticed Kenny giving me a dirty look, so I turned my back to him, spinning on the bar stool to face Dex slightly.

"No necromancer around to control it?"

I shook my head. "He'd passed in his sleep. Heart attack. The vampire got loose somehow. Started attacking anything that moved. The guilds lost three people trying to corner it. Then they got all wrapped up in the logistics and paperwork. While they were trying to figure out all of that, two more people died. I tracked it to an empty warehouse and put a stop to it once and for all. Sometimes, us poachers are more efficient than a big guild."

"I'm not arguing that." Dex reached across the bar, picked up a bottle and poured a shot. "People might not like it, but freelancers are needed. There are places we can't go, jobs too small to be worth hiring out that solo folks like yourself can handle better. Personally, I think we ought to subcontract that work out to registered agents. That'd satisfy people's need to regulate and feel safe working with outsiders. Protect freelancers, too. You get your freedom to operate and the people get their problems solved. I make a little on the side."

"That's just it, though. Why should you get a portion of the pay for the job I do?"

He shrugged. "Ideally? It'd be in exchange for legal protection. Say that vampire killed someone on your watch and the relatives wanted to take it out on you. A subcontractor relationship would mean that I've vetted you, and that legal shitstorm would fall on me."

"So the guilds would be what? Insurance?" I shook my head. "No thanks. It sounds too complicated to be beneficial. I don't like the idea of answering to anyone."

"Yeah, you don't strike me as the dependent type." He picked up his glass, toasted me, and downed it, wincing after. "It's just an idea, though. Something I'm working on."

"You don't have anything against poachers?" I asked.

"I prefer freelancers. Bet you do too." He refilled his glass. "And I don't have anything against anybody unless they earn it. I've been an outsider looking in more than once. I know it ain't easy, doing what you do. Gotta get lonely out there."

I raised an eyebrow. "And I suppose you're going to volunteer to keep me company? No offense, but I'm not looking for company to-night."

He smiled and touched his chest, pretending to be wounded. "Ouch, my pride. And here I thought we'd made a connection. Where'd I go wrong?"

"Is it cliché if I say it's not you, it's me?"

"A little, yeah."

I pressed my lips together and rose, tossing some bills down on the bar. "Well, sorry to disappoint you, Cowboy. I'm sure your pride will recover in time."

"Cowboy," Dex mused, running a finger along the rim of his hat. "I think I like that."

I left the bar with a sour taste in my mouth, and not just from the potion I'd choked down. The rain had slowed to a mild drizzle, but it was still coming down. Puddles marked potholes and low-lying areas on the roads. In the distance, worn neon signs flickered in and out of existence, announcing the closure of every business in Atlanta.

I hurried down the street and into the

lobby of a small motel where a young woman with piercings in her eyebrow manned the counter. She looked up from the book she was reading and frowned, looking me over. "We're booked up."

"Really?" I gestured to the wall of guest room keys hanging behind her.

She glanced over her shoulder before turning back, a slightly more apologetic expression on her face. "Ok, so we're not, but... One of the Marauders was just in here. Paid me not to give you a room."

"You're serious?"

"Deathly."

I'd been turned away plenty of times, but most people at least tried to hide it. "Because I'm a poacher?"

She shrugged.

I sighed and opened my wallet. "How much did he pay you? I'll double it."

"It's not really about the money. Dex and his people, they're local heroes. Dex is basically a legend here in town. A staple. If I let you stay, and they find out about it, they're going to charge me extra next time I need help."

I frowned and added another bill to the pile. Maybe Dex had a point. This whole lone hunter gig was getting kind of expensive. "How about now? That should more than cover any extra fees they charge."

The girl eyed the pile of cash, took it,

counted it, and pocketed all but one bill before retrieving a guest key. "Lucky room thirteen. Up the stairs, around the corner. Second door on the left. Enjoy your stay."

"Thanks, I guess." I took the key and moved further into the musty smelling hotel.

Worn, felt-like carpet lined the stairs. They creaked loudly as I climbed up to the second story. Old photographs hung on the walls, images from a different time and place preserved in a dingy motel. There were smiling people in front of skyscrapers, people in costumes at a convention down by the old shopping mall, a couple kissing on a glass skywalk that overlooked Peachtree Street. Some edges were worn and brown from the passage of time, but the photos were displayed proudly on scratched walls. Brass numbers hung on most of the doors, though room thirteen seemed to be the exception. The numbers were missing, but someone had been kind enough to write the room number in sharpie.

I sighed and slid the key into the lock.

The room beyond wasn't much. I had stayed in nicer, and in worse. It was a ten by fifteen space, modified from whatever the room had originally been to be just large enough to fit a bed, dresser, mirror, and a small folding desk. A few rusty wire hangers hung on a wooden dowel rod that served as a closet. To my right was the bathroom. A shower curtain around it provided the only privacy, but at least there was running water. I pulled back the paper-thin comforter, pleased to see no bugs flee the light. Running water and a bug-free mattress? Maybe the place was worth the price of admission after all.

The springs squeaked noisily as I plopped onto the end of the bed. My reflection stared back at me in the streaky mirror hanging on the wall. I looked like a drowned rat. A drowned rat with bloodstains on my shoulder. I turned my head to see if I could assess the damage, but that required taking my shirt off first. I peeled the wet shirt off, wincing when it stuck to an old wound across my stomach.

An old wound... Funny way to describe a bunch of crystals growing out of the cut across my midsection. I draped the shirt across the back of a metal chair and rose, examining the crystals. They glistened, a deep indigo. Each one was no bigger than a marble, pressed into a line as thick as a pencil just above my navel. In another era, it would've passed as some form of body jewelry or body modification, but they weren't. The crystals had been growing out of my skin for almost five years, slowly spreading. One day, even the antigen potions wouldn't be enough to stop the spread. I could already feel that the effects weren't lasting as long. When that happened, the crystals would grow unchecked. They'd invade my blood and vital organs, solidifying them to rock hard crystals. If I were lucky, I'd die before they grew in my brain. I'd seen what that could do to a person, and it wasn't pretty.

The infection was a death sentence, but a slow-moving one as long as the potions worked. Illegal potions weren't the worst of my worries, though. People didn't understand the infection, and they feared what they didn't understand. There were misconceptions that the infected could spread it to others by touch. Some believed you could catch it like a cold just by being in the same room as an infected person.

But it didn't work like that. Even if someone were to touch the crystals growing in me with their bare hands, it would never jump from me to them, not unless they had an open wound on their finger or something. They needed blood to take root and grow.

Not that anyone would listen. If anyone found out about the infection, every city would close its gates to me forever. Average people who didn't know any better wouldn't see the difference between me and the mad crystal-eating heretics who lived in the outlands. To them, I'd be just another dangerous monster to be put down before I killed someone else.

But there was nothing I could do about the crystal growth. At least, nothing now.

I turned around to get a better view of the gash on my shoulder. An angry red line streaked from the shoulder blade toward my spine. *Better clean it up.*

The shower was lukewarm, even with the knob turned to hot. I put my shoulder under the shower head, watching the water go from clear to pink to red, and back again as it trickled down the drain.

Dex had seemed nice. Easy to look at, too. I closed my eyes and leaned my forehead against the shower wall, conjuring up an image of him in my mind. Him and his dumb, lopsided smile. I let myself wonder what it would be like not to be infected, to have this secret that isolated me.

Would I have taken him up on his offer? Probably not. Casual sex just wasn't me, even before. I'd practically been a child at eighteen when I got the magicite scar, and the man I had loved, the one I thought I would spend the rest of my life with... He was gone. Swallowed by the rift. I'd never even gotten to tell him the truth about how I felt.

Now, nobody would touch me. Even if they thought they might want to, I couldn't go through with it. I couldn't let anyone see the jagged line of indigo teeth growing in my stomach. I was a deformed monster, and that meant I had to be alone.

Once I'd cleaned my shoulder with soap, I dabbed some rubbing alcohol onto the wound and bandaged it as best I could. It didn't need stitches, but it'd probably leave one hell of a scar.

My wounds seen to, I sat down cross-legged on the creaky bed and spread the newspaper's classified section out in front of me. The jobs section was pretty extensive, but most of them were for general laborers. Atlanta had two major guilds, and any important work would've gone straight to them without ever seeing a day in the paper. The few jobs posted that required a hunter's expertise didn't pay particularly well, but I'd take what I could get. A few jobs, and I might make enough to get myself another potion.

Let's see here. I tapped the flat end of a marker on my chin. There was a bakery with an unspecified infestation. No thanks. I'd grown up doing odd jobs like that as part of my training. It was likely a giant spider, or maybe some dire rats had gotten into the larder. If they were really unlucky, they had a sugarplum fairy problem. Those things were a pain to get rid of.

Further down the page, a farmer was looking to hire a few were-folk as farm hands. It was a good deal, especially since he was offering pay and lodgings, but I wasn't a were-anything, so I had to pass.

I scanned the first page and turned it over. *Hello, what's this?* My finger stopped on a wanted ad I had nearly passed over.

WANTED:
Ten to twenty expert hunters. Must travel.
Must provide own equipment. Not guild
sanctioned. Pay discussed. Meet at Red's Tavern

in the Old Fourth Ward if interested.

It sounded perfect. Well, everything except the ten to twenty hunters part. I rarely worked with other people for obvious reasons. Still, a non-guild sanctioned hunt? What sort of prey could they be after? Guilds usually only took jobs hunting creatures that were local nuisances. They didn't travel, and they didn't hunt for sport, though sometimes individual guild members would. Sport hunts were for trophies, fame, or cartloads of cash, usually hunting the biggest, most dangerous creatures. I'd heard of hunts that'd captured and killed chimeras, mad witches, or even dragons. While I didn't care about the trophies, a job like that would pay well enough I might not have to work for months at a time. I could relax a little and still have enough potions to keep myself alive.

Even better, the meeting was supposed to take place tomorrow afternoon. I couldn't have timed my arrival better if I tried.

I circled the job twice and placed the newspaper beside the bed before turning off the light and settling in.

The next morning, I checked out of the crappy motel just before noon, giving me just enough time to get to Red's.

Red's Tavern was one of those buildings that had begun its life as something else and been transformed by time and necessity. The bottom half of the building was brick mixed with concrete, and the top dark treated wood. Christmas lights hung from a wooden awning and over a hand-painted sign that swung in the light breeze. It sat on the side of a small hill, and had been built to embrace the hillside rather than to fight against it, with a street-level entrance and a set of stairs leading to a basement door. A smaller sign announced the meeting room was below, so I took the stairs.

I opened the basement door. Several burly men moved out of the way, but there wasn't far they could go. The whole room was full of people standing under a low ceiling. Each man had a sword, daggers, or wore arrows on his back. The room stank of body odor, ale, and damp oak. Dark walls drank in the light coming from the front of the room where a man paced, speaking to the crowd of hunters. From the back, I couldn't see him, especially since I was shorter than almost everyone in the room, even when I stood on my tiptoes.

"… I'll be candid. This is a dangerous trek," said the voice in the room's front.

That voice… I pushed through the crowd, sliding through small spaces toward the front. *I know it, but it can't be.* I leaned around people, tried to jump up for a better view, but I just couldn't see, and people packed in too tightly at the front.

Of all the times to be the shortest person in

the room.

I spied a pile of barrels on the other side of the room that'd be easy to climb up and made a beeline for them. As I pushed between two men in matching blue shirts, a hand shot out and grabbed my wrist. I spun, ready to defend myself, only to find it was Dex that had grabbed me.

He flashed a big smile. "Well, if it isn't the freelancer. Fancy meeting you here, Ember."

I pulled my arm away. "What are you doing here? I thought you had your own guild? The sign said this wasn't a guild sanctioned hunt."

"I've got my reasons. Didn't figure you for a team player."

"I've got my reasons." I repeated and turned my back to slide through the last few people before he could press me further. The pile of barrels was a short distance away. I grabbed the first one and pulled myself up.

"... I cannot overstate the danger those who join will face. We are going into territory that has been reclaimed by wild magic and hungry rifts. Ravenous beasts stalk the forests and mountains. Cultists capture the unwary and bandits prey upon the weak. Dozens of open rifts stand between us and our destination. Hundreds have died making the attempt at capturing this legendary beast. But should we succeed—and we will succeed—the spoils of this hunt will make all who take part rich beyond your wildest dreams," continued the familiar voice. "Our prey is none other than the elder dragon of Black Mountain."

I nearly fell from my perch. And not because he'd finally revealed the details of the hunt.

The man at the front of the room. I recognized his sharp, angular features, his dark, curly hair, his sparkling quartz-gray eyes. I knew him. I also knew it couldn't be who I thought it was because five years ago, I had watched a rift swallow him alive.

Chapter Three

Five years ago...

"EMBER!" Ash's voice was distant, like he was underwater.

I knew he couldn't be more than five feet behind me, caught in the wild winds of the widening rift. My hair whipped around my head. Rocks and other debris tore at my exposed skin, and still I couldn't move. The rift reflected in my eyes, glowing on the edges like the sun.

From a distance, the center had always seemed little more than a black hole, ready to swallow anyone who got too close. But with the rift right in front of me, I thought I could see something more, something big and wonderful waiting on the other side. It felt as if I stood on the edge of a cliff overlooking a valley of understanding and truth. Everything I had ever wanted to know waited on the other side of that rift. All I had to do was walk through it.

With the rift shining in my eyes, I reached

for what lay beyond.

And the beyond reached back.

“Ember, no!” Ash’s powerful arms wrapped around me. In one decisive move, he pivoted, yanking my feet from the ground, and threw me away from the rift.

I hit the ground face first. Fire bit into my stomach as the jagged edge of a magicite crystal sliced open the skin. The pain brought me back to reality, the weight of what I had been about to do pressing in from all sides. I pushed myself up, holding onto the bloody line the magicite had carved in me, and turned around. “Ash!”

The light of the rift swelled, making him look like nothing more than a shadow. He looked up at the rift as it closed in, then over his shoulder at me. His lips moved, mouthing something I couldn’t catch.

“Run, you idiot,” I screamed, knowing it was already too late.

Ash turned back to the rift, threw his arms wide, and let it swallow him whole.

****

Ash was dead. He had to be. There was no denying what I had seen, and no one came back from whatever was on the other side of the rifts. Everyone knew that. Monsters came through, but even they didn’t go back.

Yet there he stood, in the dimly lit basement of an Atlanta tavern, a crimson cape over one shoulder, revealing a new sword at his side, and new people at his back. The small crowd of men and women surrounding Ash all wore the same colors as him and had a pin shaped like a dragon on their sleeve.

A guild? No, this wasn't a guild sanctioned hunt. Who were they then?

I suddenly felt eyes on me and lifted my head to scan the rafters above. Two pairs of blood-red eyes peered back. The eyes belonged to the emaciated, hairless, humanoid bodies of vampires. The silver circlet with a single glowing stone meant there was a necromancer somewhere in the crowd controlling them.

Or someone on stage. I studied the people's faces again, searching for someone concentrating just a little harder than the rest. An unshackled vampire was little more than a feeding machine. It would've torn through that room in seconds, killing everyone. Under the control of a trained necromancer, however, vampires were docile with no will of their own.

A dark-haired woman with lipstick that matched her red cape turned her head slightly and met my eyes. She wore a matching silver circlet.

Gotcha. I stared back. She would've been able to see through her vampires' eyes too, giving her a prime view of everyone in the crowd. Guess they were Ash's private security.

I glanced away from her and back to Ash. *Looks like you've come up in the world since getting eaten by a rift. Who are you now? Where have you been all this time?*

There was a sudden pang in my chest. How long had he been back? Had he even looked for me? All this time, he'd let me believe he was dead. And to find him in the company of these strangers... Something about it all left a sour taste in my mouth. More than that, it hurt. It felt as if he'd rejected me, although I didn't know that was the case. For all I knew, Ash thought I was dead. That day five years ago seemed like it had happened in another life. For him, maybe it felt even longer.

Ash stepped to the side, picking up a paper scroll that he held for all to see. "Anyone interested can step forward now and sign up."

"What's the catch?" someone from the crowd yelled. A chorus of agreeing grunts and nods followed.

Ash lowered the paper. "The threat of death isn't enough?"

The small crowd at Ash's back snickered.

Ash maintained his grave expression and paced to the center of the stage. "I asked for twenty good, armed men for a reason. I fully expect that less than half who embark on this expedition will survive it. Make no mistake. We are going into hostile territory to hunt a beast that has already claimed dozens of lives. Looking around the room, just getting to the dragon's lair will be too much for some of you. Guild life has made you soft. Weak. You Atlantians are used to escorting mail trains and clearing gnomes from the park. Safe work with guaranteed pay. I'm offering you greatness, but that comes at a price. Anyone who puts his signature on this page had better be right with his God."

A disgruntled murmur swept through the crowd. Several of the hunters looked at each other, shook their heads, and shuffled toward the door. They were probably the smart ones.

I scanned the room to see who had stayed and spotted Dex's white cowboy hat, his feet planted firmly where I'd left him, arms crossed. He watched the stage with a distrustful frown, calculating and weighing losses and gains in his head.

"You haven't told us where we're going," said another man. He was an average height guy, with silver hair and a goatee. No, not silver. He was too young to have gone gray naturally, and the guy was built like a tank. His hair was snow white.

Ash's eyes focused on the man. "Ike, is it?"

The man shrugged. "You can call me Commander Tolliver."

"A good, powerful name. Generations of monster hunting in your blood. Yet you still need your hand held." Ash sat on the table, gripping the edge with both hands. "You're not the only guild leader who's crept in here. Do you know what would happen if I were to tell everyone exactly where we were going and how much it paid? You and Dexter Cavalieres would run back to your respective guild headquarters, raise a group of your own hunters, and head out to give me competition. I don't like competition." He lifted the page again, raising his voice. "Anyone who puts his name on this page today will get that information, and a small retainer just in case you need to purchase some gear. Questions?"

The room was silent.

I looked around. There were over twenty people still in the room, but some of them looked like they wanted to bolt as soon as people started moving.

Ash placed the paper on the desk with a pen and stepped aside, waiting.

Dex glanced around, lowered his arms, and pushed his way through the crowd. Silently, he picked up the pen and affixed his name to the page.

Ash nodded to him when he put the pen down and Dex stepped back into the crowd.

Dex stopped in front of Ike and gave a salute. "See you out there, Commander."

Ike grunted, watched Dex take his place at the back of the room, and went to the table to add his name. Another five people broke to follow Ike while most people headed for the door.

I got in line.

As the line moved forward, my palms

dampened with sweat, and my heart pounded in my ears. Would he recognize me? Maybe he'd lost his memory. Maybe I'd changed too much. Why else wouldn't he have looked for me when he got back? We'd been inseparable the day he went into that rift. Surely that much hadn't changed. He'd saved me. Even if he didn't return my feelings, that had to mean something, didn't it?

A dozen different scenarios ran through my head. What would he say when he saw me? What if he hated me? It was my fault he'd gone into the rift. If I hadn't stood there like an idiot, we might've both been okay.

"Ember?"

I looked up. The line had cleared in front of me, though I hadn't moved. My heart jumped into my throat. *There he is. Touch him. Make sure he's real.*

"Ember Dixon, is it really you?" He rushed around the table and stopped just in front of me, as if he were suddenly unsure again.

I swallowed and shrugged, but my voice was still tight when I said, "Who else would I be?"

His grave face faded, replaced by smiling eyes and upturned lips. The five years we'd been apart melted to nothing, and he put his arms around me, squeezing the air out of me. "I can't believe it's really you. After all this time…" He stepped back from the hug, but kept his hands on my arms, giving me a good look up and down. "God, it's good to see you! How are you? What have you been doing?"

The guy behind me cleared his throat.

Ash's face fell, and he pulled me out of line so we could talk. "What are you doing here?"

"I could ask you the same question. The last time I saw you—"

He put a finger to his lips. "Not here. Too many eyes and ears. But you're right. I do owe you an explanation, and you'll get one. I promise. Just… give me some time. I need to process this. You're still not in a guild?"

I shook my head. "Looks like you've started your own." I nodded to the people waiting behind the table.

"Them? We're not a guild so much as a group of like-minded individuals that share a common goal."

"And a common fashion designer. One you should fire." I pinched the hem of his cape and lifted it, only to let it fall limp. "Who wears capes these days?"

He shrugged. "They're practical. Listen, Ember…"

"Don't try to talk me out of this hunt." I wagged my finger at him. "I just found you. I'm not letting you out of my sight again. Not for a long damn time."

"Promise?" He grinned and winked at me.

Heat flooded my cheeks. It'd been a long time since I'd talked to anyone that much, and I'd forgotten how he used to be so flirty and carefree. "Don't be stupid. You've got a whole gaggle of bodyguards to watch you shave and shit. You know what I meant."

Ash shrugged again, conceding the point. "I won't stop you from coming along. In fact, I'd be honored to have you join us. It'll give us time to catch up."

"Good." I walked over to the paper sitting on the table. They had filled in all but one line of the twenty, so I took the last one.

The document completed, Ash picked up the scroll and rolled it up. "Those of you who've signed on, welcome to the hunt. Our prey is a rather famous beast some two hundred miles from here. It'll be quite the journey through hostile territory. I advise you to gather your things, settle any outstanding affairs, and meet back here at sunrise. In the meantime, I'm sure you're all dying to know about the pay. The daily standard rate of most guilds in the area runs about two hundred dollars per day base pay. Is that right?"

"Give or take." Ike nodded.

"I'm offering four hundred," Ash said, "plus whatever you can carry back. Dragons have many organs with magic properties. Scales sell for a week's wages. We can easily part out the dragon between us and make each of you more than a year's pay with plenty left over. That's to say nothing of the treasures it might be hoarding or the magicite crystals you can harvest and sell. I ask only that you leave me one piece. You may have everything else." He scanned the room. "But the heart is mine."

A chill ran through me with his last sentence. I'd never heard him speak with such finality before. It was almost as if someone else were speaking through him.

I dismissed the thought. Five years lost in a rift would change anyone, and Ash and I had both needed a little more confidence back then. Maybe Ash had changed for the better. He still seemed like himself when he talked to me.

"We meet back here at dawn," Ash said, and the meeting ended. He turned around, speaking briefly with the necromancer, before striding toward me.

The necromancer woman watched him go a few steps before turning her ice-cold eyes on me. If she stared any harder, her eyes would've bored two holes in my forehead. It only got worse when Ash put his arm around me and led me to the tavern stairs. "I think it's high time you and I got reacquainted, Ember."

Chapter Four

It was too early for the main floor of the tavern to be busy, though there were a few customers already seated. They had empty plates and half-full glasses of beer in front of them. My stomach reminded me I hadn't eaten since the previous morning, but the dwindling cash in my pocket meant I had to choose between food now and supplies for the road.

"Have you eaten?" Ash stopped by a table and pulled out a chair.

It took me a minute to realize that he wanted me to sit. "Careful," I said sitting. "I might get used to being treated like royalty."

"That might not be such a bad thing. After all we've been through, I'd say we deserve a little spoiling." Ash sat across from me before picking up one of the paper menus stuck between the metal napkin holders in the center of the table. "The toast and eggs are probably safe if you're hungry. I wouldn't trust the breakfast special if I were you."

I sighed and shifted my weight. "My last job was a little light. Mail runs don't pay what they used to."

"I wouldn't know. I've never done one." He pushed the menu away. "Order what you want. My treat."

"Are you sure?"

He rolled his eyes. "It's breakfast, Ember, not a six-course dinner. Get what you want."

"Okay, but only if you agree to deduct it from my pay." I grabbed the menu and scanned it with hungry eyes.

"Shall we address the elephant in the room?"

I looked up. Ash held my eyes with his intense gaze, his elbows propped on the table so he could fold his hands. Slowly, I lowered the menu, a lump forming in my throat. "Where were you? What happened? Why didn't you look for me when you got back?"

"Wow. That's... More elephants than I was expecting." He lowered his hands and leaned back in his chair with a sigh, looking around. "Where to begin?"

"How about what happened while you were in the rift. How long were you in there? What did you see?"

"I saw..." His eyes lost their focus, leaving him transfixed on an unassuming crack in the wall. He stared at it for nearly a full minute before he tore himself away from whatever memory had been playing in his brain. Ash shook his head. "I don't remember what I saw, or how long I was in there. The time I spent away feels like a dream after waking. I know it happened. The passage of that time weighs on me, ages me. But I can't grasp the memory of it. It feels almost unreal. I know I went in, and I must have come back out. The next thing I remember is waking up screaming in a hospital bed."

"Hospital?" I frowned and pushed the menu away, my hunger forgotten.

Ash nodded. "An old Coalition field hospital, if you can believe it. Members of the Institute had repurposed it."

I shuddered. That explained why he was traveling with necromancers. The Institute was short for the Institute of Undead Studies. Imagine PETA for the undead, but run by the Church of Scientology. They were part corporation, part cult, and part scientific research facility. The Institute recruited the most skilled necromancers into their ranks and rented them out to guilds as needed. Joining wasn't mandatory for necromancers, but the Institute had a way of making it seem so, especially if you were skilled.

"They had picked me up on a run into the Appalachian Outlands and brought me back thinking I was infected with the vampire pathogen," Ash continued. "I had a fever and chills, but it never developed into anything more than that.

The Institute told us to get lost as soon as they realized I wouldn't turn, and I left. Probably too soon. I wasn't well for a long time. Some people from the Institute went with me. They helped me. Nursed me back to health. It took eleven months, Ember. I fought fever and sickness like I've never experienced. I was malnourished and weak." He lifted his hand and watched his fingers flex. "I had to get strong again so I could find you."

"So you looked for me." I folded my hands on the tabletop and leaned forward.

Ash shrugged. "I tried, but have you ever tried looking for one person in this messed up world? I checked the guild directories in every city, in every kingdom or province I traveled to. I even asked about traveling caravans. No one knew an Ember Dixon."

That wasn't surprising. I wasn't famous, and most of the jobs I did were so mundane or low-profile, I wouldn't expect most people to remember my name if they had worked with me. Record keeping was also spotty outside of government agencies and the Institute. Short of pulling my official record somewhere I had worked, or seeing my name on a sign-in sheet, there was no way he could've found me. It was pure luck that we'd ever run into each other again at all.

The tavern server wandered over with coffee and took our order. He was a balding man with a thick Georgia accent, the kind only rural folk had. There weren't too many rural people around anymore. Cities were safer with their high walls, their guards, and their guilds. It made me wonder about the life he must've left behind to wait tables in a dingy Atlanta tavern. After I put in my order for toast and eggs, he scurried away, sliding into the back of the bar to prep the food himself.

"What about you?" Ash asked, drawing me back into the conversation. "I thought you would've joined a guild, or started your own by now."

"We always talked about that, didn't we? Starting our own guild?" I fidgeted with my fingers, not looking at him.

How could I tell him the truth? What did I even say? That I was dying, slowly but surely, thanks to the crystals that had infected my blood the night a rift swallowed him? What would he think of me if he knew? Part of me wanted to trust him like I always had and tell him the truth. The old Ash would've hugged me and promised that we would figure it out together. But this new Ash... He was older, maybe more practical. He had a hunt to run, and if he found out I was infected, he might leave me behind.

I couldn't let that happen. I'd already lost him once, and Hell would freeze over before I let it happen a second time.

I shrugged. "It just didn't feel right without you. I've been doing odd jobs ever since, just going from place to place, trying to make a living. Which reminds me... Running a hunt this size is pretty expensive, Ash. Is the Institute funding it?"

"No." He wrinkled his nose as if the very idea repulsed him. "No, I'm funding it. After I came back, I lucked into a few lucrative jobs. I've got a sizeable nest egg stored away, and big plans for it."

"You still want to start that guild?"

"Please," he scoffed, picking up his coffee. "That was a child's dream. I have bigger plans."

"Bigger?" I arched an eyebrow. "What could be bigger than founding your own guild?"

Ash smirked and leaned in, his voice a whisper that made goosebumps form on my arms. "How about founding your own *kingdom*?"

I almost choked on my coffee. What he was talking about wasn't impossible, I supposed, though it was close to it. After the fall of the United States government, the Coalition of the States kept the east coast united until it, too, fell apart. Now, everything had been split into twelve independent kingdoms or city states. The kingdom of Atlanta stretched from the southern border of the Chattahoochee Forest to the water-logged ruins of Jacksonville in the south. There was an unofficial western border where the old state line between Georgia and Alabama used to stand, but most of Alabama was overgrown. It was all forest and swamp land down there.

To the north was the Virginia Commonwealth. East was the Kingdom of Carolina. West of the No-man's-land of old Alabama was Texahoma and so on. Somebody had claimed most of the land. Anything that was left was an undesirable mess full of monsters, deadly rifts, and overgrown land. Founding a kingdom meant negotiating with existing powers, building a city from the ground up, and somehow enticing people to come live in it. Others had talked about it, but the effort and financial capital required was out of reach for nearly everyone. Even if Ash had sizable savings tucked away, there was no way he could've had that much cash.

"You're not serious," I said, still shocked.

"It's a long-term plan," Ash said. "But it's like you always said. Shoot for the stars. Even if you miss, at least you tried, right?"

I put my coffee cup back on the table. "Ash, do you have any idea how difficult that will be?"

"Anything worth having is worth fighting for. You said that as well."

"Yeah, but I was talking about dinner or a place to stay, probably. Not ruling my own kingdom. That sounds—"

"A little crazy?" He met my eyes and held them. "I can promise you I'm quite sane."

"That's just what a crazy person would say," I muttered and shifted in my seat to keep from staring at him.

"I don't think it's crazy to make big plans. You and me, we grew up with nothing but each other until Old Jim took us in and taught us how to use a sword. He taught us that nothing was impossible if you will fight for what you believed you were entitled to. We've bled for this world. Nearly died a dozen times over. Hell, I fell into a rift trying to scrape together enough money to..." He trailed off and sighed. "Is it so horrible to dream of owning a small patch of the world we've bled for?"

"No, I suppose not." I stared down into the dark brown liquid in my coffee cup.

"This hunt is the first in a series of jobs I have planned to raise the funds and attention I need to make it happen, Ember." He reached across the table to put his hands over mine. "And now that I've found you, I want you right there with me while I make it happen."

I stared at his hands overtop mine, a heavy feeling in the pit of my stomach. If he knew the truth, he wouldn't have held my hand like that. "It's been five years, Ash. You don't know what I've been doing, where I've been."

"I don't have to. I know *you*. I want your wit, and your sword, on my side." He retracted his hands. "But you don't need to answer now. Take some time and think about it. For now, the hunt is plenty to keep us busy."

I grunted in agreement. "Yeah, just don't go expecting me to call you Lord Ash or anything."

Ash laughed. "I was thinking *Emperor* Ash."

"Dream on."

Our food came. It was just eggs and toast, but it might as well have been a feast as hungry as I was. I dug in, completely focused on clearing my plate while Ash barely touched his food.

"These other guild leaders, Dex and Ike. What do you know about them?" Ash asked.

I shrugged and swallowed a mouthful of eggs. "Not much. I just got into town last night. Actually, I ran into Dex. Guy's got an ego the size of the Atlantic, but nothing to back it up that I could see. He runs this crappy bar. He's a smooth talker. A people person, I guess you could say. Or maybe he really just likes to hear himself talk."

"Good to know. And the other one?"

"Ike?" I chugged down the rest of my coffee, which had gotten lukewarm. "Don't know anything about him."

Ash frowned and ripped his toast in half to dip it in his eggs. "He's a Tolliver. They're practically royalty in the guild world. It was his ancestors that founded the first guild, you know. Fought the Coalition when they tried to shut them down. Odd that he'd want in on this hunt. As I understand it, he's a stickler for rules and regulations. His guild, the Iron Company, is one of the largest, most well-respected guilds in the South, so he doesn't need the cash. He certainly doesn't need the fame. Why do you suppose someone like that would sign on?"

I shrugged and swallowed the last of my eggs. "Goodwill? I mean, just because he's monster hunting royalty doesn't mean people like him. Maybe it's a P.R. ploy. Imagine the draw of being able to hire the guy who killed a dragon."

"Maybe. And maybe he's got ulterior motives."

"Now you're sounding paranoid." I put my fork down and pushed my empty plate away.

Ash smiled. "Well, a man in my position can't afford not to be. Listen, Ember... It's not widely known that I've been through a rift and back. I'd like to keep it that way. If someone like Ike were to find out, he might tell someone else, and they might tell someone else. I'm sure there are people out there who'd love to capture me and dissect me to find out how I survived. I'd rather not go through that."

I nodded. "Sure. Of course. Your secret's safe with me."

Ash sighed, relieved. "Thank you."

A memory flashed through my mind. Ash and me as kids, sitting on the ruins of a rocky garden wall overlooking a murky pond. Icy wind bit at my cheeks and pulled my hair, but it was Ash who'd been shivering. Tears trailed down his muddy cheeks as he repeated, "Please don't tell Old Jim! I just... I just wanted to hold it."

I frowned at the broken crystal in his hand.

When he found out, Old Jim was going to be furious. It took him weeks to craft them into something useable, and each one was a special order someone put in at his shop. The magicite crystals were worth more than a house, and Ash had shattered it when he knocked it off the workshop shelf.

"It's okay." I put my arms around Ash and pulled him into a tight hug. "I won't tell."

And I never did. I took the blame for breaking the crystal and got stable cleaning duties for a month. The worst month of my life, except for, of course, the month after I lost Ash through the rift. I would've cleaned a thousand stables if it meant I got him back.

Now, here he was, right in front of me like an answered prayer. I couldn't help but smile a little at the thought.

"What?" Ash tilted his head slightly. "You're smiling."

"Just remembering something. You were such a crybaby when you were a kid."

Red flashed over Ash's cheeks. "And you were a bully. Always blackmailing the other kids or bossing them about. Remember Old Jim's face when he found out you'd been threatening Yarah with a sword?"

I burst into laughter. "I thought his head was going to explode!"

"If you're gonna go waving that damned thing about, you best learn to use it so you don't kill yourself," Ash said in his best Old Jim imitation. "Do you remember what you said?"

I nodded. "I already know how to use it. You stab them with the pointy end!"

We shared another loud laugh, drawing the eyes of other patrons in the tavern. Normally, that much attention would've bothered me. I always tried to be as inconspicuous as possible. It didn't matter to me as long as Ash was with me. Having him back, it almost felt like the weight of the world had lifted and we were kids again. I could breathe again.

"You're still good and sharp with the sword, I presume?" Ash asked.

"Better than ever." I stood. "But speaking of, I have to go run some errands before tomorrow morning if you want me at my best."

"Of course. Just... Where are you staying?"

I opened my mouth and quickly shut it, not knowing how to answer. I couldn't afford to go back to the crappy motel I'd spent the night in, not if I wanted to stock up on supplies. Initially, I had planned to find a covered corner somewhere and grab a few hours of sleep in the open air, but that sounded less appealing as time went on.

"Nowhere yet," I answered after a moment's hesitation.

"Then you can come and stay with me." Ash dug out a small paper card and held it out to me. "I've booked an entire block of rooms at the old Omni. I'm sure there's an empty one somewhere for you. Wouldn't want you sleeping on the ground the night before we set out on a big hunt."

I frowned at the offered card. "I can't afford to pay you back, Ash."

He shrugged. "Then don't. Think of it as a repayment long overdue. You looked out for me a lot when we were kids. Now, I get to return the favor."

I took the card and carefully tucked it away. At least now I could be sure I wouldn't lose him again, though I was hesitant to leave his side. I still couldn't believe this wasn't real, and that if I looked away, he would disappear again.

Ash must've sensed my hesitation. He smiled. "Don't worry. I'm not going anywhere. At least, not until tomorrow morning. Promise I'll see you again later today? After you've run all your errands?"

I nodded emphatically. "Pinky swear it." I held out my pinky finger, and he hooked his on mine, just like we used to do when we were kids.

Chapter Five

People flowed through the streets, and into the beating heart of Atlanta's merchant district. There, the air smelled of iron smoke and freshly baked bread. Peach pies, still warm from the oven, sat on display, with yellow ribbons tied around them. Vendors stood with their small carts piled high with sweet Vidalia onions, blueberries, or potatoes as big as a fist. They called to passersby, urging them to sample their wares. Textile merchants smoothed their hands over simple cotton or silk brocade, the spinning wheels whirring in the shops behind them. An old man slept in his chair next to a cart of dusty Coca-Cola memorabilia, a worn ball cap pulled down over his face.

I sidestepped a pair of kids chasing each other through the narrow streets with swords made of sticks. A haggard-looking woman grabbed them by their collars and scolded them loudly. Nostalgia tugged at my heart, a memory of a time when I was one of those kids. Except

I hadn't had a mother to scold me and set me right. Maybe if I had, I'd have chosen a sensible career instead of monster hunting.

The mother licked her thumb and cleaned coal dust from her daughter's cheek. I turned away, hand on the hilt of my sword, and followed the clang of the blacksmith's hammer. There were several shops on Smithy's Row, and each of them had a fine collection of swords, armor plates, and other items to choose from. The largest shop in Atlanta, Falcon's Forge, had a small stage out front where the owner demonstrated his weapons on target dummies. The act attracted a large crowd, and probably lots of money. I passed through the crowd as they erupted in cheers and laughter, watching an actor stab a wooden troll. If only it were that simple to kill the real thing.

At the end of the row, around a corner and just off the main thoroughfare of Smithy's Row, I found a shop more to my liking. There were no demonstrations, no cheering crowds, no gold-plated suits of armor out front to attract customers. Just a three-legged stool propping up a bearded dwarf while he sat, arms crossed, frowning at his apprentice. The dwarven apprentice hammered the blade he'd been working on one last time and held it up, still red hot. Sweat darkened the scarred apprentice's collar as he scrutinized his piece. He grunted and plunged it into a waiting vat of oil.

The dwarven master grunted in response before eyeing me. “Canna help ye, *dytheirn*?” His words slurred together as one, but not because he was a drunk. His hands were too steady for that. I’d met enough dwarves to expect the fast-paced, slurry speech.

I untied the sword at my hip and placed it on the crowded wooden counter next to the old dwarf.

Without a word, he rose and drew the blade from its scabbard, eying it with dissecting eyes. “Aye, seen finer days, she has.”

“My last run-in was with a rock troll,” I explained.

He clicked his tongue and shook his head. “Canna go playin with the trolls an what expect a fine time of it. Look here, lass. You see these teeth? Like some gremlin’s done had it for breakfast, it is. She’s fixin’ to shatter with another strike.”

I nodded. “I’m in the market for a new one, but I don’t have time for something custom forged. I’m leaving town tomorrow morning to hunt big game.”

“Aye, nor the coin for it, one supposes?” He wrinkled his nose and gestured to barrel holding half a dozen swords. “As you fancy, *dytheirn*.” That was all the help the dwarf offered me before he returned to his apprentice’s side, mumbling instruction.

I approached the barrel of pre-made

swords and picked one out at random, testing its weight and balance. A custom sword was always better, of course, one crafted and fitted to my needs. However, I had never owned one. Either it had always been out of my price range, or I just didn't have the time to wait around for one to be crafted. If I did, though, I'd have hired a dwarf to make it for me. They were the finest craftsmen in the kingdoms, well-known for their attention to detail.

I unsheathed three different swords, peering down the blades at expert craftsmanship. They weren't fancy; they were sturdy and well made. Yet none of the ones I picked up and tried felt right in my hands.

Frustrated, I slid the fourth sword back into its sheathe and placed it carefully back into the barrel. I was about to pick out a fifth one to try when I spotted a sword leaning against the wall in the corner. Dust covered the hilt, and several generations of spiders had built their webs over it, meaning it had been there for a very long time.

I glanced over at the blacksmith, ready to ask about the forgotten sword, but he was deep in a demonstration with his apprentice, showing him the proper technique for hammering something out.

What can it hurt? The thing's clearly been sitting for ages. I dusted away the spider webs and lifted the sword. Something sparked in me the moment I held it. The weight was perfect, and the grip might as well have been made for my hand. The blade practically sang as I drew it from the plain leather scabbard. I expected to find a dull sword, worn down from disuse. Maybe even nothing more than a rusty blade. Instead, the blade was a beautiful blue steel unlike any I had ever seen before.

I ran my thumb along the blade and quickly jerked it away with a small line of red on my skin. Still sharp.

I took a few practice swings and knew. This was the sword I was looking for.

The dwarven blacksmith patted his apprentice on the back and nodded, letting him take over.

I held up the sword I had discovered in the corner. "How much for this one?"

The blacksmith's eyes widened. "That one… How is it you've got it?"

"I found it in the corner there." I gestured to the web coated corner. "Won't make you any money just sitting there, you know."

He stared at me as if he hadn't understood what I said. Maybe I'd spoken too fast. Maybe I'd insulted him somehow.

I looked at my reflection in the sword blade. It was perfect, but I wasn't willing to insult an entire subculture just to have it. I slid the sword back into its scabbard and held it out to the dwarf. "I'm sorry if I wasn't supposed to touch it."

He raised his hands and took a step back, as if the sword would bite him. "No, no. It's yours. Take it."

"I don't understand. I meant nothing by what I said." I took a step toward him, but he retreated further.

"Just take the bloody thing and get out!" His voice shook, and his eyes were wide with genuine terror.

I didn't know what to do. Dwarves could be a superstitious bunch, but I'd experienced nothing like that. I lowered the sword, took two steps back and pulled out my wallet, leaving a generous amount on the counter. The last thing I needed was to be accused of stealing.

Then, with one last worried look at the cowering dwarf, I ducked out of the shop.

"Wait," called another voice.

I turned back to find the apprentice had followed me out.

"That sword is cursed," he said. "At least, that's what my father believes."

I lifted the sword and frowned at it. It didn't seem cursed, but what did I know about magic swords? "What do you think?"

The apprentice shook his head. "I don't know about all that, but I can tell you that is no dwarf-forged steel you hold in your hands, *dytheirn*. It is elven. I've seen that same blue alloy worked by their smiths. Elves are a vicious bunch. I would be careful trusting an elvish blade with my life."

I pulled an inch of the sword free, just enough that I could see the strange blue steel shining in the afternoon sun. I didn't even know if elves were real. People talked about them, but I'd met no one who'd actually seen one. There were always rumors, though, of strange fletched arrows cutting through the dense trees, the swift shadows of unusually tall men always just out of sight. Remnants of ruins in the woods, and statues too strange to be human. Curses, elves, and magic swords... It all seemed pretty far-fetched to me, and I hunted monsters for a living.

I closed the sword and tied the blade to my hip. "I appreciate the warning, but I think I'll take my chances with the sword."

"As you fancy." The apprentice nodded and went back to his master.

I went about the rest of my shopping, acutely aware of the sword at my side. Maybe it was the dwarf's warning, or maybe his superstition that stayed in my mind. Either way, it was forgotten by the time I spent the last of my cash from the mail run, and I turned to my next big problem.

A long trek hunt like the one I was about to embark on meant making sure everything was in good working order. That meant I needed to repair a few leaks in my tent and inspect my mattress. Then I'd have to pack it all up nice and neat, small enough it would all fit on my back or in my duffel bag.

I found a quiet spot outside of town and set up the tent, going to work with my needle and thread in a quick patch job.

It was late afternoon, and I was almost finished when I heard the clip-clop of hooves slow in front of my tent. I ducked through the opening.

Commander Tolliver, the man who'd challenged Ash at the tavern for more information, slid down off his chestnut mare. He was tall and broad shouldered, the kind of person who would've been able to push boulders around like they were nothing. He struck me as the sort of person who might do that for fun.

He wasn't alone. He'd brought a dwarf with him. Unlike the two I had encountered at the blacksmith shop, this dwarf sported a bright red mohawk and faded blue tattoos on his face.

"Commander Tolliver," I said, standing and dusting some dirt from my knees. "To what do I owe the pleasure?"

Tolliver hesitated a step after climbing down from his horse. "You've got me at a disadvantage. You already know my name, but I don't know yours."

"Don't pretend you didn't look up everyone on Ash's list the minute you got back to your guild headquarters."

He glanced back at the dwarf for a moment. "I find it's important to know who I'm working with and for, Miss Dixon."

"Just Ember," I corrected.

He nodded. "I'm Ike."

I crossed my arms and planted my feet. "Why are you really out here, Ike?"

"My records say you're a poacher, that you don't do group jobs, especially not big ones like this."

I smirked. "Come to talk me out of it? Encourage me to give up my spot for my health?"

"Careful, *dytheirn*," warned the dwarf, his hand resting on the blade of a black dagger. "I can drop a fly at a hundred paces."

I was confused until I realized I had put my hand on the hilt of my sword. I forced my hand back to my side. "It's been less than two days since I was staring down a troll, so if you want to intimidate me into backing out of the hunt, you're going to have to work a lot harder."

"I'm not here to convince you to back out," Ike said. "I want to know everything you know about Ash Harrison."

"Let me guess. There's nothing in your files." I laughed. I couldn't help it. "Sorry, but I can't help you." I turned away.

He grabbed my wrist and turned me back to face him. I glared at him.

"People don't come from nowhere," he said. "They don't suddenly show up with enough money to finance a major hunt like this with half a dozen soldiers and Institute necromancers at their backs either."

"Don't like competition?" I yanked my arm away.

"I don't enjoy walking into a dragon's den blind," he growled.

"Well, you signed up for it, pal. Nobody made you. You can always change your mind and spend your days relaxing in your cushy little guild office, telling grunts what to do. Now, if you'll excuse me…" I gave him an exaggerated bow and started back to my tent.

"Why does he want the dragon's heart?"

I sighed and stopped. "I don't know. Ask him."

"I have. I've asked him about the hunt, about our route, about many specifics that should have been made public to those of us going on this hunt. Yet he will take no questions and give no answers. The only responses I get are platitudes. I am placing lives in this man's hands. I need some assurance that it's not reckless to do so."

I spun back around and eyed the commander. "Why did you sign up for this hunt if you're so worried about it? You have money, fame, influence. Anything you and your guild stand to gain from a hunt like this, you've already got it, so why bother?"

"My reasons are my own," he ground out.

"Talk about cryptic non-answers."

Ike stepped closer, close enough I could smell the horse stable on him. "I'm bound by oath not to tell you more, and I'm a man of my word. Know this. I have no choice but to be on this hunt. No matter what happens, I must see it through. It doesn't matter to me if I come back whole, but there are other people on this hunt. Innocent men and women who are just looking to make enough to take care of their families. They don't have a voice. I want to make sure this is a legitimate hunt and not a front for something else. There are rumors...

"Rumors? What rumors?" I glanced at the dwarf.

"There are whispers this is an Institute grab for power," explained the dwarf. "They say Ash is an Institute puppet, that he's being controlled by the necromancer. They say the Institute wants the dragon's heart for its experiments."

"So what if they do? What do you care?" I glanced up and down at the commander standing in front of me. "Wasn't it your ancestors who founded the Institute to begin with?"

His throat worked. "That was a long time ago. Generations of bad blood. The Iron Company has nothing to do with the Institute or its people. We oppose them on principle."

"Neither do I, and neither does Ash. He would never work for them."

"I hate to ask, but how can you be sure?"

asked the dwarf. "How well do you really know this Ash fellow?"

"We grew up together. I've known him since we were kids. The Ash I knew couldn't even squish a spider."

The commander nodded and stepped back to his horse, satisfied with my answer.

The dwarf, however, snorted and spat on the ground. "Be careful judging men by their behavior as boys, *dytheirn.* This world isn't kind when it makes boys into men." He nodded to his commander. "I will wait for you at the stream," he said before riding off.

"He seems nice." I gestured to the backside of the dwarf's horse.

"Foggy means well. It's difficult being a dwarf in a human world." He cleared his throat. "I feel like we might've gotten off on the wrong foot. I have no interest in making an enemy of you, Ember. Allies are far more useful where we're headed. I'd rather have a friendly sword at my back, if possible."

I nodded. "Funny way to forge an alliance, interrogating me out in the middle of nowhere and calling me a poacher."

Ike repositioned his horse to follow the dwarf, but didn't take off. "Very well. What do I need to do to convince you we should work together? Name your price."

"Trust is earned, Commander. Not bought." I crossed my arms. "You want to convince me you're not just some asshole trying to get under my skin, maybe get off your high horse and start treating me like your equal. We're both grunts in this hunt, you know."

He nodded, expression unusually grave. "I understand that."

"Do you? Because you almost seem like you want to run this hunt and not Ash."

"I don't want to run the hunt. I only want to make sure it's run well. This is dangerous prey we're after. The only chance we have of succeeding is if we can all work together. When people are keeping secrets... It makes that impossible. All I want is honesty, transparency. Honor. Those are the principles the Iron Company is built upon. Since I have to be involved, I want to make sure this will not stain my reputation, or needlessly cost lives. Is that so much to ask?"

"You sound like a control freak."

Ike chuckled. "Foggy would call me a worrier. Look, Ember, I'm only here because I'm trying to look out for everyone involved. I don't want animosity between us, or a feud with Ash. I respect what he's trying to do. I just wish I knew more about where we were going and with whom."

"Sometimes, the best laid plans go awry, Ike. You're just going to have to trust that Ash knows what he's doing."

Ike climbed up onto his horse. "As you said, trust is earned. I look forward to working with you, Ember."

"See you tomorrow, Ike."

He circled my makeshift camp once more before riding off after the dwarf. His horse kicked mud all over the side of my tent.

I sighed and hung my head. And here I thought I was almost done cleaning and packing.

Chapter Six

It was dark by the time I found myself downtown, standing in front of the ruined Omni hotel. The original building had been an oddly shaped rectangular creation of reflective glass, concrete and steel. That building had long ago fallen, the glass shattered by a concussive wave of magic that had blown through the area years ago. Like most of the rest of downtown, it had stood abandoned for years after, letting nature reclaim it in part. Flowering vines twisted around the metal carcass of the old hotel, their white petals shimmering in the moonlight.

In the shadow of magic's destruction, we built new wonders.

The new omni may have only been two stories tall, but it was even grander in its construction, forming a circle in front of where the old building had once stood. Wooden arched observation bridges wove across the top floors. Ivy and moonflowers clung to everything.

I entered the lobby and had to turn full

circle, taking in the building's beauty. Marble floors and an indoor garden, complete with a waterfall, made it feel like a temple to some forgotten god of beauty, comfort and commerce.

"Ember! You made it!"

I turned around just in time for Ash to embrace me.

He squeezed tight and stepped back. "I was worrying you'd changed your mind."

"And miss all this? I'd have to be crazy."

"It is beautiful, isn't it?" Ash put an arm around me and led me past the front desk. "Perhaps magic should've destroyed the original downtown years sooner. Can you imagine what an eyesore it would've been back in the day? Truly, a blessing in disguise."

"Well, except for all the people the magic wave killed."

"Obviously." Ash paused in front of the stairs. "Where are your things?"

"Everything's right here." I patted the duffel bag in my hand. "Everything I need to survive."

"You've always been a light packer." He gestured to the stairs, but we went up together.

"Well, it's not like I travel with a big convoy or anything," I said. "Honestly, if I can make it or find it along the way, I try not to pack it. These days, I do more with a knife, some cloth, and a bit of string than anything. Simple is better."

Ash smiled. "Old Jim would be proud."

I stopped on the landing in front of the second-floor door and stared at the crimson carpet beneath my shoes. "I still miss him, you know? He was a good man, and he deserved a better, easier end than he got. What happened out there..."

Ash put a hand on my trembling shoulder. "Jim didn't blame you. He made his choice, Ember. We all know that every hunt, every bounty, every day might be our last. We must live prepared for death. It's the life we chose."

"You didn't have to come back to it." I met his eyes.

He looked shocked. "Ember..."

"When you came back, you could've done anything. Honestly, you've surprised me, taking up this hunt. I was always the one who wanted it so badly. You were just... along for the ride. Why come back to being a bounty hunter? Why not just go live the good life with your second chance?"

Ash smiled a chiding smile and took my face in his hands. "What sort of life would I have without you? I came back so I could find you, Ember." He planted a gentle kiss on my forehead.

I blinked, warmth spreading over my nose and cheeks. My legs practically turned to jelly so that when he let go of me, I swayed slightly.

He laughed at me and winked. "Come on," he said, opening the door and going through. "I'll show you your room."

Come on, Ember. Get yourself together.

What's wrong with you? Did you forget about the deadly crystals growing in you? Stop this before it goes too far. If Ash finds out...

What would he do? Would he recoil and reject me? No, not the Ash I knew. The old Ash would have gently chastised me for not telling him, and then promptly moved on to plotting out a solution. But maybe everyone was right, and he wasn't the same person I'd known. Five years was such a long time to be gone. I knew I had changed in that time. Why wouldn't he?

We weren't kids anymore, and I couldn't afford to let my life fall apart just because Ash was back. His return wasn't some magic fix-all. I was still dying slowly, and I still needed the antigen to keep myself alive, which meant I needed this job, and many more. I'd be working until the day I died. Ash had other dreams to chase, and it wouldn't be fair for me to get in the way of them. If he found out, he'd give up on his dream to take care of me. I couldn't let that happen.

For one moment, our lives had intersected again, but it would be cruel for me to let him think it could be more than that. I'd have to set the record straight.

It could wait until we were on the road, though. I didn't want to give him the excuse he needed to leave me behind again.

Ash walked me down the hall to room two-twenty and handed me a key. "Open it." Light glimmered in his eyes. He looked like a kid about to show off his newest artwork.

I slid the key into the lock and carefully pushed open the door.

The room beyond was a far cry from the dingy motel room where I'd slept the night before. The air smelled like moonflowers, sweet and magical. On the immediate left was a small wardrobe while another door to the right opened into a bathroom with a large, round bathtub. An unbroken line of bottles waited on the counter, everything from shampoo to body wash to exotic lotions. Further in, I found the biggest bed I had ever seen with a mattress that might as well have been made of clouds as soft as it felt when I sat on it. There was a desk with paper and pens, a free-standing floor to ceiling mirror, and a basket of chocolates.

I sank into the bed and looked around, shaking my head. "Ash, this is…"

"It's everything we dreamed about as kids." He gestured around the room. "Imagine this all the time."

I sighed. "It's too much."

He chuckled. "Well, don't get used to it, of course. We won't be traveling in this sort of luxury. Although, the dragon may surprise us. I imagine he needs a rather enormous bed."

"No, Ash, I mean everything. You, this trip, this room… It's too much."

Ash's proud smile faded. "What do you mean?"

I shrugged. "I mean this morning, when I woke up, I still believed you were dead, that I'd never see you again. Now, here you are. Everything's changed. It's like five years didn't even happen, though I know they did. I'm not the person I was five years ago. Something about you has changed, too. You've got all this money, and the necromancers... And this hunt. It's like you're you, but not really. It's almost like you're someone else pretending to be you."

He crossed his arms and paced to stand with his back to the mirror. The room itself seemed to darken with his movement. "I was afraid of this. You don't think I'm the same person I was five years ago. You don't trust me, do you, Ember?"

I shook my head and put a hand on his arm. "I've spent the last five years reliving that day at the rift over and over, trying to find some way for you to have survived. I read everything, asked everyone. They all agreed that once a person goes into a rift, they don't come back. I look at you and I wonder how you can really be you. Are you?"

"Ember, please."

"I need to know, Ash. I have to."

The bed shifted as he came to sit down next to me, staring at the wall. "Okay, how can I prove it? You want me to tell you something only I would know about you? What about that time you took the blame for when I broke Old Jim's brand new earth magicite crystal? I must've cost him a month's wages, replacing the thing. You took the blame, though. And he made you clean the stables for a month."

I wrinkled my nose. "Worst month of my life."

Ash laughed. "Or what about that time with the sugar plum fairies in Mrs. Keller's basement? Only time I ever saw you afraid of anything."

I shuddered. "All that sugar in ninety degree heat and Atlanta humidity? I thought for sure we'd die down there."

"But we didn't." Ash put his hand on mine.

"Yeah, only because Old Jim came down with that fire mage and a hose. I wonder how long it took Mrs. Keller to get all that sugar off the walls."

"Months, probably."

We shared another laugh.

"Okay, I believe you," I said.

"Are we good now?"

I stared down at his hand over mine. "I don't know. It's just... I don't know if things can just go back to the way they were, like the last five years didn't happen, you know?"

"But I don't want to go back to the way things were," he said and pulled his hand away. "Why would you want that? We were children. We were stupid and weak and full of fear. You could fit our understanding of the world in a thimble. You and I spent our days working and our nights afraid of what the day would bring. The best we could've hoped for was to be accepted into a guild and work our way up, dying at the hands of some monster, just as our parents did. I don't want that. I never wanted that." Ash had worked his hands into trembling fists resting on his knees.

I put a hand over one of his fists and held it there until he relaxed.

Ash sighed and closed his eyes. "There was so much left to do when the rift swallowed me, Ember. So much left unsaid. My greatest fear used to be dying like my father did, alone and forgotten, his name stricken from the guild roster for his cowardice. Now..." He gripped my hand tightly and met my eyes, his expression pained. "The only thing I fear is facing what comes next without you."

I looked down at our intertwined fingers, the memory of him being swallowed by the rift flashing through my mind. In an instant, I relived the months of loss that followed, the mourning, the pain of knowing I had lost a part of myself too when that rift closed. A part I could never reclaim. It wasn't his fault, but I couldn't, wouldn't let him back into my life just to die on him. The pain I felt when I lost him would only be worse for him. I had to end this before it ever got started.

I pulled my hands away and swallowed the

beating heart that had made its way into my throat. "Sounds like somebody's been reading too many paperback romances again."

He laughed. "Guilty, though they've been more difficult to find of late."

I smiled and gave him a gentle shove. "Do you remember what Old Jim said when he found them hidden under your bed?"

Ash frowned. "Threatened to burn them, if I recall."

"You convinced him they were worth something, and he wound up trying to sell the lot of them. They offered him a dollar for his troubles."

He let out a small snort. "Is that all? I bought them back for twice that and had to endure his teasing." Ash sighed.

"He meant well," I said, patting his arm.

"I know. He just never understood. I never read them for the romance. It was the places, the people. I always dreamed of going to some faraway land, meeting kings and their courts. I wanted to be anywhere but there. And then I got my wish. I went somewhere no one had ever been." He hung his head. "I wish I could remember it more clearly, but all I get are flashes, like a nightmare in my waking hours."

I patted his arm. "For what it's worth, I'm glad you're back."

A tired smile lit up his face. "So am I."

We sat with each other awkwardly for a

moment, not knowing what to say. There were so many words left unsaid, so many things I had meant to tell him. I'd spent the last five years living with my regret, thinking all the time about how I should've said this or that to Ash. Yet now that he was there with me, all those trivial things had faded. Every moment felt too important to waste on words, knowing we might not get another.

His brow furrowed, and he looked down at my hand on his arm. "Ember, I know I've been gone a long time, but I hope… I hope you don't resent me for what happened."

"No," I said a little too quickly. "Never. You saved my life, Ash. I'll forever be grateful for that. Why would you think I'd resent you?"

Ash shrugged. "I don't know. It's just that… Well, I thought things would be different once I found you. Like they used to be."

"We're still friends, idiot," I said, punching his arm again.

He rubbed his arm. "Just friends?"

I sighed. "It's been five years, though. Maybe it felt like only a few months and a long sleep for you, but I've had to live every day. I've changed. The world's changed. Hell, you've changed. The Ash that went into the rift never would've been able to organize all this. We just need some time, is all. To get used to each other again."

"Maybe." He fixed his vision on the mirror in front of him, staring past his reflection at something else, something only Ash could see.

"I'm tired," I said, rising. "It's been a long day, and tomorrow is going to be even longer. I think it would be best if I turned in early. Don't you?"

Ash sat on the end of the bed for a moment, a shocked expression coloring the edges of his features. In a beat, he collected himself and rose. "Of course. Dawn comes early. I'll see myself out."

Part of me wanted to stop him, to grab him and apologize for being such a bitch and shutting him down. He deserved better. But that was why I couldn't let him fall for me, and I couldn't let myself fall for him. For anyone.

Ash paused at the door and turned back. "For what it's worth, I'm sorry, Ember. I never meant to leave you. I would change it if I could. I…"

Don't say it. Just leave, you idiot. Don't make this harder than it has to be.

He swallowed and lowered his head with a sigh. "I'm always here if you need me," Ash said, and left, closing the door gently behind him.

Chapter Seven

I tossed and turned all night in a bed far too big for one. The darkness was too dark, the pillows too cool and soft. I didn't belong in that room.

When exhaustion eventually overtook me, I dreamt I was running through a forest covered in an early morning fog. A twig snapped behind me and I spun, bringing up my sword just in time to catch the claws of a great horned beast as it swiped at me. The creature had to be at least nine feet tall, with antlers that stretched as wide as the boughs of a tree. His head was a stag's skull housing glowing magenta eyes. The skull grinned at me, and the creature retracted his claws before stretching to his full height. His body creaked as wood bark grew over him like armor. Black smoke raced along his outstretched arms. When the smoke cleared, the creature held a sword whose blade stood as tall as a man. The smoky blue steel practically glowed as he lifted the sword high.

I woke with a start, my knife pressed to a stranger's throat in the dark. The sudden gasp of the intruder was the only thing that kept me from slitting his throat. A bright white smile illuminated the dark, followed by Dex's voice. "Now that's a close shave."

I kicked him away from the side of the bed. He grunted as his back hit the wall.

I sat up quickly, holding the knife out in front of me. The first pink hues of dawn colored the sky outside the window. "What are you doing in my room, Dex? How did you even know where I was?"

"Ok, I can explain." He held out his hands in front of him.

"You'd better."

"I'm trying. I'm just trying to think of a way to phrase it so it doesn't sound so... bad."

I rose from the bed, the knife still out in front of me. "Just say it."

"Okay, I've been following you since Red's. Well, not me. I had things to do. But I've had someone tailing you ever since you left the tavern yesterday."

I gritted my teeth. "You'd better have a good explanation for why."

"If I tell you, will you promise not to stab me?"

I looked down at the knife in my hand and lowered it slowly. "For now."

Dex exhaled and lowered his hands. "Yesterday afternoon, some guy approached me. Expensive suit, cheap cologne, shiny badge. He flashed it too fast to read, but you know the type. I'm pretty sure he was DEMO. He's offering a lot of money for information about Ash."

DEMO—the Department for Ethical Magical Operations—was the one remnant of the old Coalition government that had held on. They regulated magic across the twelve kingdoms, and investigated magical crimes. At least, that's what they claimed. There had been rumors ever since the fall of the Coalition, though, that DEMO was involved in some shady business. People pointed the finger at DEMO for assassinations of public figures, accused them of orchestrating economic collapses, and making all kinds of mysterious things disappear or reappear without explanation. Kingdoms rose and fell in power based on their interactions with DEMO, and guilds were at their mercy if they wanted to continue operating.

Whenever they got involved, trouble followed.

"What does DEMO want with Ash?" I asked.

"No idea." Dex shook his head. "But what he was offering was enough that, when I saw how close you and Ash were, I figured you must know something."

I lifted a doubtful eyebrow. "So you thought it would be smart to sneak into my room while I was asleep?"

"I couldn't very well go through your things while you were awake now, could I?"

I sighed and lowered the knife. Dex wouldn't be any trouble, not now that I had him cornered. "Only an idiot would admit to searching through my stuff."

"Really? I find honesty is the best policy. People threaten me less."

I grabbed him by the collar and pulled him away from the window, dragging him toward the door. "What were you hoping to find, anyway?"

"Not really sure. The DEMO agent didn't specify. But I figured if anyone knew anything, it'd be you. I mean, I could've broken into his room, I guess, but he has guards posted. Armed guards. Did I mention I don't like the idea of being stabbed?"

I let him go near the door. "Did it ever occur to you that if you wanted to get to know him, you should just talk to him?"

He shrugged and reached up to adjust his stupid cowboy hat. "No offense, but he didn't exactly strike me as a guy who'd willingly spill his guts. Besides, what was I supposed to say? Hi, I'm Dex. Glad to meet you. DEMO is paying me to get information about you. What's your favorite color?"

I sighed again and slid past him to open the door. One of Ash's people was waiting outside, obviously standing guard. He hadn't told me he was putting a guard at my door, and the realization that he had just made me angrier. I slammed the door shut on the bleary-eyed guard before ever shoving Dex out.

Then I turned and put my back to the door, giving Dex a questioning look. "If there's a guard outside, then how did you get inside?"

He rolled his eyes. "Please. You're only two stories up. I could scale that wall in my sleep. Not that I would. Not that I should've. I mean, I'm clearly in the wrong here, but you can't really blame me for Ash's crap security. Although, I guess it's not his job to secure the hotel, is it? Or maybe it is? You know what? I'm going to stop talking now because the look you're giving me says it'd be good for my health."

I marched past him to the window, which was secured and locked. Had I checked the locks before I went to bed? Probably not. I'd been so distracted dealing with Ash and worrying about the hunt that it hadn't even crossed my mind.

Just the same, I opened the window and peered down a sheer stone wall where all the vines had been cleared away. If Dex had scaled that wall, climbed in through the window, and searched my room all without making a sound, he had some serious skill. I wasn't a light sleeper.

"So, I heard you spooked Jesker yesterday. The dwarf blacksmith? What did you say to Jesker that left him so spooked?" Dex asked, shifting closer.

I shrugged. "Nothing, really. And it's none of your business, either."

"See, this is why nobody just asks people stuff. You could be polite, you know."

I grabbed Dex and pushed him to the window. "You can go out like you came in. And if I see you before we get on the road, I'm going to knock out your front teeth. Understand?"

He leaned over the windowsill, looking down with a cringe. "If you insist." He gripped the sides of the window and thrust his body through it with a spin.

I immediately leaned out the window, expecting to find him cradling a broken arm or something on the concrete below. Instead, he landed with all the grace of a professional acrobat, rose, saluted me, and ran off.

"What a character." I shook my head and made sure I locked the window behind him.

Downstairs, I grabbed a quick slice of buttered toast and rushed out to meet the rest of the hunting party. Everyone was already there, tightening saddle straps or taking inventory. Horses stamped impatient hooves against the pavement. Three wagons full of provisions and their driving teams stood in a line, waiting for the signal to go.

Ash rode up on the back of a beautiful white stallion, pulling along a smoky gray mare with black legs and a black muzzle. He smiled, dismounted, and walked the mare up to me, handing me the reins. "I noticed you didn't ride in on a horse last night. Ember, meet Scorch."

"She's beautiful." I patted the horse on the shoulder.

Scorch shook her head.

I frowned. "But Ash, I can't accept it. I know how much a horse costs."

"It's less a gift and more an investment," Ash replied. "Otherwise, you'd have to ride with the wagons, and I'd much rather have you at the front with me where your skills can do some good." He smiled, nodded, and returned to his horse.

"Well, I suppose I should know better than to look a gift horse in the mouth," I said to Scorch. "You know, I never really understood that saying."

Scorch shook her head as if to say, "Me neither."

Eyes burned on the back of my neck. I turned and found the necromancer woman from the day before staring me down. She held her vampires on leashes made of chain and sturdy, studded leather. She narrowed her eyes at me and then stormed in my direction.

Scorch shifted, uneasy with the vampires' approach. I moved to place myself between the horse and the vampires. "Hi, I'm Ember Dixon."

She halted three paces away, making no move to greet me. "I know who you are, Poacher."

"I'm on this hunt just like everyone else."

"But you're not, are you? Like everyone else?" She gestured to Scorch. "First the hug at the tavern, then the room, and now a horse? He's quite taken with you, isn't he?"

"It's not like that. We know each other from before. Besides, it's not like I asked for any of this. I just want to help."

She took two steps forward, dragging her vampires along with her. I had to put a hand on Scorch to steady her.

"Let's get one thing straight, Poacher," said the necromancer. "Ash doesn't belong to you. His job is to lead this hunt and my job is to ensure that he's effective at his. If you so much as bat your pretty little eyelashes at him and distract him..." She smirked and leaned back. "Well, let's just say a lot of bad things can happen to an unprepared poacher out here. Wander off at night and they might never find the body."

I smiled and laughed because what else could I do? "Are you jealous or something? Because, Honey, you don't need to threaten me."

She snorted. "Jealous? Of you? Please. I have more power in my finger than you do in your entire body."

"Look, Ash is a big boy, and he can do what he wants with whomever he wants. Not that I'm that person. Like I said. I'm just here to hunt."

She wrapped the vampire chains once around her fists. "That had better be true. Just know that I don't trust you. I'm watching you,

Poacher. Don't screw up." She turned and walked away, pulling her vampires behind her.

"I see you've met Anastazia," Ash said from behind me.

"Yeah, she's a real charmer." I adjusted Scorch's saddle and started packing my gear into saddle bags.

"Zia means well," Ash said with a shrug.

I stopped packing and turned to Ash. "Why even have an Institute necromancer and her vampires along? How are they going to help take down an elder dragon?"

"Zia is more than just some institute necromancer to me, Ember. She was there when I woke up and she hasn't left my side ever since. She's part of the Institute, yes, but I also consider her a friend and protector. I wouldn't have found you without her help. As for how she and her vampires will help... Well, they can go places that would be too dangerous for us. Vampires make excellent scouts."

"Until that mind-control circlet falls off or breaks," I mumbled. "Then Zia loses control, and the vampires slaughter us all."

Ash smirked. "Have a little faith in other people, Ember. Zia is a professional, one of the best. She knows what she's doing. Let her do her job, and you do yours. We'll all get along better that way."

"As long as she and her vampire dogs stay the hell away from me." I hooked a foot in the stirrup and pulled myself up onto Scorch's back.

On horseback, I scanned the crowd of people behind me and spotted Ike on his chestnut mare alongside Foggy, his mohawked dwarf friend. On the far side of the courtyard, as far away as possible, Dex leaned lazily in the saddle of a spotted white Appaloosa. He grinned and winked at me when he saw me looking at him.

I made sure both my sword and knife were within reach.

Ash and his horse trotted up and down the main line, conversing with the wagon drivers and a few others before he rode quickly back to the front. "Hunters!" His voice rang clear and strong through the courtyard. "First, I want to thank everyone here. We have a long and arduous journey ahead of us. I know it's difficult to ask you to leave your homes, your families, your guilds for such an extended hunt. I promise you the spoils will be well worth it. When you next set foot in the Kingdom of Atlanta, it will be with more than extra cash. When we slay this beast, you will be heroes. They'll write songs about this hunt and tell the tale in every corner of every kingdom. You will return as legends."

Zia thrust her fist into the air and shouted, "For fame and glory!"

The sound of dozens of swords being drawn and thrust into the air at the same time rang through the courtyard as everyone echoed her words.

I kept my blades where they belonged, tucked neatly inside their sheathes. The pep talks were all for show. I didn't need the theatrics to get me pumped up. Besides, all the excitement would wear off by mid-day when we picked through dense forest in single file, the heat and humidity bearing down on us.

"We ride for Black Mountain!" Ash turned his horse and spurred it forward, leading the charge out of the courtyard.

Zia followed, but not before shooting a smirk in my direction.

Whips snapped. Wagon drivers whistled and wooden wagon wheels groaned with effort. Hooves thundered out of the courtyard and into the streets of Atlanta, carrying hunters and their supplies, necromancers, mages, and would-be heroes.

I rode with them, wondering how many we'd lose on the way there. Hunger, thirst, difficult terrain, raids by bandits, monsters, sickness... Many things could dwindle a hunting party that size down to just a few good men by the time we reached our destination. No wonder Ash had enlisted so many.

A vision of the creature from my nightmare flashed through my mind. It had felt so real. I swore I could feel the thing's breath on my face as it charged.

I shook my head and closed my fist around Scorch's reins as we crested a small hill overlooking the city gates. For five miles beyond the city, there was nothing. All the trees had been cleared so that the city watch could keep the place free of monsters. Beyond that waited a no-man's-land of mountains, monsters, and magic. Hungry rifts grew unchecked, waiting to swallow any of us foolish enough to wander too close. Trolls, dragons, ogres, and even the undead hid in those trees, standing between us and our prey.

Focus on what's real, Ember. There are plenty of nightmares waiting for you out there. No need to invent your own. I nudged Scorch to move faster and joined Ash at the front of the procession.

Ahead, the city gates opened with a groan that shook the ground.

Ash glanced over and smiled. "Ready?"

I smiled back. "Last one through's a rotten troll egg," I said and urged Scorch even faster.

Chapter Eight

The first day's ride was always the easiest. People were still eager, full of excitement. The road and rough terrain hadn't yet worn them down, partially because we didn't hit any rough terrain for several hours.

After passing through the initial clearing around Atlanta, we moved into a forest. The trees were sparse at first, but became thicker the further in we went. Eventually, the trees were so plentiful and their trunks so thick, the only way to pass was in single file. Branches full of whispering leaves blocked the sunlight from striking the forest floor. In the canopy above, birds sang, and other small mammals moved from branch to branch, watching us with curious eyes.

I peered up at the intertwined branches and wondered at the age of the oldest trees. The area had been home to trees and forests long before the Cataclysm—the appearance of the first rifts. Littered among the trees, however, were the ruins of suburban life, buried for generations.

When the rifts opened, and the walls went up, people abandoned the unprotected suburbs in droves. Nature reclaimed the land, driven in part by the strange magic that invaded the world. After the Cataclysm plants grew faster, larger, and stranger.

Ivy and kudzu dripped off the frame of a three-story plantation-style home off to our right. Doves had made a nest in the uppermost window. Little white flowers bloomed in a coil around an old mailbox, the address too rusted to read. Broken chain-link fences became latticework for creeping vines, abandoned playgrounds gardens for exotic weeds. Banks and schools, libraries and shops, trailers and mansions... Nature didn't care. Given time, vines and moss tore it all down. Plants were patient creatures.

I looked at the world around me and wondered if our ancestors believed they'd tamed the land they lived on. Could they have imagined how easily nature would reclaim it?

The gobble of a pair of wild turkeys drew my attention to the other side of the procession. I had never loved turkeys for their looks, but this pair was particularly ugly. They were larger than a normal turkey, with patchy feathers and sharp teeth. When they opened their wings to warn us away, it revealed sharp barbs on their wings.

We rode by them, paying them no mind. Nature hadn't changed those turkeys as much as the magic had. I wasn't educated enough to understand the why and how of magic's effects on indigenous species. As long as it wasn't bothering us, though, I was content to ignore it. We'd run into worse along the way.

By midday, the hunting party had stretched into a long, single file line with several gaps. There were clear divides between the group traveling with Ash, Ike's people, and those with Dex. Those divides only widened as the day went on and stayed visible even when we stopped to make camp for the night. Dex's people stayed with him, Ike's with him, and Ash's people around him.

Rather than choose a group to stick with, I set up my camp at the edge of the small clearing where I could see everyone coming and going. I had just finished rolling out my bed roll and arranging things inside my tent when I heard two men arguing. I climbed out of the tent and stood up, bracing my back with both hands.

Well, surprise, surprise, I thought as I watched Kenny—Dex's man—try to stare down Foggy, Ike's dwarf friend.

"Now, look here, ya brick-headed loon," spat Foggy, pointing to the ground. "I put my lines down first. It's clearly marked. You've got to leave a bloody path!"

"I was here first!" Kenny shouted. "You're taking up more than your fair share of space."

"My fair share?" Foggy puffed out his chest and crossed his arms. "I'm usin' the same space as everyone else."

"Yeah, but you're half the size of everyone else, so you only get half the space." Kenny bent over to yank one of Foggy's tent stakes out of the ground.

Foggy retaliated by stepping on Kenny's fingers, pinning his hand to the dirt. "Ya best rethink putting your dirty fingers on my gear if'n you want to see sunrise, *dytheirn*."

Kenny gritted his teeth and snarled up at the dwarf, his free hand sliding toward the knife hidden in his boot.

I rushed to intervene, but they were still far away. If Kenny drew his knife, I'd never make it before he stabbed the dwarf. Ike and Dex also stopped what they were doing and moved toward the altercation. It was Ash who got there first, arriving with his hand already resting on the hilt of his sword.

Ash eyed Kenny and then Foggy. "What's the problem here, gentlemen?"

"No problem," said Foggy, withdrawing his boot. "Just a polite conversation with a human about the best way to put down tent lines. Wouldn't want any of our people tripping over them in the dark."

"Is that so?" Ash directed his question to Kenny.

Kenny grinned widely and wiped dirt from his hand onto his shirt. "Just a friendly conversation."

Ash didn't seem convinced. His eyes darted back and forth between the two before turning around to address Dex and Ike, who'd crept up closer. "I want to make something clear. I realize there's some rivalry in the ranks that pre-dates my arrival, but in the interests of the entire group, you must put that aside. Out here, we are all relying on each other to survive. Division at any level can grow into something fatal."

"Don't preach to us like we've never been out here before." Dex crossed his arms and leaned back.

"We know what's at stake," Ike agreed.

Ash took two quick steps forward, moving to stand toe to toe with Ike. "Do you?" He spoke in a voice near a whisper, but there was a certain darkness to the way he said it, as if he knew something the rest of us didn't.

I shivered and moved out of the deep shadow, into a pool of evening light coming through the tree canopy.

Ike said nothing, choosing instead to stare Ash down.

"Control your men," Ash eventually said, stepping back. "Or send them home. We're still less than a day's ride from Atlanta." He stormed away, leaving Ike stewing.

Kenny rubbed the back of his head. "Sorry, boss."

Dex shook his head. "Just move your damn tent lines, you idiot. And next time you've got a problem with someone, bring it to me, okay?"

Foggy grunted. "That's right. Run to your master."

Kenny moved as if to charge the dwarf, but Dex held him back with a hand on his chest.

"That's what I thought." Foggy spat on the ground between them. "Forget about moving your tent lines, *dytheirn*. I'd rather be upwind of ye, anyway." He began collecting his tent spikes.

"Feel free to step in anytime," Dex gestured to Ike.

"Gladly." Ike pulled up a tent spike and quickly helped Foggy move his tent closer to the Iron Company side of the camp.

I sighed and trudged back to my tent. If this was how things were going to go, it was going to be a long march to Black Mountain.

For the rest of the evening, I kept to myself, arranging my things and setting up a self-sustaining camp with my own little cook fire. Dex and his Marauders did the same while Ike and his people put up a whole kitchen tent at the edge of camp. Ash and his people built a large fire and put a big iron pot over it. They left the path clear for anyone who dared come to investigate, an open invitation that no one took them up on. We all sat in our respective camps, separated by pathways that wound between tent poles.

It was full dark when the music started.

I looked up from my crackling fire, a renewed lance of worry in my heart. The music was clearly coming from the Marauder's side of the camp. It was late enough that someone from the Iron Company side was sure to object to it interrupting their sleep. I stood and made my way over, expecting a fight.

Kenny had propped himself up against a tree, strumming an old guitar and humming a slow tune.

"Do you really think that's a good idea?" I asked.

He shrugged. "And why not? Who doesn't like a little after dinner music?"

I opened my mouth to respond, but before I could, Foggy stomped to a stop beside me.

"What in the bloody kingdoms is that awful tune?" Foggy ground out.

Kenny kept strumming. "What? They don't have music where you come from, dwarf?"

"Aye, they do, but whatever you're playin' sounds like a dying cat."

"You want something more lively, is that it?" Kenny finally stopped playing long enough to shift his posture and his hold on the instrument. "I don't take requests."

The tension in the air was palatable as Ike approached the camp and Dex ducked out of his tent, both men frozen as they waited to see what Kenny and Foggy would do next. Foggy glanced at Ike behind him, at me, and then lifted the leather sack he'd brought with him. He ripped the bag away to reveal another stringed instrument, this one longer and bearing only two strings. From the back of the instrument's long neck, he lifted a bow that he worked gently back and forth over the strings.

The sound the instrument made was unlike anything I had ever heard, deep and layered. He played a few quick notes before Kenny started tapping his foot, nodded, and echoed the notes when Foggy paused, adding a few of his own. Foggy echoed the added notes. Back and forth they went, speeding up with every trade of notes until they were both playing at the same time. They fell into a harmony of impromptu music, as if they had somehow known the song before either of them started playing. When their tune ended, the crowd that had gathered erupted into applause.

Foggy grinned, unhooked a flask from his side and tossed it to Kenny. "You can play almost as well as you can run your mouth, *dytheirn*."

"Thanks. You're not half bad yourself." Kenny unscrewed the lid, took a drink, and immediately coughed, shooting the dwarven drink out of his nose.

Foggy let out a roar of laughter and slapped his knee. "Dwarven ale. Burns just as much coming up as it does going down."

"No kidding." Kenny wheezed and handed the flask back.

Still laughing, Foggy raised the flask and declared loudly, "A toast!"

"To what?" Kenny asked.

"Drink! What else?" The dwarf upended the flask and emptied it into his mouth, gargling it loudly before swallowing.

The crowd cheered and more bottles appeared, passed from person to person without regard for which camp he was with. Foggy and Kenny turned back to playing, working their way through several familiar tavern tunes about drinking, barflies, and the like. Whatever barriers there had been before disappeared, wiped away by drink and song.

A bottle came to me, and I passed it on without partaking, but only because I wasn't sure what was in it. As I handed it to the next person, I felt eyes burning on the back of my neck. I turned around and found Zia glaring at me from Ash's camp. Ash stood near her, but closer to the crowd, the shadow of a smile on his face. Zia, however, wore a scowl.

I took a step toward them, but Zia broke and stomped back to her tent. Guess she didn't feel like talking.

"It looks like they finally found some common ground," I said to Ash when I was next to him.

His dark eyes moved over the crowd. "As long as they don't get so drunk they slow us down. I made sure both Ike and Dex understood they were to work out a watch and patrol schedule, one with sober patrols."

I nodded. Last thing we needed was for some monster to wander into our camp while everyone was passed out drunk or hungover. "Better here than a few days down the road, though, right?"

Ash shrugged. "I suppose it's relatively safe here, but Zia is about to do some scouting for me, just in case."

"You mean Zia's vampires." I hugged myself. "She's letting them off their leashes."

"There's no reason to fear them, Ember. Zia has complete control."

"If you say so." I rubbed my arms to warm myself just the same. The idea of vampires running freely through the surrounding forest was hardly comforting. I decided it would be best to change the subject. "Hey, Ash. Can I ask you something about this hunt?"

"Anything," he said, turning to face me.

"Why do you want this dragon's heart?"

The emotion drained from his face, turning his expression to stone. Ash pressed his lips together and turned to watch the revelry unfolding in the camp beyond. "Certain organs have magical properties, uses in spells and potions. It's not strictly illegal to part out dragons, or any other monster, but it is frowned upon, which is why I couldn't put this through the guilds."

"Yes, but what sort of potion do you need a dragon's heart for? Must be something rare and powerful."

"I didn't realize you were an expert in potions," he said, turning to me.

I bit my tongue. He was right. Most people didn't know the first thing about potions and tinctures. I'd only had to learn what I knew out of necessity. Unscrupulous alchemists sometimes tried to cheat me out of a proper dose of antigen. I needed to know what I was buying was pure, and that meant learning a certain amount about the product.

I couldn't reveal all of that to Ash, though. I couldn't risk telling him the truth. He wouldn't understand.

I shrugged. "You learn a thing or two when you do this on your own."

"I know it will fetch a good price, enough to help me finance what we talked about before."

I lifted an eyebrow. "Founding your own kingdom? You were serious?"

"Why not? Even if I fail, it's better to have tried, isn't it? That's what Old Jim used to say."

"True." I could almost hear him saying it from beyond the grave. "I suppose Ike wouldn't have understood that, would he?"

Ash snorted. "He's the least likely to understand any of my motivations. Don't forget, Ember. It was Ike's grandfather that erased my dad's name from the registry, leaving me with nothing."

He had a good point there. Usually, if someone in a guild died on a mission, their families were taken care of financially. There were whole pools of cash inside guilds set aside to look after the orphaned children of their members, or their widows. It was one of the core benefits of belonging to a guild. You could go off and hunt dangerous monsters and never have to worry that your family wouldn't be taken care of if something happened to you.

Unless you screwed up a job so badly, they kicked you out posthumously. Then the family got nothing.

I didn't know the specifics of what Ash's father had done to earn the boot from the Iron Company, and I didn't want to upset him by asking. When we were younger, Ash had insisted that the whole thing was a cover up and they had made his dad take the fall for someone higher in the guild. His father had become a scapegoat, and Ash wound up on the street because of it. The story was a painful one for Ash, so I never brought it up.

"Yeah, but that was his grandfather," I pointed out. "Ike isn't much older than us. He would've been a kid when that happened. You can't blame him for something his grandfather did."

"That's the only reason he's on this hunt, Ember. That and you know what they say about keeping your enemies close."

I gave Ash a gentle punch in the arm. "Ike's not your enemy. He's just a guy."

"We'll see about all that." Ash rubbed his arm, frowning. He turned and took a step back toward his tent.

I followed. "Where are you going?"

"To Zia's tent."

"Oh really? I turn you down and you've already got someone else lined up. That was fast."

He rolled his eyes. "It's not like that. Don't pretend to be jealous, Ember. It doesn't look good on you. No, someone has to watch her body while she's riding the vampires and looking through their eyes. When she works her magic, it essentially leaves her vulnerable. I agreed to watch over her. You're welcome to join me." He paused on his trek back to the tents.

I cast a longing glance back at the party going on in the rest of camp. Drinking, singing, and dancing sounded a lot more interesting than watching a necromancer space out, but I wanted to spend time with Ash. We still needed to catch up, make up for lost time. Besides, I didn't trust Zia and her vampires any more than Ash trusted Ike. Maybe it was time for me to follow my advice and try to get to know her before making judgements.

"Come," Ash urged. "I'm sure Zia won't mind."

"If you say so," I muttered and followed him to the smallest of the two tents at the far end of camp.

Ash opened the flap of a black tent bearing the same crimson dragon symbol Zia wore as a pin. I ducked into a well-lit tent with several glowing light crystals placed on the roof. Thick chains held a pair of vampires to the center pole. Zia knelt in front of them, rubbing sunscreen on their cheeks.

"You're late. How am I supposed to do my job if you can't even be bothered to stay on schedule?" Zia's smile faded when she turned around and found me standing there instead of Ash. Her shoulders slumped. "You're not Ash. What do you want?"

"I invited her to come and observe," Ash said after ducking in the entrance.

"Well, I don't know why. I'm scouting, not putting on a show." She brought out another light crystal, cracked it, shook it, and placed it on the ground behind the vampires. Her movements were sharp and jerky.

"I've never seen a necromancer work," I offered. "Not up close, anyway."

"There's a good reason for that. The work requires intense concentration. One distraction and I might miss something important." She dragged an elaborate chair to the center space behind the pole, right behind the light crystal.

"You mean you'll lose control of the vampires?"

She stopped moving the chair long enough to glare at me. "Please. I am a captain in the Order of the Crimson Dragon. Don't insult me."

"I'm sorry," I said, looking to Ash. "I don't know what that means."

He opened his mouth to answer, but she spoke for him. "It means I'm very good at what I do. I don't lose control of my vampires."

While she grunted, fighting to get the chair in the perfect position, Ash leaned in and explained, "The Order is a very exclusive part of the Institute, a sort of elite group within the Institute. Their training focuses on covert operations with a militaristic background. Not only are her vampires powerful weapons, but Zia herself is an expertly trained combatant."

"I'm fully bonded to my vampires." She stood, dusting off her hands before gesturing to the creatures before her. "Observe."

Zia raised two fingers on her right hand and both vampires mimicked the same expression.

"So, they're like puppets," I said.

"Puppets don't feel," Zia corrected. "They don't eat, or sleep, or shit. Nobody has to clean up after their puppets or rub sunscreen on them to keep them from getting burned by residual sun rays bouncing off the moon. My vampires are both living creatures and an extension of my will."

I shrugged. "You sound very proud of them."

She gave a small, disdainful grunt. "People like you will never appreciate the power of a vampire. Not until you need one."

"That's enough, Zia. Ember doesn't mean you any harm. She's here to learn, just as I had to."

"Learn, you say?" A smirk crossed Zia's painted lips as she sank into her chair, treating it like a throne. "Then let's begin your first lesson. Unchain the vampires, if you would?"

"Unchain them?" I glanced at Ash and then back to Zia. "But they're your vampires. Shouldn't you do it?"

Zia sat up straighter in her chair. "The first and most important lesson for co-existing with vampires is not to fear them. You must conquer your fear, or it will conquer you. There are no other outcomes in this battle. Unchain the vampires, Ember."

Ash nodded.

I trusted him, didn't I? He wouldn't encourage me to do something that would cost me my life. Even being in the same tent as a vampire was dangerous, though. Their condition was highly contagious, and one hundred percent fatal. One drop of infected blood or saliva and I would become one of the undead.

I swallowed and approached the first vampire. A low, gurgling sound escaped the creature's throat as it watched me with dead, cloudy eyes. Why were they white like a dead man's eyes? I could've sworn they were blood red when I saw them in the tavern. Maybe I'd been imagining things.

My hand shook as I reached for the clasp at the vampire's collar.

Zia's smirk widened.

A tiny drop of red appeared in the center of the vampire's dead white eyes, spreading like blood in water until the vampire's eyes were pure crimson.

I hurried to unhook the vampire and stumbled back a step.

The creature stood up on its emaciated legs, sniffed the air, and grinned at me. It opened its mouth "See?" It said with a distorted version of Zia's voice without ever moving its lips. "That wasn't so hard, was it? Now, free the other."

I looked to Zia, seated in her chair. A silver sheen had passed over her eyes. Though I was sure it was her who had been speaking, she didn't move her mouth.

The first vampire watched closely as I freed the other. Then, without a word, the vampires scurried to the tent door and out into the night.

I shuddered and hugged myself tight, moving closer to Ash just to feel the warmth of something living. "Now what?"

Ash put an arm around me. "Now, we wait. If Zia sees anything through her vampires' eyes, she'll let us know."

I watched the silver eyed necromancer work, her fingers curling into the wooden arm rests of her seat. "What happens to her if something happens to her vampires? Does she feel it? Can she hear and see us when she's in their heads?"

"No," Ash said, shaking his head. "Her body may be here, but the rest of her is out there, with them. That's why I agreed to watch over her. If something happens, she feels it as if it were happening to her. And if a vampire dies while she's inside its head... They call it whiplash. Sometimes, it's fatal. Sometimes, their brains break and they never recover. Comas, aneurysms, stroke... All are possible. It's why they're trained to sever that connection in an instant if needed. But doing so a moment sooner could leave the vampire free, and that's equally dangerous."

I suddenly felt a pang of sorrow. "It must be scary, climbing into a monster's head and leaving your own body behind."

"It requires trust in whomever you choose to be your guard. We've become very close, Zia and I, since my return. I think she's worried you'll distract me, keep me from fulfilling my promise to protect her."

I think it's more than that, I thought, watching her. Zia wouldn't have tried so hard to warn me off if that was all there was to it. She wanted Ash in the same way he wanted to be with me, and he was too blind to see it.

I smiled. "She obviously doesn't know you as well as she thinks. The Ash I know would never break a promise. You'll keep her safe, no matter what. She should trust you more." I stepped away from Ash, moving to the door.

"Where are you going? I thought you wanted to see how it worked?"

"I think I've seen enough for one night. You've got this handled. We'll catch up in the morning."

He nodded. "Okay. Goodnight, Ember."

"Goodnight, Ash." I walked out of the tent, still hugging myself, a new pain growing in my chest next to my heart. Ash needed to move on, but he would not do that as long as I was hanging around. This job had to be the only one we did together, for both of our sakes.

I felt eyes on me from above and glanced up into the boughs of a nearby tree. Blood-red eyes blinked back. Zia, through her vampire, watched me for a long moment before the vampire turned and leapt deeper into the forest.

Chapter Nine

Fog settled on our small camp and stayed until morning. Even as we packed up and re-formed our convoy, it clung to the low-lying and darker areas. The sun shone through the treetops and made the shadows dance in the fog.

Among the men, there were clear signs a few had taken the drinking and revelry too far. Slow, sloppy movements, the wincing at the sound of metal striking metal or loud voices... The hangovers would wear off by mid-day, but Ash wasn't pleased. He rode through camp on his horse, eying everyone with Zia at his side. The wheels in his head turned, making lists, noting names, faces, collecting information.

When they came to me, he spoke a few quiet words to Zia before she nodded and moved on without him.

"Does she ever sleep?" I asked, adjusting the strap on one of my saddlebags.

Ash closed the distance. "When she can, like the rest of us. Not all of us can afford to get drunk and pass out on the first night of a hunt."

"Cut them some slack, Ash. At least no one's fighting anymore."

"United by their shared mistakes." He sighed and shook his head. "It's comforting, at least, to know most of the drink is gone and there won't be any repeats."

"There are worse things than a little drinking and singing, Ash." I finished with the saddle, patted Scorch down, and climbed up into the saddle. "You know, you've been almost all work and no play since you showed back up. Makes me wonder if all that time away didn't turn you into someone serious."

Ash's frown faded gradually as we rode for the front of the line. "Maybe you're right. It's just that out here, even the smallest mistake can be costly. Drink makes men slow, clumsy, even a day after."

"We won't be running into the dragon soon."

"True, but that doesn't mean we're safe out here." He scanned the tree line as if searching for threats.

"Did Zia find anything on her scouting trip last night?"

"Signs of a raiding party about two miles out, moving parallel to our path," Ash said, his tone grave. "I don't think we're being followed. We're using an old trader's route, but one that hasn't been used in several years."

I shook my head. "Raiding parties wouldn't take on a convoy of this size, not if they knew what was good for them. We've got twenty armed fighters and a handful of support folk, wagons full of weapons and supplies that'd be easier to get elsewhere. If they have scouts like most raiders, they've already seen us moving through the trees and decided on easier prey. Did she actually see the raiders?"

Ash sighed. "No, just the remains of a campfire. They were smart enough to mask their scent with crushed mint leaves. She tried to count the tracks, but they'd done a good job sweeping those clean too."

"They're not stupid, then. All the more reason for them to avoid our convoy."

"Desperation makes people take foolish risks." Ash fixed his gaze forward, focusing on something in the distance. He was quiet until we neared the front of the line. "I spoke with Dex and Ike, encouraging them to move their hung-over people toward the middle of the convoy, around the wagons. At least then we won't have to worry about stragglers getting lost. Ike is moving to the rear today to monitor things there. I'd like you at the front with me."

"You sure that's where you need me?" I glanced over at Zia.

She sat silently in her saddle, watching me with her hawk eyes.

"Need? Maybe not. I'm being selfish. Indulge me a little?" His serious expression finally broke, and Ash finally cracked a smile.

I smiled back. "If you insist."

We joined Zia at the front. Ash gave a whistle and a shout, ordering everyone to form up into a line. After a brief wait, we set off. Riders moved two abreast, which put Zia behind Ash and me. I thought she'd protest, especially after our confrontation the day before, but she said nothing. When I looked back, she rode alone with a small gap between her and the next pair of riders. Guess I wasn't the only one who got creepy vibes from the necromancer.

"Where do you keep your vampires during the day, Zia?" I called back to her.

"They're in the wagon, sleeping," she replied. "Vampires and sunlight don't get along."

"Is it true they'll catch fire in the sun?"

She laughed. "Absolutely not. No, the vampire pathogen causes them to lose most of the melanin in their bodies, leaving them susceptible to UV rays. They don't see well in bright light and get easily sunburnt. Exposed to enough sunlight, they'll develop skin cancer and have to be put down. Considering the expense of collaring and caring for a vampire, that's something most of us would rather avoid."

"They're really quite harmless," Ash assured me. "They even snore when they're asleep like children. I dare say they're almost cute in the right circumstances."

I gave a small snort. “Now that’s a stretch.”

“It’s all right, Ash. I wouldn’t expect a jock like Ember to understand the delicacies of magic. We’d be better off discussing it with the dual mage.” Zia sat up straighter in her saddle.

I raised gave her a doubtful look. “A jock? Might be the first time anyone’s called me that.”

Zia shrugged. “You strike me as mostly brawn.”

“Ember’s got plenty of brain to back it up,” Ash said.

“Oh, I don’t doubt it. But in a battle, there are really only two types of fighters. You have your brawny fighters, the ones who’d rather hack and slash their way through a problem, and then you have the brains who know better. Brains survive longer.” She smiled to herself.

“Not if they keep insulting the brawn,” I pointed out.

Her smile faded, curling into a scowl.

“I think people are more complex than that,” Ash said. “To wield a sword takes a certain level of intelligence. You have to be able to predict your opponent’s next move, anticipate attacks that could come from any angle. You need to understand complex angles of attack, calculate appropriate force, speed, and depth. It’s the same with magic, really. Many people seem to think it’s effortless to conjure a flame or a little rain, but even doing that requires a basic understanding of how the world works. You need some education in physics, the elements, and your own limits. Boiling people down to either is an oversimplification, Zia."

"I know that," she snapped back. "Of all people, I should know. People look at me and they see a necromancer, an Institute soldier."

"That's because you are both things," I said.

"I'm more than the sum of my parts, just as you are," Zia replied. "In fact—"

Ash pulled his horse to a sudden stop and held up a fist, cutting Zia off with the command for silence. Behind us, the convoy slowly came to a halt. Wagon wheels creaked and horses stamped their hooves at the ground, irritated at the sudden stop.

Scorch shifted under me and shook her mane. I patted her neck and turned to Ash. "What is it?"

"Do you hear that?" Ash whispered.

I listened and heard nothing but the sounds of our convoy. The forest had gone completely quiet, which was always a bad sign.

A sharp stabbing pain suddenly struck my stomach, right where the crystal scar was. I winced and grabbed instinctively at the injury, drawing a concerned look from Zia.

Something flew out of the woods and struck the man on horseback behind me. I twisted in the saddle only to realize it was a hatchet and it had embedded itself in the side of the man's head. His eyes rolled back in his head, and he slid off the horse.

Ash drew his sword. "We're under attack!"

A battle cry went up from the forest on either side of our convoy and people appeared from behind every bush and tree. There must've been thirty or forty men and women dressed in torn clothing. Some charged the convoy wearing old gas masks as helmets. Others ran in wearing little more than loin cloths and battle scars. Wielding axes, swords, and clubs, they rushed in and grabbed several of our people, pulling them down from their horses and beating or stabbing them. Huge four-legged creatures with fangs and patchy fur leapt out with them, snapping their jaws at the horses and sending them into a panic. Wargs.

I drew my sword as a flaming lance of magic narrowly missed my head and broke formation to charge the nearest invader. With a swift downward stroke, I cut into his shoulder, a fatal blow. He barely seemed to notice, grabbing my leg and gnashing his rotten teeth at me.

No, not rotten, I realized. Those weren't teeth at all, but a mouthful of jagged crystals, just like the ones growing in my stomach. They were everywhere on him, growing out of his cheeks, the top of his head, the joints of his arms.

A shock of magic traveled from him and into my leg where he'd grabbed me. The surrounding air made a loud popping sound. Scorch reared and dumped me to the ground. The impact knocked all the air out of me and left me stunned. A moment later, the infected man dropped to the ground beside me, finally having bled out from his wound.

I pushed myself up, sword in hand, ready to fight the next one.

The forest was chaos. Horses without riders trotted in circles off the path. Our people clashed with the invaders, all of whom had strange crystals growing under their skin. Fire magic spun out of control, striking the trees and setting everything ablaze.

Ash rode by the infected man who'd tossed the fire spell and took the raider's head from his shoulders with one decisive strike. "Heretics!" Ash shouted. "Protect the wagons!"

The nearest wagon had pulled off to one side, the driver picking off infected invaders from his seat with a crossbow. Three heretics rushed to him. I ran for the wagon, even knowing I'd never make it in time. It was too far, and the magicite scar in my stomach was on fire. I tried not to let it slow me down, but the pain was brutal.

The heretics reached the wagon and grabbed the driver. A massive steel hammer smashed into the back of one of the heretic's head. Runes carved into the hammer lit up a brilliant crimson and the heretic's head exploded. The body teetered for a moment before falling over. Two other heretics who'd been harassing the driver looked over as Foggy pulled the hammer back. The same crimson light from the hammer flowed out of his eyes and from the tattoos on his body, reaching into the air around him as an extension of their bodies. Foggy let out a bestial roar. The two heretics dropped their weapons and fled into the forest. Satisfied, Foggy turned and swung his hammer, striking another heretic in the chest.

I reached the driver and stopped, ready to defend him. "Are you okay?"

The driver blinked, reloaded his crossbow. "Think so."

"I've got this one covered, lass," Foggy said. "Go to the others."

I shuddered under the dwarf's glowing gaze, oddly glad to get away from him. I was pretty sure he could handle himself.

I hurried to the second wagon back and found Zia slashing at several heretics from the back of the wagon with a pair of curved knives. Another heretic climbed up onto the wagon behind her, unnoticed. I rushed around the other side and jammed my sword into his calf just as he raised a sword over Zia's head. The heretic grunted, grimaced, and brought the sword down. The sound he made as I stabbed him was just enough warning to let Zia tumble out of the way. She came up and sliced open the heretic's face.

I pulled my sword free and carved at the back of the heretic's legs, severing tendons. He tumbled to the ground. "You okay?" I asked Zia, climbing up the rest of the way.

She let out a breath and nodded once. "My vampires are inside."

"Should you let them out?"

She shook her head. "Too much blood. Too risky. I just need to make sure no one else does."

"I've got this." Dex climbed up onto the wagon with us, tugging on a pair of white gloves. The one on his right hand bore a red triangle, and the left a blue diamond. He snapped the fingers on his left hand and drew in the air with his finger. A wall of blue ice sprang up around the wagon, growing higher with every second.

I hopped down from the wagon's roof before the ice sealed me in and turned my attention to the last wagon. The bulk of the remaining heretic invaders had gathered around it. Only Ike had made it to the third wagon's defense. The driver was missing, probably dead, and Ike was surrounded. Not only that, but Ike looked to be unarmed. His sword lay on the ground with the heretics blocking his path to it. One warg charged at him, fangs first.

Ike caught the creature by the jaws, straining to hold its mouth open while claws raked at his armor. The gathered heretics watched, gripping their weapons, but not intervening. The beast trembled and gained ground. It looked like

Ike was about to be warg food until there was a sudden crack. The warg's bottom jaw fell limply out of Ike's hand and the creature reared back. Ike tugged a blacksmithing hammer from his belt and struck the monster's skull, crushing it.

One heretic, armed with a sling, spun it and cast a large stone at Ike. It struck Ike in the side of the head, and he stumbled.

I let out a battle cry and charged the group. Magic buzzed by my face an instant before I buried my blade in one heretic's chest. I kicked another away and yanked the blade free, slashing a third from shoulder to hip. The blade bounced off of metal armor, leaving the heretic untouched, but providing an opening for me. I slid into the circle to stand with Ike and his hammer.

"Buy me thirty seconds," Ike said and bent to pick up the rock that'd been flung at him.

I slashed at the closest heretic, but found only air as he dodged. A snarl made me turn my head just in time to see another warg charging. I lifted my arm to keep it from biting my head. Fangs sank deep into the meat of my forearm. I let out a pained cry and slashed at the creature's neck, but I didn't cut deep enough into the muscle to kill it. It was enough to get the warg to release me, though. A club struck the back of my leg and I fought not to go down, spinning and swinging the sword at my new attacker.

"Hurry, Ike!" I glanced over to see him

stacking more rocks upon rocks, carefully arranging them. "Now's not the time to play with your stones!"

"Almost ready. Just a few more seconds."

"This had better be worth it," I ground out from between clenched teeth and swung the sword at the warg, keeping it back. My arm screamed in pain. Blood dripped from the hole the warg had ripped in me.

There was a sudden *ting* sound beside me. I twisted my head for a quick look at what Ike was up to and watched him strike the pile of stones again with the hammer. A blinding blue light rose from the rock pile. I had to shield my eyes from it. The warg snarled and retreated to the safety of the shadows. All the heretics took a half step back.

Beside me, the sound of rocks cracking, crumbling and falling atop one another drowned out all the other noise of battle. It sounded like I was standing next to a rockslide.

When the noise stopped and the light dimmed, Ike and I were no longer alone in our defense of the wagon. A ten-foot-tall golem of stone stood next to us. The golem swung out with both arms, knocking three of the heretics back at once. They retreated as the golem took two steps toward them. Arrows and magic flew at Ike's golem, but they might as well have been paper for all the damage they did. The golem stomped forward, reaching for the nearest heretic. He tried to run, but he wasn't fast enough to escape the golem's grip. The golem picked him up and squeezed him in a fist, crushing the heretic's ribcage before discarding him like a broken doll.

I let out a shaky breath and gave Ike a worried glance. "How well can you control that thing?"

Before he could answer, the team of horses yoked the wagon behind us let out a loud cry. The wagon jerked forward. We spun around to find three heretics had climbed up on to the wagon while we were distracted with the golem. The wagon lunged forward and took off through the rough terrain.

Zia let out a shout as a warg charged at her, knocking her off the top of the wagon she was defending. Two heretics grabbed her and held her limp body. Blood dripped from a head wound. She must've hit her head when she fell.

I tried to get to her, but the heretics tossed her up on the wagon and sped off.

With a victory shout, the last of the heretics let up their attack and fled into the woods after the wagon. Their remaining wargs howled and raced to follow.

Chapter Ten

The wagon containing vampires trembled. Inside, the vampires snarled and hissed, scratching at the doors to get out. With their mistress unconscious and gone, they would be little more than mindless killing machines.

"We have to go after her!" I searched for Scorch, but she was back toward the front of the procession. I took a step forward and staggered under the renewed ache in my stomach and the flash of burning pain in my forearm.

Ike kept me from falling. "You're not going anywhere until you've seen a healer." He nodded to my bleeding arm.

Ash rode up, still on horseback. "What happened?"

Before answering, Ike lifted his hammer and struck the golem on the back. It collapsed loudly. Now that the magic was gone, it was only a pile of rocks. He tucked the hammer back into his belt. "They took the wagon and the necromancer."

Dex slid off the middle wagon. His ice shield had melted into a puddle, turning the ground around the wagon to mud. "We won't catch them on foot, and we don't know what we're going into."

"We can track them back to their camp." I pointed to the trail of broken branches and disturbed forest floor the wagon and the army had left in its wake.

"There's no need." Ash dismounted and walked several paces toward the middle wagon, where he found one of the injured heretics lying on the ground. The heretic was bleeding from a large gash in his arm, but the injury was unlikely to be fatal. Ash yanked the heretic up by the scrap of netted shirt he wore. "Where is your camp?"

The heretic grinned, showing a mouthful of blue and red crystals instead of teeth. More of them protruded from his neck, his elbows, and the backs of his hands.

I restrained a shudder at the sight of him and instinctually put a hand over the aching crystal scar on my stomach. Left unchecked, my infection would grow out of control. Even with the antigen, it was still growing, albeit slowly. Is that what would become of me? Would I one day have magicite bursting through my skin? I couldn't imagine the pain he might've been in, though the heretic didn't seem to show it.

When the heretic didn't answer, Ash slammed his back into the wagon. "Where did they take her?"

"I've nothing to say to you," The heretic spat at Ash and tilted his head back, laughing like a madman.

Ash wiped a sleeve over his cheek. "We'll see about that." He pressed his hand against the man's chest. A black, shadowy mist swirled under Ash's hand.

Magic.

Magic? Since when had Ash had any magic?

Before he fell into the rift, he was just another nobody like me. Neither of us had grown up with magic. Old Jim insisted we learn to use a sword for exactly that reason.

All the blood drained from the heretic's face, leaving his skin bone white. The whites of his eyes turned red and bulged. He gasped for air, but could find none.

"Where is your camp?" Ash demanded. He removed his hand from the man's chest so the heretic could answer.

The heretic blinked, letting bloody tears fall. "You..." He lifted a trembling hand and touched Ash's face. "You have seen the Black City! I can smell its taint on your skin. Do you hear the whispers of the gods? They call to us. We are brothers, you and I."

Ash drew a dagger from his hip and slit the man's throat before he could say anything more. He stepped back, releasing his hold on the heretic.

The heretic dropped limply to his knees, grasping at the blood flowing from his neck. He looked at Ash, his expression a mix of awe and terror, before falling over dead.

"What a waste," Ash remarked, cleaning his blade on his cloak.

"Why'd you kill him then?" Dex moved around to stand between Ash and the dead heretic. "He might've been more useful alive. Could've traded him back to his people for the necromancer."

Ash's head snapped to the side, sizing up Dex. "Had many dealings with these heretics, have you?"

Dex swallowed. "Well, no, but—"

"Then let me explain the difference between a heretic and a normal bandit. They eat the magicite. They cut their bodies and plant it in their blood to take root on purpose, knowing it will turn them into raving, violent madmen. And they do it all because they believe the rifts are portals to the realm of their gods, and doing so will allow them to speak to those gods." Ash leaned in, almost nose to nose with Dex. "They're rabid madmen with magic powers. There's no negotiating with a heretic, Dex. None."

Dex lifted his hands in surrender. "Okay, okay. Sorry. I just thought—"

"Then don't think. I didn't hire you for this hunt to think."

Dex clenched his jaw and narrowed his eyes, stepping forward. "You know, if I were a lesser man, I'd think of that as a challenge." He clenched his fists, his enchanted gloves still on. For a moment, the surrounding air seemed to buzz and crackle with magic. Then Dex leaned back and shrugged lazily. "Of course, I know better. You don't seem the sort who'd go around fighting with his own hired men. That'd get you a pretty awful reputation, you know? The sort that'd make this your only hunt. Ever."

"I have no intention of wasting my time with you." Ash slid his blade back into the sheathe on his hip. "I have other uses for your skills. I'm told you're a skilled tracker and competent at remaining out of sight. That makes you ideal for retrieving both Zia and the wagon."

"We could just follow the tracks to their camp," Ike suggested. "Ambush them. Take them all out so they'll never prey on anyone else in this forest ever again."

Ash shook his head. "I doubt the battle would go in our favor. We're a large force, and they'd likely hear us coming. They'll execute Zia if they hear us coming."

"I'm going with Dex," I said. "You need at least two people to pull this off."

Ash gestured to my injured arm. "You're not going anywhere until that's seen to."

"Dex, get enough provisions together for three for two days. Just in case. Be ready to go when I return."

Ash frowned, but didn't object. He put his arm around me and nearly dragged me up the line to the first wagon.

I shrugged his arm off. "There's no need to make a big fuss over all this. I'm fine."

"It could be infected. Those creatures, they're all exposed to the magicite. Even something as simple as a bite could spread their infection. If that happened… If you got infected I…" He ground his teeth. "I'd never forgive myself, Ember."

I turned away. Whether the heretic's wargs were infected didn't matter. I already had the same poison in my blood. It wasn't like I was going to get infected again. "Just let me bandage it myself, Ash. I promise, it's really not a big deal. I've had much worse."

"Nonsense," was all he said.

We reached the front wagon, which held most of the medical supplies. Foggy was still there, leaning against the side of it, enjoying the contents of his flask. The glow that had engulfed him earlier had faded, leaving him looking a little more tired than usual. His massive hammer hung on his back. The thing was nearly as large as he was.

Foggy saw us coming and raised his flask in a toast. "Good to see you're not dead."

I glanced around, realizing that we had a few injured sitting around. A few workers had dragged a pair of bodies into the clearing.

"I'm amazed we didn't lose more. They surprised us," I said.

"Something they'll only get away with once," Foggy assured me and took a drink.

Ash opened the back of the wagon and pulled down a set of wooden stairs. He offered me a hand to climb them, but I declined. I was perfectly capable of getting up three little steps all by myself.

The inside of the wagon was dark and had a slightly musty smell. They had organized boxes and bags in nets attached to the walls and ceilings. There wasn't much room to stand, so I had to slide onto the bench on one side.

While Ash searched the netting for the right supplies to bandage my arm, I started peeling off layers. I'd never been one to wear big, bulky plates of armor, and I couldn't afford good Kevlar, so I just put on layers of thick cloth and leather. I winced, shrugging off the aged leather jacket, but the next layer in was worse. Some of the blood had dried, holding the woven fabric in place. Tearing the fabric off opened another part of the wound that had previously closed, sending several drops of blood to the floor.

Ash turned around with his kit and sat on the bench across from me. "Quit moving it. You'll just make it worse."

"You can't very well patch me up if I'm still wearing all these layers."

"Well, it's a good thing younger me didn't know all it took was a warg bite to get you to take off all your clothes."

My face flushed, and I fumbled with one of the ties. "You keep saying things like that, Zia's going to hate me even more. She seems to think she's more your type."

"I don't have a type," Ash said with a sigh. "And if I did, Zia wouldn't be it."

"Really? Why not? She's powerful, beautiful…" I carefully rolled the sleeve up on my undershirt, inhaling a hiss of pain at the sight of the bite. The skin was broken, bruised, and bloody. I'd had worse, but that was definitely going to leave a scar.

"Don't be ridiculous. Zia is a co-worker, nothing more." He opened a small vial of clear liquid and took my arm gently by the wrist.

"Then why is she hell bent on keeping me away from you?" I flinched and grimaced as he poured the liquid over the wound.

"Come on now," Ash chided. "It's only water."

"Well, it hurts!"

"I saw you fighting off dozens of heretics and you're going to complain about a little water?" He set the water aside and used a white towel to wipe the wound clean. "As for Zia, she views herself as my protector. Don't ask me why. I have no idea what I might've done to inspire such loyalty, and she's not very forthcoming with her explanations. Zia's a puzzle. You're better off not trying to understand her."

I bit my lip and turned away as he finished cleaning the wound.

"This doesn't look good, Ember. Might need stitches."

I swallowed and looked back at the arm. "Nah. Throw some butterfly tape on it, wrap it up real good, and I'll be fine."

"Are you sure? It could get infected."

I tilted my head to the side. "Give me some credit. I know how to care for an open wound. Besides, it's not my sword arm."

"All right. It's your arm." He shook his head, doubtful, and pulled down more supplies.

I watched him work, carefully applying the butterfly tape with gentle fingers, a far cry from how he had treated the heretic earlier. He almost didn't seem like the same man.

"What was that magic you used earlier, Ash?" I asked quietly.

He hesitated halfway through opening a package. "I… It's complicated to explain."

"It happened while you were in the rift?"

Ash nodded slowly and went back to work on my arm. "When I came back, I found I could do certain things, manipulate the world in a way I couldn't before. It was why the Institute took me in at first. They wanted to study me, Ember. But I didn't want to be a lab rat. Zia helped me get out."

He lifted his hand and stared at his palm. A deep black shadow enveloped his fingers, dancing on them like a dark flame. "I don't remember what happened to me in there, but I know it's changed me. It's in my blood, the same way it's in the heretics' blood. Except it's not making me sick or driving me insane."

For a moment, I considered telling him the truth, showing him the crystals growing in the scar on my stomach. Maybe he'd understand. The rift had changed us both.

Then I remembered how brutally he'd executed the heretic outside. Ash hadn't even treated him as human. One look at the truth, and he'd think I was one of them. I couldn't tell him. Even he wouldn't understand what was happening to me. I barely understood it myself.

"I need this to be our secret, Ember," Ash said as he finished bandaging my arm. "No one besides you and Zia knows what I've been through, and I'd like to keep it that way. Dex and Ike wouldn't understand. To them, I'd be no different from one of those heretics. I'd be less than human. A monster, driven mad."

"Maybe not all heretics are so bad, Ash."

He let out a bitter laugh. "Right, and I'm the queen of Atlanta. You saw them, Ember. They're crazy. They attack anyone they come across, drag them back to their camp, and force feed them magicite until they become just as insane and deformed as they are. Why do you think they're called heretics in the first place?"

I shrugged. "Because they worship the rifts as gods."

"The rifts are deadly portals created by black magic seeping from another world into ours. They're not gods." Ash dumped the last of the water over his hands, cleaning my blood from them. He turned to cleaning up the mess, picking up open packages and discarding them in a drawstring bag he found in the corner. "I'm not like them, Ember."

I hesitated, looking up from examining his handiwork. "Why would you say that?"

He shrugged without looking at me. "Just promise me... If you ever look at me and see no difference between the madmen who attacked us and me, that you'll stop me. Don't let me become like that. Ever."

"Sure, I guess. But that won't happen." I flexed my fist. The arm still hurt a little, but not as bad as it had before.

Ash placed a hand gently on my bandaged arm. "Ember, without Zia, this hunt may be forfeit. We need her vampires to scout the dragon's nest." His voice was strained, his expression desperate. What he wasn't saying was how much he needed her by his side.

I couldn't pretend to understand the strange bond between the two of them, but I would not let her suffer at the hands of madmen. "I'll bring her back to you, Ash. I promise."

He nodded, relieved by the promise.

I stepped out of the wagon to find Foggy, Kenny, and several others working to reenforce the doors to the vampire wagon. The whole thing rocked precariously back and forth.

"How long will it hold?" I asked as I approached the wagon.

Foggy grunted and spat a nail into his fist before hammering it into place. "As long as it has to. Don't worry about things here, lass. You do yer part an' leave us to do ours."

"There's a steel cage on the inside," Ash said. "This is just an extra precaution. I'm more concerned the creatures will tear themselves apart trying to get out, or that it'll affect the morale here. The sooner you and Dex can bring Zia back, the better."

"We'd best get going then." Dex walked up carrying two leather packs. He'd gathered a length of rope around his middle like a belt and stuffed his gloves into his pocket. "You ready? I tossed some extra gauze and tape in your pack."

"Where are the horses?"

Dex shook his head. "No horses. You want to track, we go on foot. Might take a little longer, but we're less likely to miss signs or spook any scouts they might have out. They took one of ours, so they probably expect us to mount a rescue. They'll be looking for us. I intend to be invisible." He slid on a pair of sunglasses.

"I'm sure the sunglasses will help." I

winced as I slid the pack onto my back.

"Laugh if you want, but I'd rather be over-prepared than under."

"Just a second." Ike jogged up with a small leather pouch in his hands. He held it out to me.

Turning the pouch over, I realized it wasn't a pouch at all but a holster for a gun. "I don't really use guns," I said and tried to give it back to him. Firearms were as deadly as they'd ever been in history, but less reliable for taking down monsters. I'd carried them in the past, but never felt comfortable with them.

"It's a flare gun," Ike explained. "If anything goes wrong and the two of you get captured, fire it straight up. We'll mobilize another search party to find you."

I couldn't very well say no to that, so I looped the holster onto my belt, thanked Ike, and hurried off to join Dex.

He shifted the weight of his pack and we started off from the main group.

I cast a look behind me as we stepped into the thick foliage crushed by wagon wheels, but Ash and the others had already turned their attention back to the wagon. *I hope they're right about how sturdy that wagon is,* I thought and ducked under a thick vine, leaving the convoy far behind.

Chapter Eleven

"So, you and Ash." Dex pushed aside some vines that had nearly been chopped in half when the wagon passed through.

The heretics had done little to cover their tracks. Either they weren't concerned about us mounting a rescue mission, or they were counting on it. I was banking on the latter. The crystals in their blood might've poisoned their minds beyond all reason, but they weren't stupid. Their ambush on our convoy was organized, well planned. They hadn't just grabbed whatever they could carry and run off. To me, it seemed like they had chosen their target, but why Zia?

"What about it?" I gave him the side eye.

Dex shrugged. "Just wanted to know if that was a thing."

"What sort of thing would it be?"

"You know," he made a vague gesture with his hands. "A *thing*."

"You mean a romantic thing." I stepped over a fallen log, moving parallel to the wagon tracks where foot traffic had stomped down leaves and bushes. "No. We grew up together. You'd hardly know it now, but Ash used to be a gentle soul. He was terrified of spiders. Why? You think you might have a chance?"

"With you?" Dex shrugged again. "Always good to know what my options are."

"That's interesting. Yesterday, I was a poacher your people were happy to turn away and today I'm a potential romance."

He lifted a fallen branch out of the way, searching the ground. The broken section of the bough still held some green, and it looked like someone had deliberately placed the branch to cover the wagon tracks. "I told you I've got nothing against poachers. Truth is, the Marauders are a small guild. We can't take every job. Even with Ike and his Iron Company snatching up most of the high-paying work, there's more to be done in and around Atlanta than both our guilds can handle."

"Seems like the rest of your people disagree with you."

"You mean Kenny?" Dex offered a hand to help me climb over a log that had been dragged onto the path to slow our progress. "Kenny's like a brother to me, but he's got no idea how to run a guild."

I put my hands in his and let him balance me as I slid over the log. "And you do?"

"I suppose time will tell, won't it?" He let

go of me and perched his hands on his hips, advancing slowly while frowning at the ground. "Seems they changed their minds and are making more of an effort to cover their tracks. Think they know we're coming?"

"I think they're expecting some kind of response."

Dex nodded, and we moved further from the path, keeping the line of broken twigs and uprooted bushes just in sight. When we lost track of the wagon's path, we had to stop and pick through the bushes, but we eventually found it.

At dusk, we lost the tracks again and spread out. I was rooting through a thick berry bush with bright yellow buds when Dex whistled, giving the signal for us to regroup. I left the bush alone and navigated through a line of thick trees, almost stumbling into him on the other side. There were no signs of the wagon, but Dex squatted in front of a pair of stone statues. Time had worn the features from the statues' faces, but there was no mistaking their humanoid shape. They stood like sentries, spears out.

Beyond the statues stood an ancient-looking ruin of moss-covered stone. Vines curled around arches and through broken stained glass. The building itself seemed to have been uprooted and turned onto its side from the strange angle at which it sat. I couldn't see past the broken wall, but the flicker of light and the chatter of voices told me there were people in there.

"What is it?" I asked.

Dex pointed off to the right. The wagon was there, hidden under a pile of branches.

I squatted beside him. "Okay, so what's the plan?"

"These are elven lands." He spoke in a reverent whisper. "We shouldn't be here."

I gave the place a second glace. It didn't look like any elves had been there in a long time. Then again, I had no idea what an elvish settlement would look like. Like most humans, I had never seen an elf. Many believed they were just a myth made up to scare people away from deep forests, but I'd always thought there were too many stories for them to be completely false.

I leaned around the statues for a better look. "We don't really have much of a choice. If the heretics are here, then that's where we go."

"We're going to have to get closer to see."

I nodded.

We crept forward, keeping as low to the ground as possible. I put my hand on my sword. As we closed on the broken wall, Dex carefully slid on his gloves.

A loud voice boomed out of the destroyed building. "... For the covenant demands we drink of the blood and eat of the flesh of the gods so that, one day, his prophet will rise. And the nonbelievers will cower in his presence, crying out in awe at his wondrous works."

We reached the building and crowded a

small crack in the wall to see through. Zia was there, chained to an old iron cross. Heretics had gathered around her on their knees with their hands folded as if in prayer before her. And not just the ones who'd attacked us earlier in the day. There were women and children among them, all of them deformed by the crystals growing in their blood.

A man walked down the line of gathered heretics with a silver chalice. Actually, he might've been more magicite than man. An enormous lump of green crystal protruded from his left shoulder, making him walk lopsided. Another group of crystals grew out of his eye sockets, leaving him blind. Yet he didn't seem to have any trouble finding his way. Scraps of white clothing hung from his body, which was covered in knotted, scarred skin. He offered the cup to each of the heretics, who took a sip before handing it back. Armed guards lined the walls, looking on.

Zia struggled against her chains.

"What are we going to do?" I asked Dex in the quietest whisper.

There was no way we'd be able to take on everyone in there, but we had to get to Zia before they did anything to her.

The heretic priest limped from the line of worshippers to where Zia stood, strapped to the cross. "I say to you, any woman who drinks the blood will be purified. Through death or transformation, I say this is the day you will meet your maker." He shoved the cup at her face.

She turned her head away, refusing. A guard stepped away from the wall, grabbed her head, pinched her nose, and forced her jaw open. The priest poured a glowing crimson liquid into Zia's mouth while the guard held it closed.

The moment the guard let go of her jaw, Zia spat the tainted liquid back at the priest. "Fuck you."

One worshipper rose to offer the priest a dirty scrap of cloth to clean his face.

He took it, mopping up the liquid. "You reject salvation?"

"I'd rather die than drink your disgusting blood," Zia snarled, and fought against her imprisonment.

"Then you are not yet penitent. And yet the gods speak to me. You have been chosen. One doesn't have to be willing to bear the fruit of the gods." The priest gestured to the guards who came forward and lifted the entire cross out of the pedestal on the ground. And Zia with it. "Take her."

Zia fought, screamed, and cursed as they carried her away.

While the deformed priest turned back to his congregation, I crept around the side of the broken church, clinging to the shadows. A pair of massive wooden doors swung open, and the guards carried Zia out. I pressed my back firmly against the stone wall and held my breath, watching. *Think invisible thoughts.*

They carried her down a small hill and into another dilapidated building leaning to one side. I exchanged a look with Dex. We could take out two guards easily enough. Then we just had to free Zia, grab the wagon, and ride back. We could meet up with the main group by sunrise.

Dex nodded and removed his sunglasses, clipping them to his shirt.

We crept along the hill, watching the broken church and the dilapidated building both, but no one came out of either. The building where they'd taken Zia was a long, shotgun-style house that had once been two stories high. The top floor seemed to have been ripped off and tossed carelessly into a shallow lake nearby, leaving the upper floors exposed. The elements had rotted all the exposed carpeting and what few bits of furniture remained. Wind blew through the open stairway, almost sounding like a scream.

One guard stood just inside the front entrance, but I couldn't see the other. Charging them from the front porch would be stupid, especially since we didn't know where the other guard was. He could run off and sound the alarm and we'd have the entire camp on us.

Carefully, we changed positions so that we could see if there was a way in through the back. There was a door and two windows, but all three appeared boarded shut.

Dex and I sank into the shadows behind a large boulder.

"Okay," he said, "I think the best way in is going to be through the second story."

"I don't see anywhere to climb up except the old drain pipe, and that'll be too noisy."

"There are plenty of places. Just follow me and stay quiet."

I tried to tell him to wait, that we needed more of a plan than how to get into the house, but Dex pushed himself out from behind the rock and tiptoed to the nearest side of the house.

The old vinyl siding had mostly fallen off, and most of the silver insulation was gone. They had put a few boards up to keep out the worst of the weather. Dex grabbed some invisible handhold and hauled himself up with ease. I tried to mimic his movements and use the same handholds, but I was much slower. Dex pulled himself through a hole in the wall and stood on the second floor while I was still only about halfway up.

"Uh... Hey, Ember?" he called down.

"Just a sec. Almost there." I grunted and pulled myself up. No sooner had I stood up than I found a blade at my neck.

The second heretic guard, along with another we hadn't even known was there, were waiting for us.

I raised my hands in surrender, scowling at Dex. "Brilliant plan, Dex."

Something hard struck the back of my head, and everything was suddenly black.

***

I woke to drumming and a rhythmic throbbing in my skull. Every mallet strike echoed inside my head, a ripple of pain. I winced and opened my eyes. Flame danced in my vision and strange, crystalline people danced around the fire, spinning and singing in deep, throaty voices.

"What the hell?" I blinked, trying to make sense of what I was seeing.

"Oh, you're awake, are you?"

I turned my head at the sound of Dex's voice next to me. "Dex? What happened?" I tried to lift my hand to my head, but found it tied behind my back. When I found out I was tied up, I turned my head to Dex for an explanation, but my words caught in my throat. It was the first time I had ever seen him without that stupid cowboy hat on. At first, the pointed ears sticking up out of his shaggy hair seemed fake, but why would he have fake ears? "Dex, your ears."

"What? You didn't think I wore a hat for the fashion?" He shrugged.

"You idiots are the worst rescuers ever," Zia said on the other side of me. Her hair was disheveled and there was a line of dried blood on her forehead, but she otherwise looked okay.

"I find that hard to believe," quipped Dex. "Technically, this is no longer a rescue mission.

The only question left is how we're going to die."

"Does it matter?" Zia growled.

"Actually, yes. If they toss us in the fire, it'll be unfortunate for the two of you, but I stand a chance. Of course, that depends on how hot it is and if I can still work magic through the pain of being burned alive."

"Silence!" The heretic priest waved a feathered staff in front of our faces. Tiny misshapen skulls rattled on the end, hidden inside the feathers. The drumming stopped suddenly as the priest turned his back to us and lifted his staff. "We have gathered here tonight to witness the purification and transfiguration of these blasphemers, that they may be remade in the image of our lord."

A cheer went up from the crowd.

I exchanged a worried look with Dex.

He winced and tried to twist his hands free to no avail. "This doesn't sound good."

The priest held up his staff again, and the crowd fell silent. "Blessed is he who bows before the ashen throne!"

"May the prophet show us the way," the crowd responded in a monotone.

"Blessed is he who looks upon the Black City! Tremble before its power. We are but ants before him. It is our honor to be called into service that we may convert the non-believers, turning them to his loving embrace." The priest lifted the same chalice he'd used earlier, placed it upon a flat rock, and held his hand over it. A curved black blade shimmered in the firelight as he drew it over his palm. Blood flowed from his fist into the chalice, tainted blood to which he added a pinch of ground magicite, just to be sure.

One drop of the tainted blood and Dex or Zia would be just as infected as me. I, however, would be immune, at least to the effects of the magicite. Who knew what other diseases the priest's blood might carry? The idea of swallowing it made my stomach churn.

The priest lifted the chalice and approached me, the crystals in his eye sockets shimmering. "Will you accept salvation, sister?"

"Get away from me!"

"Hold her."

Heavy hands gripped my jaw and pinched my nose. Rough, calloused fingers wrenched my jaw open and held it. The priest lifted the chalice to my mouth. I gagged on the putrid smell of blood and magic as he tilted the chalice up.

A flaming arrow suddenly sailed out of the shadows and pierced the priest in the neck. He opened his mouth, spitting blood onto my face, before tumbling to one side and lying still in a spreading puddle of his own blood.

The heretics drew their weapons and turned to face the new threat, but they were met with a hail of flaming arrows. They lit up the sky like angry stars for a moment before falling, each one finding a mark.

I flinched away from one that pierced the corpse at my feet. Miraculously, none of the arrows struck us.

Those heretics who survived the initial attack rose with torches and blades to rush whatever lie in wait for them at the edge of camp. I squinted into the darkness, trying to see, but the shadows were too deep. The only thing to come out of the shadows were the pained screams of the dying heretics as whatever was out there tore them apart. If I strained, I could pick out the flash of something silver, the spray of blood as it sliced a heretic from stomach to chin in one move.

Genuine terror churned in the pit of my stomach. "What are they?"

"Elves," Dex breathed.

"I thought elves were supposed to be beautiful and graceful," Zia whispered.

"The same is true of venomous spiders and snakes." Dex struggled against the ropes that held him. "We need to get out of here. Now." He closed his eyes and let out a breath. A long tendril of flame shot out of the fire before us, curling around to set his ropes aflame. With a grunt, he pulled his hands free of the burning rope. As soon as he untied me, a blade lowered against his throat.

I felt the same bite of steel pressed against my neck and chanced a look at the creature holding the delicate sword to my throat. He stood taller than the tallest man I had ever seen, his face hidden behind a helm of the same gleaming blue steel as my sword. Glowing, ice-blue eyes stared at me, as immovable as a mountain.

Dex slowly raised his hands in surrender. “We’re unarmed.”

“You’ve still got both your arms as far as I can see.” Another elf strode out of the darkness. He removed his helmet and handed it to the slightly shorter elf at his side. In the right light, he might’ve been mistaken for a human, but only if one didn’t look closely. While the elf’s features resembled a human’s, they were slightly off in every way. His cheek bones were sharper, more pronounced, and his eyes an unnatural shade of purple made brighter by the dark war paint streaked over his face. Sharp ears, pointed like a lynx’s, rose through platinum hair. Bloodstains colored his white armor. He gripped a sword with a pearl hilt.

Dex seemed to relax a little, letting his hands fall slightly. “*Savidad, Laseran.*”

The elf seemed unimpressed. “Your Elvish is almost as bad as your stench, *pherlon*.”

Dex’s hands shot back up as the sword to his throat shifted. “Come on, Laseran. You’re not going to kill us.”

“I could. You *are* trespassing, after all. The *Telmara* made it very clear that you were not welcome.” The elf looked us over, his eyes hard and sharp. They seemed to peer beneath my skin, leaving me chilled under his gaze.

"I didn't come here on purpose," Dex ground out, leaning away from the blade.

"We only came to retrieve our friend, who the heretics kidnapped," I nodded to Zia. "Let us go and we'll be on our way."

Laseran narrowed his eyes at me, scrutinizing. After a long moment, he gestured to another elf, who cut Zia free.

The ropes holding me in place tightened before releasing. I stepped away from the tree they had tied me to, rubbing the rope burn on my wrists and eying the elf behind me as he put his knife away.

Zia stumbled forward a few steps before falling to her knees. She looked up at me, her eyes unfocused, and wrapped her arms around her stomach before vomiting loudly.

The elves near her took a step back.

Laseran frowned. "It seems your friend is unwell. She drank from the chalice?"

"They made me," Zia managed, and spat. She turned around and blinked. Tears of blood flowed from the corners of her eyes. She gasped once before she fell over, convulsing.

Dex shifted as if he would go to her side, but the blade kept him in place. "She doesn't deserve this! Help her!"

"Why?" Leseran lifted his chin. "I've saved your worthless life and set you free. The only reason I did that much was because I was eager to see the heretic stain removed from this place.

Consider yourself lucky to be leaving with your life. Be gone from this forest before dawn or I may change my mind." He turned his back on us.

The sword moved away from Dex's neck, and he went immediately to Zia's side, touching her forehead with the back of his hand. "She has a fever. They've infected her. Leseran, I know it's in your power to help! Don't make me beg."

The elf paused before slowly turning around, a dark smile touching his thin lips. "Actually, that might be quite convincing. Would you be willing to fall on your knees before me and beg for the life of your comrade? I might be swayed if your plea is moving enough."

Dex ground his teeth. He stood, clenching his fists.

I put a hand on his shoulder. "Don't play his game."

He shrugged my hand off. "I have to. She's innocent and doesn't deserve to die because he wants to lord over me." Dex walked over to stand in front of Leseran before dropping to his knees. "Please, Leseran, I beg you… Save Zia's life."

Leseran smirked. "Your elven blood must be more diluted than I thought. A son of the Telmara would never kneel to save a *dhalethein*."

I suddenly spied my sword sitting in a pile of all our gear just a short distance away. I lunged for it, prompting the nearby elves to ready their blades. I brought my sword up and slid closer to Zia. "If you're not going to help her, then back away!"

Leseran's eyes widened. His nostrils flared. "That sword... It is an elven blade. Where did you get it?"

I gave Dex a worried glance, but he seemed just as confused as me. I shifted my grip on the sword and swallowed, trying to project more confidence than I had. "Help her and I'll tell you whatever it is you want to know about it."

Leseran stepped forward. The blade of my sword made a small sound as it struck his breastplate. His eyebrow twitched. It was all the movement I saw before I was on the ground next to Dex, cradling my sore wrist. My sword was in the elf's hand. Leseran had disarmed me so fast I didn't even see him move.

He held the sword up into the night and watched the reflection of the heretic's fire burn in the blade. "There is nothing you can tell me about this blade that I have not already heard. But what is a *dhalethein* doing with it? That story, I would very much like to hear."

I swallowed. "I bought it from a dwarven blacksmith in Atlanta." The blacksmith's apprentice had told me it was cursed, and clearly Leseran knew more about it than I did, though he didn't fear it like the dwarves.

"You *purchased* it?" He spat, eyes blazing. "Has our history become so forgotten that we trade it for mere coin?"

"Well, I didn't exactly buy it. But I didn't

steal it either."

Leseran lowered the sword, almost smirking at me. "Perhaps there's more to you than meets the eye, *dhalethein.*" He nodded to his people. "Take the girl. Blindfold the others. The last thing we need is them leading more of their kind into our land."

Chapter Twelve

The elves blindfolded us, put us on a horse, and led us into the night.

"Don't get any ideas," I said to Dex as his front leaned against my back.

He let out a huff of breath that tickled the back of my neck. "Who, me? Never."

"Quiet," Leseran spat. "The forest has well-trained ears, and you two are already loud enough as it is." He clicked his tongue, and the horse started forward at a quick, but manageable pace.

I spent the first few minutes trying to discern our direction. We'd gone east from the convoy to find the heretic camp, and it seemed to me that Leseran's people were headed north, almost parallel to our convoy, but I couldn't be sure. Then the horse looped around a few times, and I lost my bearings completely.

The night forest was quiet but for the whisper of elves and their horses moving through the underbrush. A few of the elves mur-

mured to each other in their own language. I wished I understood what they were saying. Dex clearly knew at least a little Elvish, but he hadn't made the offer to translate.

I turned my head to whisper to him. "You know, you could've mentioned you were an elf instead of hiding it with that stupid hat."

Dex sighed. "I'm only half an elf, and not even the right half, apparently. As if that's not bad enough, Leseran is actually my half-brother on my father's side. Talk about toxic family."

"You'd think they'd be more welcoming to someone who shares their blood."

"Oh, if only." He gave a derisive snort and turned his head. "I'm a stain on our father's otherwise spotless honor, a living, breathing reminder of the time a human witch seduced a member of the Telmara."

"The Telmara?" I tipped my head to the side.

"Elves don't have kings and queens. The Telmara is a sort of ruling council, but it's more than a governing body. Their word is law, and their honor beyond reproach. Well, usually. They're sort of like town elders, role-model celebrities, and living gods all rolled into one. Traditionalists like Leseran worship the ground the Telmara walks on."

"The Telmara are not gods, nor are they infallible," Leseran growled from somewhere ahead and to our right. "But they are honored elders, and our people would rather not be reminded of past dishonor."

"Is that really what happened?" I asked Dex, ignoring Leseran. "Your mother was some sort of powerful witch?"

"My mother was a prostitute," Dex said matter-of-factly. "She had a bit of magic, but to claim she overpowered an elf, let alone a powerful elder in his prime, is a bit of a stretch even for me." I felt the weight of his shoulders rise and fall. "But if that's the story they want to tell, I'm not going to argue."

I twisted in the saddle. "Why not? It's a lie. I'm sure your mother doesn't appreciate it."

Silence answered.

Leseran made a small sound somewhere between a grunt and a snort. "Humans are so fragile and only grow more so with age, don't they?"

Dex's hands curled into fists and pressed against my lower back.

I immediately felt guilty for bringing up his mother. I knew nothing about Dex, where he came from, or his history. For all I knew, she was dead. "I'm sorry. I didn't know she'd died."

"There are worse things that can happen to you *dhalethein* than death," Leseran said.

For a moment, Leseran's words threw me back in time and left me standing in front of an expanding rift, screaming Ash's name. Wind spun and twisted the air, drowning out my cries. Eerie greenish light glowed in the center of the rift, so close I could almost touch it.

I shook my head and came back to the present. Maybe it was better if I said nothing at all.

We rode in silence for a long time. I don't know how long, or how far we went. Blindfolded, and in unfamiliar territory, it was impossible to tell. By the time anything changed, my lower back was screaming from the uncomfortable ride, and Dex's extra weight against me. He'd fallen asleep shortly after I stupidly brought his mother up and was snoring gently. Despite the awkward position I occupied in the saddle, his presence was at least a little comforting.

Eventually, new sounds and smells joined the constant chirping of birds and the forest scents. I inhaled the familiar smells of campfires and imagined the last embers of the night's fires fading into a foggy morning. Goats bleated. Wooden spoons scraped the bottom of iron pots. Low voices and light footsteps. We had made it to the elven camp.

The horses stopped and someone lifted my blindfold. I squinted into the morning light at first, but as I got used to it, I realized it was barely light out. The creatures I'd mistaken for goats earlier were something else, as large as an alpaca but with ram's horns, thick fur, and the udders of a cow. Most of them wandered around lazily inside a wooden pen while a pair of elves worked to milk the creatures.

Dex slid off the horse before me. His feet

hit the ground with an audible squish, and he winced. "Lovely. Nothing like stepping in orzalope shit first thing in the morning." Dex muttered to himself as he desperately tried to scrape his boot through the grass to clean the feces off. He got too close to one orzalope and it let out a loud bleat before spitting at him. Dex sighed and wiped his face off with his shirt.

I was careful to dismount in the other direction. As I did, I noticed several elves carrying Zia on a stretcher toward a large smoking hut at the center of camp. "Hey, wait." I rushed to follow where they were taking her.

Leseran moved to block my path. He held my sword in a fist. "You and the half-ears will come with me."

"Like hell I will. I'm staying with Zia. Someone's got to watch over her."

He sighed and rolled his eyes. "I am a man of my word. The Sinera will draw the poison from her blood if they are able, but that will take time, and your presence will be little more than a distraction to our healers. I must take you before the Telmara. They're the only ones who can decide what to do with you."

"Do with me?" I looked to Dex, who was only a few paces behind me. "What do you mean? I've done nothing to you and your people, yet you're treating me like a prisoner."

He lifted an eyebrow. "Elves do not take prisoners. If I wished you dead, it would be so.

Now come. I grow tired of speaking your corrupt tongue." He put a hand on my shoulder and pushed me toward another building standing on a small rise.

I went, but only because I didn't know what choice I had. The elves in the camp had all stopped to stare at me. After his performance back at the heretic camp, I knew I couldn't best Leseran in a fight. Besides, he had my sword. If I wanted it back, and to get back to the wagon convoy safely, my only choice was to cooperate.

Dex joined Leseran and I on our path up to the large, round building, walking backward. "What does the Telmara want with her?"

Leseran didn't even look at Dex. "I haven't summoned them yet."

"Then how do you know they'll even want to speak to her? Look, if you want the sword, I'm sure we can come to some sort of agreement. You bought it, right, Ember? Would you part with it for an honest price?"

Leseran stopped walking and sneered at Dex. "It is not the sword that troubles me, nor that this *dhalethein* had it. It is the timing, and the combination of the two."

"I don't understand," I said. "It's just a sword."

"And you are just a mewling sack of flesh and bone," he spat. "I will not negotiate. I know my duty. *Move!*" He gave me another shove.

The large round building at the top of the

hill was barely an inch taller than Leseran at the outer walls, though the ceiling rose higher the further toward the center. It looked to be made of many scraps of hide, tanned and stitched together. Gray smoke rose through a hole in the center of the roof.

Leseran didn't enter. He lifted the door flap and stepped back. "You can wait here. The Telmara will arrive shortly. Know that I will place a guard outside. If you attempt to flee, you will be cut down on sight without question. Do you understand?"

"And I thought the elves didn't take prisoners," I scoffed. "Sounds a lot like prison to me."

He just scowled at me. "Remove your shoes."

I kicked off my boots and placed them by the door. "They'd better be here when I get back."

Dex pinched his nose and dropped his. "I honestly don't care if mine are still there."

The tent seemed a lot larger on the inside than the outside, as if some magic were at work, changing the dimensions. I could barely see the other side in the dim light. Woven rugs with intricate detail lined the floor. Once Leseran let go of the tent door, it was even darker inside, at least until my eyes adjusted to the strange, smokey air inside the tent. At least it wasn't unpleasant to breathe. I closed my eyes and inhaled through my nose.

"Honeysuckle and jasmine," Dex said. "It's

supposed to be calming. I suppose it might be for normal folk. I don't have pleasant associations with it." He paced toward the center of the tent where a large iron stove stood. A semi-circle of carved wooden chairs sat before it, facing the door.

"What's going to happen here, Dex?" I fidgeted with my hands and moved closer to him.

He shrugged. "I don't know. Elves are protective of their heritage, but I've never seen anyone get so worked up over an artifact, let alone a sword. That thing didn't have a hint of rust on it. Besides, it's not like you desecrated an elven burial ground to get it, did you?"

"No! I found it at the blacksmith's, just like I said."

"Hm. Then maybe he desecrated the elven burial ground or something. Wouldn't put it past a dwarf. Who knows?" He tapped his chin in thought.

I sighed and sat down on the floor, wrapping my arms around my knees. "You're not being very helpful."

Dex snorted. "What? You think just because I've got pointy ears, I know everything about being elvish? I was raised human. I honestly didn't even know I wasn't human until I was seven or eight."

"You'd think the ears would give it away."

"You would, wouldn't you?" He touched

the pointed tops of his ears and sighed. "I just thought I was some sort of misshapen freak. I looked at my ears the same way most people probably look at their freckles or their twenty extra pounds. With the right clothing, I could hide them well enough."

"So what happened? How did you find out?"

Dex let his arms fall limply to his sides. He paced back and forth a minute before plopping onto the floor across from me with a half-hearted shrug. "You have to understand that I didn't grow up like most kids. For most kids, they've got mom, dad, the dog and maybe a brother or sister. They're brought up thinking family is blood. I grew up thinking family meant people who lived together in one big house. That meant I thought of all the men and women in the brothel as family. I had a mother and a bunch of aunts and uncles... But I didn't have a father. It didn't matter so much to me until some other kids started teasing me about it. We fought, and I lost, badly."

"So you asked your mom about it?" I leaned forward, waiting for his answer.

Dex wrinkled his nose. "Hell, no. I was too ashamed to admit I got beat up, so I found one of my uncles. Of course, he really wasn't my uncle at all. Just another prostitute, trying to get by. But they looked after me. All of them did. Anyway, he was the one who told me what I was.

I didn't believe him at first. I didn't think elves were real. But the more I thought about it, the more I wanted it to be real. I started to imagine what life might be like if I had a father, as well as all my aunts and uncles. I had this fantasy in my head that I could find him, and everyone would get along because they loved me, you know?"

I nodded and swallowed familiar pang of grief. I hadn't grown up as Dex had, but I'd lost both my parents when I was young. Old Jim had raised me and Ash, but I'd always known he wasn't my father. There was a time when I wanted so badly to believe that the story I'd been told was a lie, that my parents had survived the attack and were really out there, searching for me. If I looked hard enough, I would find them. It ended when Old Jim finally took me to where they were buried. It felt like my entire childhood ended that day. Maybe it did.

"Anyway," Dex continued, staring at the floor, "it didn't turn out that way. I ran away from home, tracked down my father. Long story short, he and the rest of the Telmara made it clear he wanted nothing to do with me, and that I wasn't welcome among the people."

"I'm sorry, Dex." I put a hand on his arm. "That's not fair."

"Hey, nobody said life was fair, right?" He cracked a smile. "Anyway, it's fine. Imagine if things had worked out the way I wanted. I would've had to put up with Leseran as an older brother. Dodged a bullet there. Besides, my guild is my family now. The one good thing to come out of all of this is that I learned you make your own family. Blood's got nothing to do with it."

I nodded. "I understand that. Maybe better than you know."

Light flooded the tent as someone lifted the tent flap. A tall, thin figure blocked out some of the light for a moment before it passed into the tent. Another followed behind. One by one, nine elves entered the tent in silence, their faces hidden behind beaded veils. They wore large, bulky cloaks of crimson with high collars and long trains. The cloaks wrapped around their bodies, hiding any definable features. There was no telling the gender or age of the elves who entered the tent. All of them were blank walls of crimson and silver veils.

The only one to stand out was one who walked with a large, iron staff made to look like a gnarled bit of wood.

Dex and I rose as Leseran entered and closed the tent flap behind him, standing guard at the entrance.

The procession of elves moved around the outskirts of the tent, meeting in the middle to stand one before each chair. The elves stood there, silent and unmoving, waiting for some unseen signal before they all sank into their seats at the same time.

The elf in the center seat lifted their staff

and brought it down three times against the carpet. A wave of red magic exploded from the end of the staff and struck me, pushing the air out of my lungs. My skin burned as it washed over me, but the pain was short lived.

"The Telmara shall come to order," said the leader in the center with a voice that was neither purely masculine nor feminine. "Bring forth the *Gwœ́tach Mhor*!"

Leseran left his post by the door to come and kneel before the Telmara, kneeling to present my sword to the leader with a flourish.

The leader elf took the sword, rose, and pulled the blade from its scabbard.

Light flooded the room, reflected off the blade from nowhere. A pulse of dark magic followed. An inhuman scream echoed in my ears. I gasped and fell to my knees, holding my head as visions flooded my mind.

The Telmara tent faded, and I was thrust into a foggy forest alone. Dew clung to the underside of the leaves, and spiders scurried around on their webs.

And there, grinning down at me from behind his stag skull helmet, was the giant, tree-armored creature from my dream. Black smoke billowed around my feet, turning into hands, grasping at my ankles. I tried to kick them away, but there were too many. Fingernails raked at my bare skin and the ground beneath me gave way, pulling me into a grave while the creature watched.

"Help me!" I reached for the creature, my screams echoing through the forest. "Please!"

The creature lifted a sword. Shadow raced along the blame like fire and spread into the surrounding trees.

And then I understood. Whatever this thing was, it wasn't there to help me. It meant to kill me.

Chapter Thirteen

I woke to the sound of a crackling fire and the touch of a cool cloth on my forehead. The ceiling overhead was made of strange cloth stretched over spokes of wood. A hole in the center opened to a blue sky. Smoke pumped through a black metal tube protruding through the hole, keeping it from building up in the tent.

"You're awake," Dex said, kneeling next to me. "About time. I was starting to worry you were slipping into some kind of coma."

I groaned and touched my head. It throbbed from where the heretic had struck me before, but also in my temples. "What happened?"

"Good question." Dex let his forearm rest on his knee. "One minute, we're standing in the dark, and the next there's this brilliant light. You're on the ground, screaming and holding your ears, and the rest of us are standing around, baffled. At least I was. I had no idea what was going on. Leseran and the other guards snatched us up and locked us in here, presumably until the Telmara decide what it all means." He gestured to the small tent.

I sat up.

Dex took my arm. "Easy. You went down hard."

I was a little dizzy sitting up, but managed. The tent was still larger than most hotel rooms, maybe twenty feet from one side to the other, though the walls were slanted. I'd only be able to stand at my full height toward the center. There were two beds piled high with patterned blankets and pillows, and a table with two chairs. A woven rug served as the floor.

"The sword. I saw..." Images of the stag-skulled monster from my visions flashed through my mind. I shook my head, but that just made me dizzier. "They called it something *mohr*?"

"Beats me. What I know of elven lore couldn't fit in a teacup," Dex said with a shrug. "They seem to think it's a big deal. I just wish I knew if they were going to kill us or not."

I lowered my hands from my head and stared at him. "How would it help to know it in advance?"

"Because if I'm going to die sooner rather than later, I'm going to have to speed up my plan to seduce you." He smiled and winked.

I rolled my eyes and swung my feet over the side of the bed.

The door flap opened and Leseran ducked inside, carrying a sack. Dex found his feet and moved between me and the elf.

"Sit down, fool," Leseran growled. "If the Telmara wanted you dead, it would be so already."

"If I'd remained sitting, you would've told me to stand and respect my betters," Dex muttered and plopped back down. "There's no pleasing you people."

"You can't keep us here," I said. "We were supposed to return to our convoy. If we're gone much longer, they'll come looking for us."

Leseran's frown deepened. "Your convoy of big game hunters is the least of our concerns. Without one of the people with them, they'd never find this camp, anyway."

"Then you could at least tell us why we're being detained. What do you plan to do with us?" I crossed my arms.

The elf sighed and shifted the sack under his arm. "I'm here to invite you to dinner. But first..." He upended the sack on the empty bed on the other side of the room, picking up a small white bar and tossing it to Dex. "You two stink. Clean yourselves up and put on some decent clothes. I've had to estimate your sizes. Considering how short you are, finding clothes that would fit you was a task."

Dex picked up a shirt and held it out in front of him like it would bite him. "I don't understand."

"We're going to clean you up, feed you, and send you on your way with some supplies. What's not to understand?"

"What about my sword?" I asked, shifting forward.

"Ah, that." Leseran winced slightly. "The sword you were carrying was an ancient elven artifact. Normally, we'd take possession of it, as it was likely stolen from our people. It happens more often than you'd think. Dwarves and greedy *dhalethein* always find ways to break into our tombs and strip the dead. However, this sword... It has a history. Perhaps it's best if I let the *Shainach* explain. For now, just get yourselves cleaned up and changed. I'll be waiting outside." He hurried out of the tent.

"What's a *Shainach*?" I asked Dex. "I'm having trouble keeping all these elvish words straight."

"It's a storyteller."

"Then why not just call it that?"

Dex shrugged and stood. "Well, because that's not exactly true, either. A *Shainach* is a historian, a keeper of both lore and memories. When one *Shainach* dies, he passes his knowledge to an apprentice in an intense magic ritual which ensures they lose no information from generation to generation. They're more important than your average storyteller. You could argue they're the core of elvish culture and history." He pulled his shirt over his head and tossed it lazily aside.

In my line of work, you get used to seeing all kinds of things. I'd seen more blood and guts than most. With injuries comes the awkward territory of helping co-workers patch up. I did my own patch jobs, but I wasn't above bandaging the wounded if the need arose. It was in that context that I usually viewed bodies, as things that needed fixing.

There was nothing on Dex that needed fixed. He was all lean, smooth muscle. The guild work kept him in shape.

"You keep staring at me like that, I might have to put on a show," he said halfway through unbuckling his belt.

I cleared my throat and turned my back to him. "A little warning before you go streaking through the tent, Dex."

"Why? Are you going to pretend to be all shy and modest?" He snorted. "Please. You're a beautiful woman who kills monsters for a living. If you try to tell me you've never seen a naked man before, I'll eat my hat. Which reminds me, we'll have to go back and find the damn thing."

"We're not going back there just for your hat."

"I'm going through all of this because of your sword. The least you could do is help me get my hat back. But you're just trying to change the topic on me. I bet you've left a bunch of heartbroken guys in your wake."

I folded my arms. "I'm usually a little busy saving people and killing things to get horizontal, Dex."

"So, no crazy ex-boyfriends I should be worried about?"

My cheeks burned. "We're not having this conversation."

"Okay, all right. Never let it be said I made a lady do anything she wasn't willing to." He patted himself loudly. "You can turn around now. The immediate danger of me seducing you with my rippling abs and sculpted ass has passed. You're safe again."

Slowly, I turned around. He'd shed the light leather armored vest he'd been wearing and the layers of protective clothing, donning a simpler blue tunic that reached his knees and simple brown pants.

"What do you think?" Dex asked, doing a little turn. "Do I look elvish enough? I think a nice, dramatic cloak would add something to the look."

I paced over the pile of clothing Leseran had dumped, picking up a light green dress before cringing and putting it back down. I hadn't worn a dress since Old Jim took me to church, which had been so long ago I couldn't even remember it. If Old Jim hadn't liked to tell the story of how much I hated the dress, I never would've known. I passed on the dress and picked up a set of clothing similar to the one Dex had slipped into.

"Not into dresses, eh?" he said, smirking.

"If you like it so much, why didn't you put it on?" I threw it at him.

He wadded up the dress and tossed it over his shoulder. "I'm not above it, but green's not really my color."

"Turn around so I can get dressed."

Dex turned around without protest.

I shrugged off my jacket and winced at the pain resurfacing in my arm. It probably needed looked at. "You know, I don't understand anything that's happening. First, we're begging for their help. Then we're prisoners and now some storyteller is going to explain why I've got to go buy a new sword."

"Elves are a strange bunch," Dex said with a shrug. "It's even crazier from my perspective."

"How so?" I tugged on a red tunic with laces on the sleeves.

"They've shown more interest in you than they ever did me, and I've got elven blood flowing through my veins. It's almost as if they like you better than me."

"I don't know that I'd go that far. They don't seem to like me very much either."

He chuckled. "Don't be offended. They're elves. They don't like anybody."

I finished dressing. The tunic was a little big, but it worked well enough once I put my belt back on. I felt naked without it, anyway. "Be honest, Dex. What do you think this is all about?" I asked, folding my clothes neatly and placing them on the bed.

Dex shrugged and put his hands on his hips. "Honestly, I've got nothing. But Leseran was right. If they wanted us dead, we would be. I've just never seen them do a turn like this. I think you're right to be suspicious. We should stick close tonight. Don't trust anyone who hasn't earned it."

It was twilight when we stepped out of the tent. More than a day had passed since we left the hunting convoy, though it almost felt like a lifetime. I wondered if Ike and Ash were worried about us. Had they sent a search party? What had become of Zia's vampires? I never thought I'd be sorry to imagine the creatures being put down, but she seemed pretty attached to them.

The elven camp was more active than it was when we'd arrived. Men and women worked together to chop wood, peel vegetables, and mind giant iron pots boiling over a fire pit that had been dug in the ground like a trench. Older children minded younger ones while sitting in groups and gossiping, pointing at us occasionally. The eyes of the elves weighed heavily on us as we met Leseran a few paces from the tent.

He turned around, arms crossed. "Well, your smell is less offensive at least."

"I'd like to talk to this *Shainach* of yours," I

said. "I think I'm owed an explanation."

"For once, we agree. Come. I'll take you to her." He turned around and marched further into the camp.

Dex and I followed.

Leseran led us through the small encampment to the very edge opposite the building where we'd met with the Telmara. It was a smaller hut with several nets hung on the outside. A group of youngsters ran by, giggling. We followed them around the hut to the back. Children had gathered into a circle to sit cross legged before an old woman in a padded chair. The old woman leaned heavily on a cane. Mounds of silver braids were piled upon her head, each one tied with a different color. Fading tattoos marked her cheeks, forehead, and hands The woman and the children turned their heads when we entered.

Leseran put a fist to his chest and bowed. "My apologies for interrupting, *Shainach*. The Telmara asked that I bring you these outsiders."

The old elf smiled. "Be welcome, strangers. Children, say hello."

"*Savidad*," muttered the children in unison. Some of them smiled at us with gap-toothed grins.

"Come, sit. Children, make room." The Shainach gestured to the circle of children in front of her. "Leseran, you too."

Leseran gave her a tight-lipped smile and

a bow. "I'm afraid my duties call me elsewhere tonight. Perhaps another time." He turned and gave us a warning glance. "I'll be within shouting distance should you need me," he said, and went on his way.

Dex and I sat at the edge of the circle. I expected the kids to give us plenty of distance as the adults had, but they crowded in, curious.

One of them poked at Dex's ears. "What's wrong with your ears? They're so small!"

"Dexter's mother is a human," replied the Shainach.

"Thanks for the reminder," Dex groaned.

"Did you forget who you were?" The Shainach leaned back in her seat and drew out a long pipe, filling the end. "Or maybe you wish to forget, like Rychell the Small. Who can tell me what happened to him?"

The children's hands all shot up eagerly until the Shainach picked one at random.

The little boy beamed and stood up straight. "He wanted to be a warrior, but the Telmara made him a cook instead. He was so ashamed, he ran into the forest to hide."

"That's foolish," said a little girl, her arms wrapped around her knees. "You can't run away from who you are."

The Shainach nodded. "That's right, Ailara, but Rychell didn't believe it was his destiny to be a cook, even though he showed great skill at it, and enjoyed it very much. He believed that being a cook wasn't important enough. But everyone needs to eat. It was Rychell the Small who fed the people during the Great Famine. His skill made him a hero. All of us have our roles to play for the betterment of the world we live in. Even you, Dexter."

Dex's head flopped to one side with a sigh. "Please don't call me that. Just Dex."

The little girl raised her hand and rose once the Shainach called on her. "Um, how come his mom is a human? Isn't it forbidden?"

The Shainach crossed her ankles and lit her pipe, leaning back. "So is having an extra cookie, but we all sometimes enjoy one now and again, don't we? Rules exist for our protection, but even the most well-meaning rules can sometimes overreach. And there is no command that can override nature. Just like you sometimes want what's forbidden, so do we all, child. Some believe that the mere act of forbidding one thing only increases our desire for it."

"Like Orrian and the powerful magic," said another child.

The Shainach nodded. "Just so. But today we're not going to hear about Orrian and her battles against the Willow Mage."

A collective groan of disappointment rose from the children gathered.

"Today," continued the Shainach, "you will hear about the fall of the elves, about how we came to be here, and why. It is a story of many sorrows, a shameful story. But we must remember it and keep the truth in our hearts. If we forget our sins past, we learn nothing from it."

"Pardon," I said, hesitant to interrupt. "But Leseran said my sword had a history with your people and that I should ask you about it. What makes it so special? Is it cursed?"

"The history of that sword is inextricably tied to the greatest sin of the elves. Listen, and you'll hear your answers, outsider."

The Shainach sucked on her pipe for a long moment before answering. A silver sheen passed over her eyes and quickly disappeared. "Long ago, before the eldest among us was born, the elves lived in another place. Our lands stretched from the salt sea in the east to the tall snowy mountains in the west, from the wastes in the north to the Dread Forest in the south. The domain of the elves was vast and rich. Our cities rose into the sky, glass towers glittering in the sun. Magic in those days was plentiful and used without fear. Everyone was gifted with it, from the poorest child in the slums to the wealthiest lords in their towers. It was as common to us as blades of grass to you, everywhere and natural.

"But it wasn't enough. Some sought more. The lords waged wars against one another, pitting brother against brother in pursuit of more. Every great nation raced to develop new ways of fighting, of causing pain and hurt to one another. We waged war against ourselves in our endless pursuit of more."

"More what?" I asked.

The Shainach shrugged. "More wealth. More power. More land and more people. There were many small wars fought over many things. Toward the end, it was so common that war was a way of life. The people barely cared what it was for. But the war for more drove every part of their lives from their economies to who became our leaders. Whoever had more was always one step ahead in every way, and each group waged an endless struggle to take from the other."

She was silent for a long time, silver-tinged eyes looking out over the busy work going on in the camp. The gentle ting of metal against metal rang out from someone working somewhere, though I couldn't pinpoint the direction. It sounded peaceful, quiet. Almost idyllic. A far cry from the hustle and bustle of the cities I knew.

At length, the old elf spoke. "Before there was the Telmara, there were the Felmor, great magister lords among our people. It was their job to protect the elves, and to seek knowledge so to serve better. But they forgot their role was to serve and sought instead to rule. The Felmor used thieir positions to gain more power. With forbidden magic, they destroyed the peace of ages and our people descended into war."

I shrugged. "Sounds a lot like human history. We had our share of wars too."

"Our people were no stranger to war, but this war was different," the *Shainach* said. "Magic became a weapon, and each sect wielded it against the other. The Felmor became servants of death and destruction, using their knowledge to invent new magics that would kill more people more efficiently. They told themselves it would bring an end to the fighting they themselves had sparked a generation past. I do not know which faction opened the first rifts," she said, looking to the sky, "only that they didn't come here."

My back went rigid. "Is that true? The elves caused all of this?"

Humans had their theories. Some said the rifts were a natural phenomenon, opened when our reality butted up against another. It created some sort of subatomic spark and the world was never the same. That was the leading scientific theory, at least. No one knew for sure, though. Religious groups taught the rifts were physical manifestations of their gods' wrath, or a punishment from Heaven for mortal sins. Other groups said it was some shady organization that caused it, performing experiments that blended black magic and science.

No matter the story, they all had one thing in common. Humans blamed other humans for the tragedy. There was always some scapegoat, some minority group, being singled out as being responsible. In the early days, that led to mass riots and attempts at genocide around the world.

We killed more of our people than the rifts did, yet the rifts took all the blame. It was easier than admitting humans were so terrible.

Now that history was largely forgotten, humanity preferring to gloss over our own mistakes and shortcomings rather than learn from them.

If it got out that elves were responsible, I could only imagine how my people would take it.

I envisioned a large-scale war of extermination, humans hunting elves and elves hunting humans in kind. Cities burned and kingdoms fell. Millions would die.

"That is what the memories say," said the *Shainach*, nodding. "That we opened the rifts to escape a dying world, however, is only a half-truth. It must be understood that our world was only dying because we had destroyed it. Our wars killed our world. But we didn't know it when the Felmor opened the first rifts. They had decided they would invade other worlds in search of more. That is how they found the Black City."

"The Black City," I repeated, barely above a whisper. "The heretics spoke of it, too."

She nodded slowly. "That doesn't surprise me. Perhaps in their insanity, they've seen the truth."

"The Black City." Dex wiggled his fingers. "Sounds ominous."

"It was in the Black City they learned the art of summoning and binding elemental spirits to their will. The Felmor called forth spirits of all kinds and enslaved them: spirits of air, water, fire, spirits of justice, of vengeance. They bound them to their bodies and, in so doing, became something *other*. They became the first *Gwœ́tach.* In your language, Shadow Warriors."

I hugged myself tight, suppressing a shiver. "The stag-headed creature in my visions... It's one of these Shadow Warriors?"

She put her pipe in her mouth and nodded.

"I don't get it," Dex said. "How does one of these *Gwœ́tach* get stuck in a sword?"

"Dark magic that's been lost to time," said the *Shainach.* "Even the memories don't speak of it. We know only that the ancients understood the essence of a living being to be completely separate from the body. Thus, they theorized immortality could be achieved if the essence were contained in a vessel that didn't age. It was taboo magic, even then. Not that the Felmor cared. They reveled in the forbidden. It doesn't surprise me to find one inside an instrument of death. Our people have many stories about *Gwœ́tach* artifacts surfacing from time to time since the great wars. When they do, the days that follow are bleak indeed."

"So there's some type of demon inside the sword. Great." I threw my hands up.

The Shainach lowered her pipe with a frown. "Don't be so quick to demonize the *Gwœ́tach.*"

“But you just said—”

She held up a hand, silencing Dex. “Remember their motivation for going to the Black City was to end war. They believed they could fashion a weapon so terrible, the very threat of its existence would bring peace. In your history, you did the same. The atomic bomb, nuclear weapons.”

“It was a mistake.” I don’t know why I felt like I was on trial. The Shainach had just told me her people had done something even worse. At least humans hadn’t destroyed the planet by hurling bombs at each other, though the number of times we had come close was truly terrifying.

The Shainach nodded. “As it often is. Weapons do not end wars. Weapons exist to fight wars. War can only truly ever end if we lay down all arms and learn to resolve differences peacefully. The Telmara were formed with this goal. We seek to heal our people, and minimize our harm to this world as penance for the damage we did to our own.”

“So did it work?” asked one child “Did the Felmor end the war?”

“In a manner of speaking, though not how they intended. They woke something up in the Black City. Something *hungry*. Something that reached into our world and nearly eradicated us. The crystals the humans call magicite grew out of everything, corrupting the land and the people. Sickness swept through our cities, driven by the presence of it.

"The last of the Felmor magisters used his power to enter the Black City and sacrificed his life to bridge our world to a world beyond. Those who could, traveled through the rifts and came here, never to return to the world they left behind."

She slumped back against the wall of her hut as if telling the story exhausted her. "Today, our people camp near the rifts and keep to ourselves. Our scholars are working, just as the humans are, to close the portals we opened long ago. We keep to ourselves and dream of one day returning home."

"Do you think it's possible?" asked an older boy with a long braid and bright eyes. "Can we really go home?"

A heavy sigh escaped her lips. She closed her eyes. "My old bones do ache for the homeland. I wish my spirit could rest there instead of in this strange world, but even we cannot return through the rifts. Not yet. But perhaps one of you will be the one to change it."

No one comes back except for Ash. I pressed my lips together in thought. Why had he come back? How? "Say someone were to fall into a rift. What would happen to them?"

"They'd die," answered one child. "Don't you know that?"

"Hush, Jhearthe," chided the Shainach.

"So there's no magic, Felmor or Elven, that

you can think of that might let a person pass into a rift and come back safely?"

She gripped her chair and leaned forward, her brow furrowed. "Girl, if I were to encounter anyone claiming to have survived such a feat, I would be very cautious. Not everything that looks human is. It is a lesson hard learned by the elves when we faced the Felmor. Rifts are not small magic that some enchanted trinket can protect you from."

"I know. It's just…" I folded my hands and lowered my head. "I lost someone once."

"Then they are gone, and you must accept that," said the *Shainach*, putting a hand on my back.

"I have a question," said Dex. "Why did the Telmara change their tune when she reacted to the presence in the sword?"

The Shainach shrugged. "It's obviously trying to communicate with her. We don't know why, or how, but the *Gwǽtach* has chosen to speak to you, Ember. The Telmara tried to communicate with the spirit on their own, but to no avail. You have contacted a spirit that we hope will one day tell us much about the old world."

"But I don't even have magic," I said, shaking my head. "I'm nobody. I mean, I found the thing by accident."

The Shainach narrowed her eyes and pressed her lips together. "When something greater calls, you must answer. Be it fate, destiny, the gods, or an ancient spirit, we mortals can no more fight against the tides of the universe than we can stab the wind. It is the decision of the Telmara not to interfere, but to watch your progress with interest."

"From a safe distance, of course." Dex grunted and folded his arms. "A lot of help you guys are."

She glared at him. "It is not the place of the Telmara to interfere with what we do not understand. We did that once, and it did not turn out so well for our people." The Shainach rose, her hands on her lower back. "Now, children, it looks like it's almost time to eat. Play, but stay out of the way of the cooks."

The children jumped up and bolted in every direction, chattering and giggling with each other. One girl stopped to pull on Dex's ears. "Will you come play?"

He winced. "I don't think that's such a good idea."

The little girl's face fell. "Oh."

"Go, child. These two have important matters to attend to." The Shainach waved her off and pointed to the camp. "I think your friend is finally feeling better."

I rose from the ground and turned around. Zia wandered through the camp as if she were looking for familiar faces.

"Go on," urged the Shainach. "Enjoy the evening. Tomorrow morning, Leseran will escort you back to your convoy."

"Thank you, Shainach," Dex said, rising.

She dismissed his thanks with a wave of her hand. "Bah! Don't thank me. You're the idiot traveling with her. That puts you in the line of fire. Just don't come crying to me when you get burned, young man. You'll have to navigate all this without my help."

"Well, she was a laugh and a half," Dex muttered to me as we left the Shainach's hut behind. "Do you believe all that?"

I shook my head. "I don't know what to believe, but I know we can't tell anyone. If humans anywhere suspect the elves are behind the Cataclysm, even if it's only a story, they'll hunt them to the last, Dex."

He rubbed the back of his head and sighed. "You get the cool demon sword, and what do I get? Secrets to keep. Always the sidekick and never the hero. Typical."

"Cheer up, Dex." I slapped his back, and he stumbled forward a step. "They say we're all the heroes of our own stories. Maybe you just haven't met your villain yet."

"Or maybe I have." He cringed and nodded to Leseran coming down the road toward us, half-dragging Zia with him.

When she saw us, Zia broke away and ran up to us, red faced. "There you two are! Please tell this pointy-eared idiot that we need to go. Now. I've already been away from my vampires too long."

To his credit, Leseran took the insult in stride. "If you leave now, you'll be passing through Heretic territory in the dark. I didn't have the healers save your life just so you could go get killed. Besides, we'll make better time in the daylight. I'll have you back to your convoy by midday tomorrow. You have my word. Now, if you'll excuse me..." He put a fist to his chest, bowed, and took off.

Zia lifted her arms and let them fall limply to her sides. "What are we supposed to do in the meantime? Just sit around and wait?"

Dex slid behind me. "Is that a whole orzalope they're roasting over there? Well, I know what I'm doing."

"Seriously, Dex? All you can think of is to eat at a time like this?" Zia frowned.

"Well, that's not all, but my father is part of this group, and I've got no idea which of the others are my siblings. I wouldn't want to accidentally seduce one of them, would I?" He hooked his arms over our shoulders and pulled us toward the firepit.

Chapter Fourteen

The elves, for all their flaws, really knew how to live. They gathered for their meals communally and broke off into small groups to socialize and eat. I had never seen an orzalope before that day, let alone eaten one. If I had to place it, I'd put it somewhere between mutton and venison without the gaminess. They served us each a large portion of meat so tender it fell easily off the bone along with a healthy helping of purple potatoes, yellow carrots, and some wilted greens I couldn't identify. It was all perfect.

Dex, Zia and I kept mostly to ourselves, finding a small patch of grass at the edge of the small clearing. I ate and watched the elves talk and laugh amongst themselves. Occasionally, one would throw a look our way, but mostly, they ignored their guests. That was fine with me. I'd had enough of being the center of attention for a while.

"I suppose I should thank you, Dex," Zia said, pushing her meat around in the wooden bowl they'd given her.

Dex looked up from his food and swallowed. "Me? Why? What did I do?"

Zia sighed and put the bowl down. "Well, if you hadn't convinced the elves to heal me, I'd have become one of those *things*."

"It's nothing you wouldn't have done for me," Dex said, shrugging one shoulder.

She opened her mouth, closed it, grimaced, and turned away.

I got the feeling what Dex said wasn't true. If the roles had been reversed, she would've left him to his fate. *All the more reason for me to keep my situation a secret.* I cleared my throat. "So, Zia, does the Institute have files on the elves?"

"Oh, please." She rolled her eyes. "We have entire databases dedicated to them and the dwarves. While most humans are content to think they're a myth, we've spent the last few decades studying them. And of course I knew about Dex being half-elf. I did extensive background checks within the Institute databases on everyone who joined the hunt."

Dex touched the tops of his ears, a self-conscious but instinctive gesture.

"I won't tell anyone," Zia promised. "It means nothing to me, so long as you do your job."

"I'm not sure how I feel about the Institute keeping tabs on me," Dex said, frowning.

"Don't feel anything. They have files on everyone these days. Well, almost everyone." She glanced at me. "Some people's files are more complete than others."

As the eating waned, the atmosphere around us changed. People started gathering in larger groups, the conversations becoming louder and more playful. Music started somewhere, and where there's music, there's dancing, even among elves.

Dex watched the dancers move with interest, the shadow of their graceful movements flickering across his face.

I put a hand on his arm. "Are you okay?"

He forced a smile. "Me? I'm ecstatic. I mean, why wouldn't I be? For most of my childhood, all I wanted was to run away and find the elves and see what that side of my family was like. Turns out, elves are just as full of shit as humans."

"I'm sorry."

He shrugged. "It's not news to me. I've been out here before, remember?" His expression darkened. "But what we learned from the Shainach… It's troubling."

I glanced over at Zia. She was listening in on our conversation. I didn't trust her not to blab to the Institute, so I figured it would be best if I steered the conversation away from how the elves had probably destroyed the world.

I shrugged. "It could be worse. It could always be worse."

Zia snorted. "Saying something like that

invites trouble. On that note, I think I'm going to turn in. I want to be on the road at first light. The sooner we can get back to my vampires, the better off we'll all be." She stood and started back down the hill for the small hut Dex and I had been in earlier.

I watched her go, thinking about how different things might've turned out if even one detail of the last few days had changed. If the heretics hadn't ambushed us and taken Zia, I never would've learned about the creature in the sword. Meeting the elves had also given me hope that maybe the crystal infected scar across my stomach could be cured. They had extracted the magicite from Zia, after all. Maybe they knew some ancient form of healing that could help me. I had wanted to bring it up to the Shainach, but I was afraid. The elves might kick us out, or Dex might decide I was better off dead. For so long, I had kept it a secret, trusting no one. If I wanted a chance to change my future, to survive, then I'd have to trust someone eventually enough to ask, and my time with the elves was running out.

"It's amazing they could heal her," I said. "I always thought magicite ingestion was fatal."

"The heretics survive it."

"But not forever. It infects them, changes them. Once it gets in you, there's no going back. At least, that's what I always thought. Do you realize what this means? If the elves have a technique that can help people..."

Dex sighed. "It means nothing. They won't share their methods with outsiders. I wouldn't be surprised if even Zia doesn't remember what they did. Elven magic is a closely guarded secret. Yet another reason they don't care much for me." He looked down at his palm and flexed his fingers. "For most people, magic isn't innate. You have to use magicite infused items, or be exposed to small amounts of it over time. Even most humans who are born with powers have them because of exposure in the womb to trace amounts. But the elves, it's as natural to them as breathing."

"I don't understand why they'd have anything against that. I mean, it's not like you chose any of this."

He made a fist. "I was expected to suppress what I could do. Even growing up, I had to hide my ears, hide my powers. Even if mom hadn't made me, I would've done it myself. I wanted to fit in. Besides, I knew the price of having powers. If people found out, I'd get sent away to one of those magic schools run by DEMO."

DEMO was almost as bad as the Institute when it came to abuse of power, and they had offices and agents everywhere.

They also ran the magic academies, which snatched children away from their homes and families as soon as they showed signs of ability, and sequestered them in boarding schools. Of course, wealthy families could afford to send their kids to upper class academies where they were well taken care of, but I doubted that was Dex's experience. For the average kid, the academies were a grueling gauntlet of trials, tests, and training. In the end, academy kids were passed to the Institute, went to work for local governments, or joined a guild. There weren't many career prospects beyond that for someone with magical talent. At least, not legal ones.

Dex picked up a stick and started doodling in the dirt. "They eventually sniffed me out. I was the best elementalist in my class. You'd never know it, though. I learned the hard way it was better to pretend to be mediocre, so I didn't show up the human kids. Fewer black eyes that way."

"That must've been hard."

"Life's hard. For everyone. I'm not special." He shook his head and tossed the stick away. "Anyway, I don't know the first thing about healing magic. Not my area. Now, if you want a flaming inferno the size of an elephant or a wall of ice, I'm your man."

"Half a man, anyway," said Leseran. He'd sneaked up behind us, silent. He smirked and folded his hands behind his back. "I escorted your friend back to the guest quarters and put a guard on the door. Will you two be joining her or do I have to keep babysitting you from the shadows?"

"Actually," I said, standing, "I'd like to talk to the people who healed Zia."

"Why?" Leseran looked me up and down as if I'd just announced I wanted to eat his firstborn.

I lifted my arm. "I thought maybe they'd like to look at this warg bite." It was a pretense. The bite was already healing nicely aside from a little pain whenever I moved the arm, but if it got me an audience alone with the healers, I'd take it.

"Is it bothering you? I could take a look," Dex offered.

I raised an eyebrow. "No offense, but you just got done telling me you don't know the first thing about healing magic."

"Well, magic isn't everything." He crossed his arms.

"Let me see." Leseran grabbed my arm and yanked on it.

I let out a pained gasp and hissed through my teeth as he poked it through the bandage.

"Hmm. Warg bites can be serious. It looks like you could do with a change of bandages as well." He let go of my arm. "I suppose if I take you to the healers, I'll get a few minutes to enjoy the evening, provided the half-ears minds his distance."

"I'm not going anywhere," Dex muttered. "I'll just sit here like a good half-ears. No trouble at all."

"Very well then. Follow me." Leseran stepped around Dex and started around the perimeter of the post-dinner merriment.

I followed him to the far side of the clearing where a group of elves with white collars sat, just apart from the rest of the group. The collared elves moved among the people gathered—which ranged in age from the very old to the very young—and helped them with their food. Some of them needed to be fed, either because they had extensive injuries, or seemed to have some other issue I couldn't see. There were patients who were confined to chairs, elder elves who could no longer sit up on their own, and small children that barely stopped running back and forth long enough to grab a bite of food.

I immediately felt guilty for interrupting what seemed to be a regular evening. The healers already had their hands full.

A white-collared elf with stripes of silver in her brown hair came to greet us. She spoke briefly with Leseran in Elvish before beckoning to me. "Come, come. Let's have a look."

"I'm sorry to bother you," I offered as she showed me to a bench sitting away from the others.

"It's no bother if you've got a wound. Now, let's see it."

I extended my arm. She carefully unwrapped the dressing, and I winced at the sight of it. The warg bite was indeed healing, but it'd left my forearm bruised a deep shade of purple. A jagged line of broken skin marked the bite.

"My, my. That's quite a wound. Let me take care of it for you." She placed her hands gently over my bruised forearm.

"A warg bit me. One of the heretic's wargs. It could be infected with..." I trailed off as the warmth of her healing magic enveloped my arm. It was as comforting as a warm bath on a chilly day at first. Then the lightning bolt of pain struck across my abdomen. I pulled my arm away with a pained cry.

The healer was stunned for a moment until she calmly rose. "Neesa, watch the children for me. We'll need privacy. Come with me, human."

"But—"

The healer bent over and hissed in my ear. "Don't make a fuss. If Leseran and his warriors find out, you'll be dead within the hour. Now, come with me."

I pressed my lips together and glanced over at the other healers who were giving me curious looks. There was no choice but to go with her. I followed the healer to one of the white-roofed huts just behind where they had gathered for their meal. She held open the door flap for me and I slipped inside.

Unlike the other huts, this one had several sections divided into rooms by white sheets hanging from the spokes in the ceiling. She ushered me into a room and had me sit on a platform in the center.

The elven healer verified we were alone in the hut before she closed the curtains and put her back to them. "Show me."

"I…" I snapped my mouth closed and turned away. "I don't know what you're talking about."

"Don't play with me, girl. I know you've got magicite growing out of you. It's why the healing magic hurts. The more magic that touches you, the faster they grow. So, let's see it."

I put a hand over my stomach and slid to the far end of the bench, away from her. "It's not like you think. I'm not like the heretics. I take antigen potions to keep the growth in check. I'm not dangerous."

She sighed. "I didn't say you were. Go on, then. Off with the shirt. Let me see."

Isn't this why I came here? Maybe she knows how to help. Slowly, I lifted my shirt. I don't know what I expected. Maybe for her eyes to widen, or for her to gasp in surprise.

She didn't do either of those things. She simply bent over me, examining the area carefully. "How long has it been like this?"

"It happened five years ago."

"Five years." She clicked her tongue.

"Can you help me?" My voice sounded small, almost child-like in my own ears.

"You mean can I cure you?" She leaned back with a sigh. "The magicite is complicated. Once it gets into your bloodstream, there's often little even we can do. Your friend was lucky the tainted blood was simply sitting in her stomach.

She had digested none of it yet. Your situation is different, I'm afraid. The magicite has taken root in the soft tissue, but it hasn't spread. That's nothing short of miraculous. Antigen potions, you were saying?"

"Can the crystals be removed?" I'd thought about trying to cut them out myself in the past, but I was too worried I'd pass out from blood loss. I needed someone who knew what they were doing.

She shook her head. "It's unlikely we'd be able to remove it all. You know that, despite the antigen, the crystal *is* growing? It will eventually kill you."

I rolled my shirt down. "I know."

"I'm sorry." The healer sat down on the bench next to me. "I wish I had a better answer for you, but even we can't fix everything."

My heart sank into my stomach. I squeezed my eyes closed and turned away. "How long until it kills me?"

"It's impossible to say. The more magic and magicite you're exposed to, the faster the crystals will grow. Eventually, they'll move into your non-vital organs. Then they'll attack the vital organs, growing in your lungs and around your heart. The crystals will infect your blood and travel to your brain. They could affect your vision. You could hear voices. See things."

"I'll go crazy like the heretics," I said.

She nodded and rose from the bench,

smoothing her hands over her collar. "But there is another option." The healer lifted a plain white box from a shelf on the wall and opened it. Inside were two vials of liquid, one red and one clear. "I cannot cure you, but I can provide you with the power to decide your own fate. The clear vial brings on sleep. The red one ensures you will never wake. You will slip away peacefully, pain-free. Once you take them, there is no coming back, so you must be sure."

I took the red vial and lifted it, looking at my distorted reflection in the glass. It wasn't the first time I had thought of ending things. If death were unavoidable, wouldn't it be better if I could choose when and how it happened? How many years had I struggled against the inevitable, grasping at reasons to live? Even this hunt was more of the same.

But I had just found Ash, and I wanted some time to get to know him before I made my decision. There was more to learn about the creature in my sword trying to communicate with me, and a dragon waiting to be slain. They were simple reasons to live, but as good a reason as any.

I carefully placed the red vial back in the box. "I'm not ready."

She nodded. "I didn't expect you would be. But when the time comes, seek us out. Ask for me by name. I am Feylin. I will make sure you have what you need without question." She closed the box and put it back on the shelf.

"I appreciate it, but why offer it to me? I'm a human. You barely know me."

"It is true the *erimor* is normally only reserved for our people, for warriors who fought bravely and the dishonored. However, you are not just any human. I'm told you carry the *Gwǽtach mhor*. That affords you some standing. Whether the destiny of the *Gwǽtach* will lead you to great good or evil, it doesn't matter. I am a healer. My responsibility is to care, to provide peace and a pain-free existence however I can. Human, elf, or beast makes no difference to me. My oath supersedes my race."

"Thank you for the offer," I said, standing. "I suppose this means you won't be able to do much for my arm, huh?"

She shook her head gravely. "Not unless you want to advance the infection. You must avoid magic, child. Not just having it used upon you, but being near it. And steer clear of rifts as well. There is no telling how your infection will react to a rift."

"Trust me, I don't have any plans to go near a rift anytime soon." With the healer's help, I bandaged my arm again and left the tent.

Rather than immediately rejoin Dex, I wandered away from the main body of the camp. Leseran or one of his people was likely shadowing me, but I didn't care. I wanted to be alone, or at least as close to it as I could get.

I found my way to the top of a small knoll just behind two huts. I was close enough to the revelry that the music and voices were a dull murmur. The hill rolled into a thick forest which rose into the side of a mountain. Veins of something a silvery blue marked the exposed granite. As the sun sank, it struck the silver, and the mountains shimmered as if they were alive.

I sat and hugged my knees to my chest, watching the world go about its business. Thoughts floated around in my head, too ephemeral to hold. I wondered about dying, entertaining thoughts of an afterlife. There were still people who believed in that sort of thing, though I wasn't one of them. It must've been comforting to have no fear of death. For as often as I put my life on the line, I'd never truly beaten that. In the moment, when I was battling heretics, or dire bears, or trolls, I didn't really think about it. I was too busy surviving to die.

But death was coming for me sooner than he had any right to.

I thought about everything I had done up until that moment, how much time I'd wasted on meaningless things. In the grand scheme of it all, waking every day to fight for a little coin felt stupid. There had to be more to life than that. Here I was dying, and I hadn't even had time to make my mark on the world.

I can change all of that now that Ash is back. My dreams are all dead, but his aren't. I closed my eyes and allowed myself to imagine the world Ash had described, a kingdom carved out of wild land. A new city, built brick by brick to be the seat of an empire with spires that challenged cruel magic to tear it down. A city and an empire where the strong protected the weak, the wrong-doers were brought to justice, and no one went to bed cold and hungry. Wasn't that what every-one wanted? I could fight for that. I could *live* for that.

"There you are!"

I turned my head as Dex plopped down cross-legged next to me. He was carrying my sword, and he seemed to have found his hat somehow. "Your hat..."

"I come bearing gifts from the Telmara," he said, and held my sword out to me. "A group of scouts went back to the heretic stronghold to make sure it was cleared out. They were kind enough to retrieve my hat for me. As for your sword, apparently, it's yours, free and clear."

I took the sword from him. "I'm surprised they let you walk around camp armed. They seem pretty suspicious of us."

"I'm useless with a sword, and that's prob-ably pretty obvious. But you should've seen Les-eran's face when he realized you'd wandered off. He's still looking for you. Lucky I found you first, eh? What are you doing out here, anyway? Any luck getting the arm treated?"

I put a hand over the gauze wrapped

around my arm. "Turns out the magic was too much trouble. It'll heal on its own."

"That's how it is, isn't it? Magic. Pain in the ass." He leaned back lazily, and we sat there in amicable silence for a long time. "Can I ask you a personal question? Why did you join this hunt?"

I shrugged and let the sword lay across my lap. "It's been a long time since Ash and I have seen each other. I wanted to catch up."

"I feel like it's more than that, this thing between you and Ash. More complicated than a couple of childhood friends catching up and bonding over dead dragons."

"Maybe it is." I closed my eyes and focused on the feeling of the wind on my face. "I think I was in love with him once, but now... Now I don't know. He and I have been apart for so long, we've both changed. That change isn't necessarily good either. We used to tell each other everything, but now there's something I can't tell him, and I get the feeling he isn't telling me everything either."

"When I was younger, there was this girl, Jesse," Dex said, clasping his hands over his chest. "She was beautiful, talented, smart... Everything. I thought she was the one. Best of all, she didn't know where I'd come from or what I was. See, we'd met at some academy function. When she went back to her school and I to mine, we kept in touch. Eventually, letters turned into meetings, turned into midnight rendezvous. You know the story. Boy meets girl. Boy falls for girl,

girl falls for him. They kiss and make plans to live happily ever after."

I fell onto my back, looking up at the sky, and mimicked his hand placement over my chest. "Why do I get the feeling it didn't end so well?"

"Spoiler alert: I'm still a bachelor. Anyway, I proposed, and she accepted... Until she found out the truth. There are only so many situations where one can get away with wearing a cowboy hat." He lifted his hat and waved it at me.

I rolled over onto my stomach and propped up my chin, raising an eyebrow. "You really didn't think she'd notice the ears?"

Dex shrugged. "I thought I would explain it to her, and she'd be more accepting than she turned out to be. Point is, I learned the hard way that secrets are the antithesis of love. Real love is honest, but it isn't blind. If you feel like something is off, that usually means it is. Whatever it is he's hiding, it's going to come out one day and bite you both in the ass. That's just my two cents, anyway."

I grunted. "Great. What's the world coming to? I'm taking relationship advice from a perpetual bachelor. And here I thought you were trying to get into my pants yourself."

"What can I say? I'm a sucker for a good love story, even if it's not my own." He winked and sat up. "On a more serious note, I get bad vibes from that guy. Maybe I'm feeling some of what you're feeling. Ash is... unusual. There are too many things about him I don't know."

"Then why did you sign up for the hunt?" I asked.

His face sobered. He clasped his arms around his knees and looked out at the sun setting behind the mountains. "Because I want to be famous. A hunt like this, it'll go a long way to spreading my name around. Especially if I'm lucky enough to get the killing blow."

I laughed. "Why would you want that?"

"Because if you're famous, nobody forgets you." The way he said it, he sounded almost sad.

In a strange way, I understood. We only had a limited number of years to leave our mark on the world. Dex didn't want to fade away, just another guild leader in another city. I wanted to do something that mattered. We both had our own reasons for being on that hunt.

Dex stretched and stood. "Well, I think we've let Leseran sweat long enough. It's time we got back before his head explodes." He offered me a hand.

I took it and he pulled me to my feet, but didn't let go.

"Ember, I..." Dex looked down and realized he was still holding my hand. He let it go and cleared his throat before rubbing the back of his head. "I just wanted to thank you for listening and putting up with me. I know I can be a sarcastic ass sometimes. I can't talk about half this stuff with anyone and it's been... Well, it's been nice to get some of it out in the open, you know? With someone who isn't going to judge me."

"What right do I have to judge you? We're all human, Dex."

"Half," he corrected with a wink, and stepped back. "Also, it'd be awesome if you didn't tell everyone back at camp about my shitty family, sad upbringing, and failed romance. I have a reputation to maintain."

I rolled my eyes and started up the hill. "Of course, Dex. Anything for you."

Chapter Fifteen

The hut had only two beds, and Zia was in one of them, fast asleep. Dex insisted I take the last one and positioned himself by the door, propped up by a pillow. He lowered his hat over his face, but I got the feeling he wasn't fully asleep.

I thought I would have a lot of trouble falling asleep, considering my strange surroundings and everything that had happened over the last few days, but I was out almost as soon as I put my head down.

At first, I drifted in a dreamless sleep. I had the distinct feeling that I was floating down a relaxing stream, or maybe in the clouds. My body was present, but weightless and unreachable beyond a veil of foggy sleep.

I woke when someone put a gentle hand on my shoulder. It was still dark, and the night quiet, but I could just barely make out Ash's outline in the night.

I sat up. "Ash? What are you—"

He put a finger to his lips and offered me a hand.

I glanced over at where Zia slept. The bed was empty. Dex was no longer at his post by the door. "Where are they?"

"Safe," Ash said. "Please, come with me. There's something I need you to see."

My mind reached to question the situation. There were too many things that didn't make sense. How had Ash gotten there? Where were the others? Why had the elves just let him walk through their camp? But when I tried to give the questions form, they faded beyond my grasp.

I put my hand in Ash's.

We walked hand in hand out of the hut and stepped into a foggy forest.

Ancient tree trunks stretched into the sky, their boughs thick enough to block out the sky. Fog wrapped around them like a blanket, painted on reality in wispy brush strokes. Crickets sang, owls hooted, and fireflies flashed. The forest felt as alive as the two of us, and even aware.

I didn't question where the elven camp had gone. In the moment, it made perfect sense, as if I expected to wake up there.

I rubbed the chill from my shoulders. "How far are we from the others?"

"Not far. Here." Ash unclasped his black cloak and wrapped it around my shoulders. "I didn't realize it was so cold."

I hugged the cloak closer. "It wasn't earlier. It rarely gets so chilly this time of year, does it? But you didn't wake me up to talk about the weather."

"No," he said gravely. His face fell, and he took a step away, leaning a forearm against one of the tree trunks.

"What is it, Ash? What's wrong?"

He lifted his head and an ethereal green light glowed on his face, but Ash wasn't the source. I followed his gaze and found him looking up at a rift. Somehow, the forest had fallen away, revealing a mountainside. Ice clung to the silver cliffs, reflecting the ghostly light.

My breath caught in my throat at the sight of it, and I moved to take a step back. My foot slid on a patch of ice, and I fell.

Ash caught me with a hand on my back at the last second, keeping me from tumbling down the mountainside. He held me at a distance for a long moment, looking down at me. The light of the rift flashed in his eyes, illuminating some dark uncertainty I hadn't seen before. Silent wind tugged at his hair.

I swallowed, my heart hammering in my chest. "Ash?"

He shifted his grip, pulling me against him. Startled, and now overbalanced, I looked up at him. The uncertainty was gone, replaced by the old spark of mischief that had once been there. For a moment, he was the Ash I had known before we went after that last bounty, before Old Jim died, before Ash fell into the rift and disappeared for five years. He smiled that old, familiar smile and kissed me softly.

Thunder growled overhead. A thick arm of lightning arced around the rift before shooting out and striking the ground at our feet. Rocks exploded, and the world was suddenly on fire, pushing us apart. I tumbled down the mountainside, gathering scrapes and bruises as I did.

When I finally came to a stop, I groaned and pushed myself up to look for Ash, but he wasn't at the bottom of the mountain. I looked up, in the rift's direction, and found him walking toward it, one arm up to shield his face from the wind and gathering storm.

"Ash!" I screamed his name as I fought to my feet. "Ash, stop it! Come back!"

The wind rose, howling through the mountain pass. Thunder growled from the rift as if it were a living being. It was too loud for him to have heard me. Yet he paused and turned back, hesitating.

Our eyes connected. His face was a mask of regret. Without words, I understood what he meant to say, even if I couldn't understand why.

He turned around again, fighting his way toward the rift.

I lowered my head and struck the rocks with a fist, unwilling to watch him leave me alone all over again. As my hand struck the ground it changed, transforming into a shallow pool. I watched as ripples distorted my reflection. Mist curled around me, and the sounds of the forest returned.

Something let out a heavy, snorting breath behind me.

Slowly, I turned to look over my shoulder. My breath caught as I looked at the shadow warrior behind me. Red eyes blazed inside the stag-skull helmet. Talons gripped the hilt of his great sword. With every breath, smoke poured from the nostril holes of the stag skull.

I should have been afraid, as I had been the last two times I had seen it. But this time, I noticed something different. The creature's massive antlers weren't bare bone. A white flowering ivy grew over them, the petals wilted and dying. Looking at them filled me with an inexplicable sadness.

Slowly, with shaky hands, I reached out to touch the skull. The bone was cool and smooth under my fingers, as real as any I had ever touched, though I knew I wasn't really there, touching anything. "This is a dream." The forest had grown quiet. My words echoed in the emptiness. "But you're real, aren't you?"

The shadow warrior leaned into my hand. Its red eyes flickered and then faded into strangely familiar gunmetal blue eyes. Its armor creaked, receding back to wherever it had grown from, revealing the naked body of a man. After the armor disappeared, the skull came loose and fell aside on its own.

My jaw fell open in surprise at the sight of the man beneath. “Dex?”

He took a single, shuddering breath before collapsing into my lap.

I woke up back in the hut with my breath caught in my throat and sweat on my back.

Dex stumbled back a step before falling on his ass. “Damn,” he said, rubbing his jaw. “That’s quite a right hook.”

“Sorry,” I mumbled, and put my head in my hands.

“Bad dreams?”

I nodded.

“Figured. You were tossing and turning pretty good.” He stood up, dusting himself off. “That’ll teach me to wake up someone in the middle of a nightmare.”

I lifted my head. “It wasn’t a nightmare. But it wasn’t a good dream either. It was…” I didn’t know how to describe it. It had seemed so real, but so strange. Almost as if the dream were magic.

I didn’t like the idea of someone using magic to mess with my head while I was sleeping, though, so I dismissed the idea. The elves wouldn’t have reason to do that, and neither would Dex or Zia. It was easier to just dismiss it as a weird dream and move on.

Zia ducked back through the tent flap and scanned the room before scowling. "You're still in bed? Are you serious? Get up! Let's go! The sun's almost up!"

"Coming, coming." I grumbled to myself as I pushed back the blankets and got out of bed.

Leseran and a handful of other armored elves waited outside when I finally made it out there, still trying to tie the sword to my belt. "Finally," he breathed.

"Give me a break, will you? I had a few rough days to recover from." I finished adjusting the sword.

The elf gestured for his people to come forward with their blindfolds.

Dex sighed. "Again with the blindfolds? I thought we were past this."

Leseran shrugged. "It's not my policy. Not that I disagree, mind you."

After blindfolding us, the elves led us to horses and helped us up onto them. Then, with a few clicks of the tongue, we were off, moving through the forest and back toward our convoy. The early morning forest was as quiet as it'd been in my dream. A few crickets sang from the bushes and birds chirped in the branches above, but no one spoke. I listened to the sound of hooves on our horses moving through the wild land and couldn't help but replay the dream in my head. Did it mean something? Maybe not. I'd read somewhere that dreams were the brain's way of working through problems, and I certainly had my fair share of those lately.

"It'll be nice to get back," Zia said suddenly off to my right. "I hope they haven't had too much trouble with my vampires."

"How do you know they didn't put them down?" I asked. "They were talking about it as a possibility when I left."

"Ash would never… Well, I suppose if they were out of control, maybe. But the wagon was re-enforced, and I left instructions to strengthen it. Even if the wagon failed to contain them, I had contingencies and failsafes in place that would've rendered them harmless. There would be no need to put them down simply because I was indisposed. They certainly don't deserve it." She cleared her throat. "Besides, if something had happened, I would know. We share a bond, and if it were permanently severed, I would feel it."

I shrugged. "They seemed pretty wild when we took off. All I'm saying is someone mentioned it as an option."

Leather creaked on Zia's side. "What's your problem with my vampires?"

"Nothing," I answered, "except I don't like the idea of having my throat ripped out by blood sucking monsters."

"They're not *monsters*!"

"You're right. I misspoke. They're weapons of mass destruction, and the only thing keeping them from killing us all is a metal circle on your head. If that enchanted tiara falls off, they'd kill us all in an instant. I don't care what failsafes you have in place or how many. There are always ways it can go wrong. When you play with fire, you get burned and those vampires... They're an open flame next to gasoline."

"How do you know? You wouldn't know the first thing about magic. You're just a dim-witted poacher with good tits and a sword."

"I know!" I spat back. "I've seen it happen up close and personal, okay?"

"Enough!" Leseran's voice cut through the forest just ahead. "Spirits, you two are arguing loud enough, I'm surprised every madman in the forest hasn't descended on us."

I turned away from Zia, though I couldn't see her. Just the idea of being near her made me feel sick. If I could see where I was, I would've moved my horse and let Dex ride next to her.

We rode on in sullen silence for a short distance before Zia spoke again. "I'm sorry you had to see that. It must've been terrible. How old were you?"

"Does it matter?" There was less vitriol in my words and more exhaustion. Rather than argue and make things worse, though, I eventually decided I should answer. Maybe she'd understand my side of things and be more careful. "I was six. We went down to Macon for some festival or something."

"You were at the Macon Massacre?"

"Is that what it's called?" I shrugged. "I remember the quiet just before it happened. The stunned silence that stretched on and on as everyone in the square sucked in a collective breath, waiting to see what would happen. When the killing started, a shopkeeper took a bunch of us in. Said we'd be safe in the cold room under the floor. By the time we got there, it was already full. There was only enough room for me." I squeezed my eyes closed. "People say it's the screams you never forget, but there were so many. They all just blend together. It's the scratching, the way they clawed at the floorboards above us for *hours*."

"I don't remember this," Dex said. "What exactly happened?"

"A mentally unstable necromancer set himself on fire in the Macon town square," Zia answered. "His two vampires were released from control and killed almost a hundred people. But he was a rogue, not a member of the Institute. If he had been, they would've known about his condition and helped him before he got so bad. I'm sorry about what happened to you, Ember, but that's why the Institute is needed. Magic isn't a toy you toss around to solve all your problems. It's a responsibility."

I sighed. "Sorry doesn't bring my parents back, or anyone else."

The horses stopped suddenly, and Leseran

dismounted. A few seconds later, I was blinking at the light after my blindfold had been removed. Morning had crept into the sky, but it was still early. Most of the convoy would just be finishing their breakfast. If they weren't vampire food, that was.

Leseran removed the last blindfold from Zia's face. "Your convoy is about a half mile north of here. You'll have to clear the distance on foot. Hopefully, the three of you can survive half a mile on your own."

"We should be able to make it," I said, rubbing my eyes. I dismounted and extended a hand. "Thank you."

He wrinkled his nose and looked down at my hand. "Your thanks mean nothing to me. If you're truly grateful, you'll discard that sword and forget you ever met my people." He glanced at Dex, but said nothing before going back to mount his horse. He waited for his people to tie the empty horses to their own before starting to back off.

Dex watched him go and sighed before adjusting his hat. "Elves."

"Elves," Zia agreed.

The walk back to the convoy wasn't unpleasant. I spent it trying to figure out if they'd made any progress forward, or if they'd stayed in the same place for two days waiting on us to return. Ash wouldn't have been happy about losing two days. We'd have to rush to make up for it or else risk getting low on basic supplies.

We didn't spot the convoy until we were almost on top of it. Some scouts had gone into the woods to gather supplies. We stumbled on them pissing in the bushes, and they gave us an escort back to the main force.

Zia broke away and ran straight to the wagon holding her vampires. From the looks of it, Foggy and the others had spent the last two days reenforcing the outside, and the doors. They'd nailed several extra planks of wood in place. Zia was already frantically trying to find someone to pry the boards off.

"Ember?" Ash navigated his way through the gathering crowd. He sprouted a smile and threw his arms around me. "I was starting to worry something had happened to you."

"I'm fine. Thanks for asking," Dex quipped.

Ash ignored him and took a step back, his hands still on my shoulders. He wore a look of concern. "What happened out there?"

I glanced over at Dex. How much of the truth could I tell? We should've gotten our story straight.

Before I could answer, Zia swept in. "The heretics tried to poison me with some of their magicite blood. Lucky these two showed up or I would've been dead. Took a while to wrangle our way free."

"I assume the heretics have been dealt with?" Ash let his hands drop to his sides.

"They're dead," Zia confirmed. "And we're not, which means we can get back on schedule just as soon as you find someone with a hammer to open my wagon."

"We'll be just as dead as them if we keep going." We all turned our heads as Ike and Foggy stormed up. Ike grasped a handful of papers.

Ash narrowed his eyes and turned to face Ike. "What's going on?"

"This." Ike shoved the papers at Ash. "I found out exactly where we're headed. If we continue to follow this man, we're all marching to our deaths."

Kenny, who'd wandered up holding his arm, spat on the ground. "Not like you Iron Company freaks to be afraid of a little dragon fire, Ike."

Foggy frowned. "It's not the dragon fire we fear, lad. When it comes to beasts, you'll find none braver than us, but even we know better than to go fucking around with rifts!"

"I'm sure we'll give any rifts between here and there a wide berth," I said.

The dwarf gestured to Ash before crossing his arms. "You best confer with your boyfriend here about where we're headed, then. The way his maps are marked out, we'll be headed straight into the shadow of a theta-class rift. Unstable, dangerous, and deadly."

I looked to Ash for an explanation.

Ash lowered the papers Ike had thrust at

him and smoothed them out. "The dragon we're hunting keeps a nest inside the rift's zone."

I couldn't believe what I was hearing. "Ash, you know what will happen if we step into the zone. We can't even get within fifty feet of the affected area without ill effects! People will die."

"Calm down. We're not going into the affected area. Why do you think we need the vampires?" He gestured to Zia. "They can go into the zone and draw the dragon out where we can take it down a safe distance from the rift."

"So they're bait?" I looked at Zia, scrutinizing her expression.

Her face was stone. "It's like Ash said. We'll use the vampires to draw the dragon away from the rift. I don't see what everyone is so upset about."

"I put my men's lives in your hands." Ike waved a finger at Ash and leaned in, threatening. "The guilds have specific rules about who's allowed to go so close to a rift, and under what circumstances."

"Why do you think this isn't a guild-sanctioned hunt?" Ash shoved Ike's finger out of his face. "We have to get close to take this thing down, but I'm not stupid. If I were to march everyone up there and kill you, I'd be a pariah. No one would ever work with me again. Not only that, but DEMO would be on my ass for the rest of my life, and so would the Institute for putting one of their own in danger. I know how to weigh benefits and risks, Ike. Don't preach to me about how to run my hunt. If you don't like it, it's only a few days' ride back to Atlanta. You and yours are welcome to leave at any time."

"Boss?" Kenny tugged on Dex's sleeve. He suddenly looked pale. "A word?"

Dex waved him off. "One second."

"I don't think..." Kenny grimaced in pain, then doubled over and vomited blood. When he rose, tears of blood trailed from the corners of his eyes. He tried to wipe it away before anyone saw, but it was too late.

Ash grabbed Kenny before he could slip away and yanked up his sleeve to reveal a nasty cut on Kenny's upper arm. Several small crystals had already taken root in the gash. "He's infected!" he spat in disgust and pushed Kenny away.

"No, I'm not!" Kenny struggled to his knees while everyone took a step back from him. "The crystals are still small. It hasn't spread. They can still be removed, see?" He dug into his wound with his bare fingers to pry them out.

I turned away.

"The heretics must've used a powder on their weapons." Foggy shook his head. "Poor lad."

"Kenny..." Dex put a hand over his mouth and shook his head.

Kenny gasped and finally gave up on prying the crystals from his body. He staggered to his feet. "No, no. It's fine, boss. I just need a healer and I'll be back in fighting shape in no time."

"This man is a threat to the entire hunting party," Ike said, furrowing his brow.

Ash drew his sword.

"No!" Kenny shook his head and gripped his arm. He staggered away from Ash, forcing everyone on my side of the circle to take another step back. He looked down at the blood dripping from his infected arm and turned to Dex, wild-eyed. "You… You'll help me." He reached for Dex with bloody fingers.

When Kenny saw even Dex shrink away, he let his hand fall limply to his side. "You can take the arm. Cut it off. I can fight with one arm. Lots of guys fight with one arm. Just cut off my arm and I'll go back to Atlanta. I'll be healed up by the time you get back, boss."

Dex lowered his head. He was thinking the same thing as everyone else. Kenny's infection was a death sentence. It'd progressed too far to just take the arm and be done with it. The bloody vomit, the bleeding eyes… The magicite was in his blood now. It was only a matter of time before the poison killed him or drove him insane.

Of course, I knew better. He might survive with antigen, at least for a while. That too would only delay the inevitable though. There was no cure for a magicite infection of the blood. Kenny was a dead man walking.

Foggy pulled a knife from his belt and tossed it into the dirt in front of Kenny.

Kenny stared at the knife, wide-eyed.

"Make the choice, lad," the dwarf offered. "Go out on your own terms."

Kenny kicked the knife away as if it were a snake. "No! I can't! Dex, tell him! Tell him I'll be fine!"

Dex stared at the ground in silence.

Kenny searched the faces of the gathering crowd, turning a circle. "Please! Someone! One of you has to believe me!"

Ash's sword came down, swift and sure. Almost as quick as a blink, it moved in a perfect motion, separating Kenny's head from his body. The head rolled to a stop in front of Dex while the body slumped into a lifeless pile. Blood pumped into the worn ground from Kenny's stump neck.

The crowd stood in stunned silence. For a moment, I was back in the Macon town square, listening as everyone sucked in a collective breath.

Then I realized Dex was breathing hard next to me. His fingers curled into fists and he cliched his teeth. "You bastard!" He charged into the circle and landed one good punch to Ash's chin.

Several of Ash's people stepped out from the crowd to grab Dex and hold him back before he could land another blow. Others drew their weapons. In response, Ike and Foggy readied their blades and took up a fighting stance.

Ash, stunned, touched his chin and glared at Dex. His face hardened. "Someone had to do it."

Dex fought against his captors. "You had no right!"

Ash drew a thumb over his lip and rubbed the small stripe of blood between two fingers. "Dead is dead. My strike was clean. He felt only a flash of pain, and then it was over. What I did was a mercy compared to what the magicite would've done to him. You saw the heretics. Did you want him to end up like that?"

"He should have been given a choice!" Dex spat. "Kenny deserved better."

"I agree," Ike said. "This was murder, and you should have to answer for it."

"Answer to whom exactly?" Ash sneered. "This *my* hunt, and these are *my* people. Atlanta is many miles behind us. What would you do? Kill my men, put me in chains, and drag me back to stand trial? This is an unsanctioned guild hunt, which means he knew the risks. You *all* knew." He pointed around the circle before turning back to Ike. "No jury would convict me for making the hard choice that had to be made, and you know it. So, unless you plan to enact justice all on your own, your threats are fruitless." He spread his arms wide. "But if you want to take your shot, take it."

Ike looked almost ready to take the bait.

"That's enough." I stepped in and put a hand on Ash's chest, pushing him back from Ike. "Ike, this isn't your fight. Kenny was Dex's man.

And he was infected beyond help. We all saw it. Maybe he should have been given the choice, but the result is the same. Whether we all agree, it's done. More arguing is only going to make things worse."

"I can't follow a murderer into a fight," Ike said, shaking his head. "And a fight that will probably kill the rest of us at that, despite what his pet necromancer says."

"Then you may leave," Ash spat. "This is not a democracy. I lead. You either follow or you get the hell out."

Ike made a fist, turned, and stormed away.

"The rest of you, prepare to move," Ash shouted. "We've already lost two days. We'll need to make good time if we want to get back on schedule. Ember..."

I put a hand to stop him and went to Dex's side as he knelt by the body. "I don't want to talk to you right now, Ash. Just go."

His tone softened. "But..."

"Go!"

Something dark flashed in Ash's eyes. He glowered at Dex for a minute before he, too, stomped away.

I squatted and put a hand on Dex's shoulder. "How can I help?"

Dex looked from the head to the body blankly. "We can't leave him here. Like this. Kenny... He had a girlfriend and a kid on the way. They shouldn't see him like this, but we can't just carry the body around. Not with vampires. And I don't want to bury him out here where they can't come to pay respects. It's not right."

I nodded. "I'll see if I can talk Foggy into lending his ax to cut down some trees. We can build a pyre."

He looked at me, his eyes still unfocused. "But the convoy... They're moving on. We'll get left behind."

"We can make up any lost ground and catch up to them tomorrow if you still want to finish the hunt."

He stood. "I have to now. For Kenny's sake. Because this wasn't a guild sanctioned hunt, his family will get nothing. But if I can bring back something from the dragon, I can sell it. I can make sure his family is taken care of. Without that, they'll be on the street. I can't let that happen."

I nodded and put a hand on his arm.

Zia slowly stepped forward, fidgeting with a cloth draped over her arm. She'd donned a pair of black gloves.

Dex shot her a hard glance.

Her hands went up. "I know you think I'm on Ash's side, but I'm not here to take sides. As a necromancer, nothing is more sacred to me than the dead. Respectfully, I offer my assistance."

"And what would you do?" Dex shook his head.

Zia looked at the body. "The dead should be

handled with care and respect. Allow me to clean the body and prepare it for cremation. It's the least I can do after you put your life on the line to save mine. You can observe if you wish, but as a necromancer, I consider tending to the fallen as one of my duties on this hunt."

Dex looked at me before nodding. "Okay. Yeah. I... wouldn't know how to do that."

She nodded and knelt carefully. We watched as she positioned the body, carefully placed the head back in place and pressed her fingers to the severed skin on either side. Zia closed her eyes and magic flared. A moment later, Kenny's body was whole again. Zia rose, carefully draping the cloth she'd brought with her over the body. "I'll have a small tent erected and my supplies brought down from the wagon."

"Thank you," Dex said, almost sheepishly.

Zia bobbed her head. "I am, and always shall be, at Death's service. Wherever He goes, we follow."

The Institute slogan usually felt hollow and cheap, but when Zia spoke it, she made it sound like a prayer.

I linked my arm in Dex's and forced him to turn away. "Come on. Let's go see if Foggy will help us."

Dex cast one more long glance behind him before coming with me.

Chapter Sixteen

Foggy and Ike cut down a handful of trees and asked nothing for it. They worked in silence, jaws set, axes swinging, sweat on their backs and brows. I had the distinct feeling they were imagining swinging their weapons at Ash instead of tree trunks.

The convoy moved on without us, leaving behind only the wagon with the vampires for Zia to follow. It was a somber moment, standing in the woods while the wagons rolled out of sight against the sound of axes chipping away at trees. I told myself I'd catch up with them later, but part of me didn't want to.

It would be safer for me to slip away unnoticed and pretend that Ash and I had never been reunited. He'd look for me, maybe even find me. Then what? How would I explain abandoning the only friend who'd stuck with me since childhood? Murder seemed like a good reason, but was it really murder like Ike had pointed out? It seemed like murder should've been black and white. Either it was, or it wasn't. Instead, everything had turned gray.

But if I followed the convoy, if I caught up with Ash, what then? How far would things go before I found another excuse to run? Things couldn't go back to the way they were before because I was infected and Ash... Ash had gone from shrieking at the sight of spiders to beheading men on a whim.

How certain was I that this really was Ash and not some impostor who looked like him? He had Ash's memories, and Ash's body as far as I could tell, but was that enough to make him Ash?

I glanced over to the small tent where Zia worked in the shadows, preparing Kenny's body for cremation. Dex sat despondently on a stump outside the tent, staring in, but not seeing. His eyes were unfocused, his mind wandering elsewhere while his hands turned his hat in circles. I knew that grief. He was lucky to have a body to grieve over, but that didn't make it any easier to lose a friend.

People have to be more than their memories and their bodies, I thought. *If that's all we were, we wouldn't mourn the dead.* That mourning was for the loss of something more, the things that really mattered. The smiles, the laughter, the tears. We were more... The Ash that had walked into that rift was more.

Then what is he now? I looked down at my hands. Maybe the thing that had come back through was never Ash to begin with. Maybe he wasn't completely human anymore. That was what the rifts and magicite did, wasn't it? They twisted things, wound them up with magic and spat them back out as something new, something terrible and powerful. Something fearsome.

I had to know the truth. That alone would drive me to follow Ash as long as I could stand it. It was dangerous, even more so than I had thought. If he found out what I really was, he'd kill me as fast as he'd struck down Kenny.

I pushed up from the stump where I'd been sitting and went to Dex's side. He didn't even look up as I approached. "Are you okay?"

He swallowed and shook his head. "I don't know. We came out here, knowing it could be our last job. Every job can be the last one, you know? You just kind of accept that in our line of work. But seeing that... Nothing can prepare you for that." He was quiet for a minute before he let out a bitter laugh. "You know the funny thing is, I can't stop thinking about how it might've gone differently if I was here instead of playing at being an elf."

I sat down on the stump with him. "Dex, you couldn't have known."

"I was just so damn distracted by what I wanted. I should've been here for him. With him. Then maybe..." He broke off, eyes glistening, put his hat back on, and rose. "I'm sorry. I just... I don't want company right now."

"Of course. Take all the time you need." I felt helpless, watching him walk off into the woods. For all his flaws, Dex seemed like a good person, and he was hurting. I wished I could take that pain away from him.

Ike dumped an armload of chopped wood nearby and wiped sweat from his brow. "That should be enough."

Foggy leaned on the handle of his ax and glanced over at me. "Surprised you stayed. You and Ash seemed rather attached."

"Don't be rude, Foggy." Ike stripped off his work gloves and put them in his pocket on his way over to me. "She didn't expect that any more than we did. Ash surprised all of us."

I closed my eyes. "I'm not sure that is Ash. At least, he's not the Ash I knew five years ago. He's changed, and not for the better."

"People always change." He put his ax down and sat in the grass next to me. "We're shaped by our experience in the world, the things we see and do. It happens to all of us. If you'd been together those five years, it would've happened in inches, increments so small you'd never have noticed. It's not your fault, Ember. There's nothing you could've done to change what happened. Ash made a choice, and he will have to answer for it."

My eyes snapped open, and I frowned at Ike. "You heard him. Even if you tried to handle things through the courts, he'd barely get a slap on the wrist."

"You assume Kenny's murder is his only crime." Ike opened his canteen and took a long, deep drink.

"What do you mean?" I spun around to face him.

"All I'm saying is that you might be right. He might not be the man you think he is, Ember."

"If you know something, you need to tell me, Ike."

Ike exchanged a worried glance with Foggy.

The dwarf sighed, picked his ax up off the ground, and swaggered over to join us with a sigh. "I told you this wouldn't work. The lass is too smart, I said. She'll catch on. You should avoid talking to her. But do you listen? No. All it takes is a pretty girl and you're a puppy ready to spill his guts. It's as if you wanted us to get caught. Bloody idiot. Well? What are you waiting for? You might as well bare your stones. She's onto us."

"Okay," Ike whispered, "but you've got to swear you won't breathe a word of this to anyone else. Especially Zia."

I crossed my arms. "How do you know I won't just break my promise?"

"Because you're a poacher. You don't have the backing of a guild, which means you've developed a reputation. Reputations are built on trust, and trust only happens when you keep your word. Poachers live and die by the bond of their word, more so than guild bonded bounty hunters like Foggy and me. I trust you to know the value of a promise. Besides, I believe you want the same thing we want."

"Which is?" I raised an eyebrow, waiting.

"To stop that bloody idiot before he kills someone else," Foggy muttered.

Ike ignored him. "You want to help Ash, even if that means saving him from himself. I respect that."

I pressed my lips together in thought for a moment before nodding. "Okay. I promise. Whatever you say doesn't go beyond us. Now spill."

"A week ago, I returned from sparring practice to find an unnamed agent waiting in my office," Ike began. "He was a strange one. He gave no name, introducing himself only by the badge he carried."

"DEMO." Foggy spat off into the forest. "Bloody spook division."

Ike nodded. "He told me he'd gotten a tip that a man going by the name Ash would soon come into my city and post a job looking for dragon hunters. I was to join the hunt. Watch. Report what I saw and find out his next moves. Initially, I refused, but the agent made it clear that my participation wasn't voluntary."

"He blackmailed you, lad. Nut up and tell

it like it is or don't tell it at all." Foggy folded his arms.

DEMO. This was the second time they'd gotten involved.

"What does a DEMO spook want with Ash?" Almost as soon as I asked, a feeling of dread swelled in my chest. I already had the answer. Ash had already given it to me when he talked about building his own empire.

"No idea," Ike said, shrugging. "I didn't ask. Wasn't much room for questions. Now that we've been traveling with him, I can see why DEMO might have an interest, though. Ash has some sort of innate magic like I've never seen before. I don't know what he did to that heretic when he was interrogating him, but it was dark magic. You don't get that from sitting around doing nothing."

"And you don't get a loyal institute dog as a bodyguard for being nobody." Foggy gestured toward the tent. "Ash is up to something no good, lass. It'd be best you shared any knowledge you had with us."

I glanced from Foggy to Ike. Suddenly, the conversation felt a lot more like an interrogation. "Wait a minute. You don't think that I'm on his side, do you?"

"Are you?" Ike's tone was flat.

I stood. "I'm not on anybody's side. I'm here to hunt a dragon and make enough money to... To live for a while. I don't know where Ash has been all this time, and even if I did, I wouldn't tell some DEMO spy."

My fingers curled into fists at my sides. I couldn't explain why I was so angry. Everything Ike and Foggy had pointed out was true. Even I had questioned Ash's motivations. There was just something about hearing other people question him that struck a nerve. They didn't know him, didn't know what he'd been through, how much we had struggled and suffered to get where we were.

This had to be a misunderstanding. There must've been something I wasn't seeing.

I stormed away, but Ike caught me by the wrist. I turned back, glaring daggers at him.

"I only want the truth, Ember," Ike pleaded gently. "If there's something at play here that I'm not seeing, help me understand it."

I yanked my hand away. "If you've got any brains at all, you'll go back to your guild and tell DEMO it didn't work out. If you decide to keep going and follow Ash and the convoy… I won't tell him about you, but I won't protect you when he finds out either. And he will find out. You two are the worst secret agents ever."

I stomped away before I said or did something I knew I'd regret.

When I was a good distance away from everyone, I plopped down on a patch of moss between two trees and flopped onto my back, staring up. The tree branches looked like veins against scaly green skin. Here and there, the midday sun worked its way through the leaves, only to be scattered by the time it struck the ground.

This had all gotten so complicated. How did I get thrust into the middle of DEMO spies, elven legends, and a would-be empire? I was just a lone bounty hunter, trying to get by until the magic claimed me for good. My life was supposed to be simple.

I closed my eyes, sighed, and listened to the birds in the trees, letting my mind drift. For a while, I hovered on the edge of sleep, resting but aware. A small part of my mind stayed awake and alert, sorting through my options.

After a long time, I sat up. Heat had settled in over the forest, held in place by the treetops. Somewhere nearby, cicadas buzzed in a dull chorus.

As much as I wanted to turn around and leave after everything that had happened, I couldn't. Part of me felt responsible for Ash. I'd been looking out for him ever since we were kids. If he was going to do something stupid, I needed to be there to stop him.

Ike and Dex carried Kenny's body to a pyre of wood and dry grass. Zia made a torch and lit it, handing it to Dex to do the honors. Dex stepped up to the body wrapped in white cloth, hesitating just a moment. He said nothing as he thrust the torch into the pyre.

I took his hand as he stepped back a

safe distance and squeezed. There were so many things I felt like I should say, but I couldn't form any of them into words.

Foggy brought out his stringed instrument and plucked a few strings, adjusting them, before he began to play. It was a wordless tune, deep and low. Each note was drawn out yet flowed easily into the next like the march of tired feet ever moving forward.

The song echoed in my mind long after he stopped playing it, even after the last flames were embers, and the five of us began our journey to rejoin the main convoy. The mood of our march was as somber as the tune had been. Zia drove the wagon at a measured pace while the rest of us walked. She would occasionally click at the horses, or say something to urge them forward, but no one said anything to anyone else.

By the time we caught up with the main force, it was edging toward evening. Normally, the convoy would slow to a stop, but Ash had given the order to press on.

I put a hand on Dex's shoulder. "Are you going to be okay?"

He nodded. "I'll be better once that dragon is dead, and we're all headed back."

I nodded.

Zia stopped the wagon and traded places with someone else, taking his horse. "I'm riding to the front to tell Ash we've returned."

"I'm coming too," I said. "I need to talk to

him."

"Ember." Ike caught my attention and shook his head. He was afraid I'd go back on my word and rat him out to Ash.

Maybe I should have reassured him I had no intention of telling Ash about his deal with DEMO, but I was still angry at him. I let him sweat and turned my back to Ike without a word.

Zia frowned down at me for a moment before offering a hand. "Okay. You can ride with me." Zia pulled me up to sit in the saddle behind her.

"Thank you for what you did for Kenny," I said, wrapping my hands around her middle so I wouldn't fall off.

"Still hate necromancers?"

"I don't hate you. It's the vampires I don't like."

Zia shrugged. "Well, we are a package deal."

"I guess nobody's perfect."

We arrived at the front of the convoy, where Ash and several of his people were. He had Scorch walking alongside him, her saddle empty. Ash's face was blank as Zia and I rode up to meet him. He glanced over at me before turning forward again. "Here for the horse? She's yours, whether you stay on the hunt or not."

"I'm not going anywhere, Ash."

He gave me another glance, gestured to his people to keep the convoy moving, and guided his horse—and Scorch—out of the way of the wagons to join us.

Zia stopped the horse, and I dismounted. “Thanks for the ride.”

“You keep thanking me and I’ll start to think you like me,” she replied with a wry smile before addressing Ash. “The others have returned as well.”

Ash frowned. “Ike and the dwarf?”

“Moping in the rear, but present.”

“Thank you, Zia.” He nodded to her.

She nodded back, glanced at me, and turned her horse around.

“Will you ride with me?” Ash gestured to Scorch.

I mounted the horse and settled in, expecting him to go back to the head of the convoy. Instead, he led me further into the forest. We kept the convoy in sight, moving parallel to it, but out of earshot of anyone in it.

“You’re angry with me,” he said at length. “Ember, someone had to make a decision. The man was dead either way.”

“It’s more than that, Ash. It’s... everything. You’ve been so different since the start of this. If I didn’t know your face, I would think you were a different person.”

He brought the horse around so he was facing me while sitting in the saddle. “What are you saying?”

I sighed and refused to look at him, watching the convoy pass in the distance instead. "People don't come back after going through rifts. Everyone knows that. I look at you, at everything you've done, and I can't help but wonder..."

"Am I really me?"

I nodded.

"I thought I already proved myself. What further proof do you require?"

I turned away, unable to answer.

Ash brought his horse around and we started forward again, albeit at a slower pace. "Suppose I'm not who I claim I am. Then what am I?"

I shrugged. "I don't know. A doppelgänger? Some spirit from another world, possessing Ash's body? Maybe you're under someone else's control and can't act freely."

His saddle creaked as he shifted his weight. "I asked myself the same questions when I first returned. How am I back, I wondered? Why am I not dead? What if I'm not me? How could I prove I was myself? The questioning almost drove me insane."

"What conclusion did you come to?" I finally turned my head to look at him.

Ash smirked. "I decided it didn't matter. I felt like myself. I had my memories, my body... Existential questions about the nature of man felt like looking a gift horse in the mouth."

"Well, it matters to me. I need to know

that you're you, that the man that I…" I trailed off, cleared my throat, started again. "I need to be sure, Ash, because you're not acting like yourself."

"You mean because I'm not afraid of my own shadow and second-guessing everything I do? Does my having found my confidence make me someone else?"

"No, Ash. That's not it. Beheading a man isn't confidence."

"It was a choice that needed to be made."

"And what if it didn't?" I spat and stared at Ash, fire in my gaze. "What if there was another way? A way that meant no one had to die? What if that were me? Would you cut my head off too?"

"Ember, I could never…"

"Well, if you wouldn't do it to me, what makes you think it was okay to do to Kenny?"

Ash was quiet for a moment, considering. He lowered his head, his voice softening. "There are a lot of things I would do with you I wouldn't do with anyone else, Ember. By now, you have to know that."

I couldn't answer at first. I didn't know how.

Ash stopped his horse, waiting.

What could I say? It was obvious how we both felt about each other. It'd been obvious even before he'd walked into that rift. The two of us had been too young and stupid to know what we had when we had it. We'd squandered our chance at being together, but he couldn't see it. Why would he? He didn't know that I was dying.

"I want you to have dinner with me," he said. "Tonight, when we make camp. Will you come?"

"Ash..." I sighed.

"Please, Ember. Give me a chance. It would mean a lot to me."

I pressed my lips together in thought. Maybe it would give me the opportunity to let him down easily. "Okay, but promise it will just be us. No bodyguards, no Zia, nobody else."

"You have my word."

I nodded. "It's a date then. Race you back to the front of the convoy?"

He smiled that familiar sheepish grin from ear to ear and took off full speed through the forest.

Chapter Seventeen

The convoy wound through the woods, the ground gently sloping upward. Rocks rose on either side, pinching us into single file along a narrow dirt path. Trees leaned in like children waiting to hear a secret. The forest was silent except for the sounds of our convoy moving through it.

Gradually, the green earth rose into equal parts rock and plant. The trees didn't thin out so much as they changed shape, shifting from poplar and maples to sturdy evergreens and oak. Root formations crawled over the rocky soil like fingers digging into sand.

By duskfall, we had reached a small grove of pine trees. Their needles coated the ground, the acidity leeching into the soil so that nothing else would grow. In the distance, the shadow of a mountain rose. It wasn't Black Mountain. The convoy was slow moving enough we wouldn't see Black Mountain for another day or so. Yet we had clearly left behind the foothills and moved into the mountains. From there, it would be tougher terrain for the wagons. I suspected by the end of the next day, we would have to leave them at a base camp and continue on foot.

That night, however, we made camp in the pine grove, circling the wagons to the center of camp where they could easily be guarded. Ash, Zia and their people set up their camp to the west while Dex, Ike, and Foggy stayed to the east. The north and south sections stayed empty, with people crowding to one side or the other.

I shouldered my pack and looked first toward Ash's camp, then toward the guild camp. I didn't want to stay with either, so I pitched my tent at the center near the wagons.

It was dark by the time I finished. One of Ash's people was making their way around camp, lighting some torches that had been placed in the ground earlier. He nodded to me as I came out of the tent. "Might want to take a cloak with you, miss."

As if to emphasize his words, thunder cracked above. I looked up, but couldn't see the sky. The way the sound echoed through the mountains left me with goosebumps.

"Storm's a ways off yet," continued the torch lighter. "But it's coming."

"Thanks." I ducked back into the tent to grab my leather jacket. I didn't plan on being out in it, so I figured it'd be good enough.

Music drifted up from the guild camp, a

slow and somber tune that almost seemed to go along with the approaching storm. Dex saw me and waved me over. I glanced over at Ash's tent, where he waited for me, and decided he could keep waiting.

"Hey, Ember." Dex offered me a wooden tankard full of beer. "We're drinking. Want to join us?"

I shook my head. "I wish I could, but I promised Ash I'd have dinner with him."

Dex's face fell. "Oh, well maybe after? Unless… Never mind. Don't worry about it."

Foggy lifted his bow from the stringed instrument and pointed it at me. "You don't let him forget us, eh? We might be hired hands, but as you can see, we're the quiet majority here." He gestured around him.

It was true. If I did a count of heads, there were more on the guild side of the camp than Ash's.

"Good luck hunting that dragon by himself." Dex sneered and took a drink before stalking off.

"I thought you weren't leaving?" I frowned at Foggy.

The dwarf shrugged. "That's not the plan, but there are murmurs of discontent out here. People doubt. They've had time to reflect on what happened, and distance. Both have given them some perspective."

Ike nodded and hooked his thumbs in his

belt. "No one doubts that what was done was necessary. It's the way it was handled, Ember."

Foggy grunted and raised his glass in a toast to what Ike had said. "I know we're on this hunt to make money and not friends, but... Well, the lad would be wise not to make enemies of heavily armed men."

I crossed my arms. "Are you threatening him?"

Dex finished his drink and threw the mug down. "Don't have to threaten. We're walking into a fight some of us might not walk away from. Might come a time when your boyfriend wished he had friends to offer a hand."

"Ash isn't my boyfriend."

"You keep sayin' that," Dex mumbled as he picked up his cup, dusted it off, and refilled it. "And then you go to dinner with him. I know better than to wait up."

"You're drunk," I said.

"Not drunk enough," he replied, and emptied his cup again.

Ike sighed and stepped between me and Dex. "The point Dex is trying to make is that disgruntled fighters can make the whole hunt unravel. If he wants this to go well, he should attempt to bridge that gap, Ember. You need to tell him that."

"And what sort of olive branch would be good enough for you?" I lifted my chin, anger swelling in my chest. Ike and Dex were in the right, but their threats were out of line.

"An apology would be a start," Ike said.

Foggy snorted. "Good luck with that. Men like Ash don't apologize. They rationalize. That's what evil does."

"Ash isn't evil. Nobody is *evil*. The world's not black and white."

The dwarf shook his head and picked up his bow.

Ike gestured vaguely with his cup. "Evil is the tree that grows from the seed of pride. All it needs to take root is for good people to look the other way long enough for it to grow. How long are you willing to look the other way, Ember? The signs are all there. He's not who you think he is."

"Nobody is who they say they are!" I unfolded my arms and balled my hands into fists. "Dex hid his half-elf heritage from all of us. You two are DEMO spies!"

Dex looked up halfway through refilling his tankard, beer spilling to the ground. "You guys are what now?"

Everyone ignored him.

"I'm not what you think I am," I said. "We're all liars except for Ash. He may be the most honest one among us. You don't get to call him evil just because you don't like him."

"Ember…" Ike called.

But I was already walking away, fuming. I couldn't excuse what Ash had done, but I would not stand there and listen to them talk about him like that. He'd made a decision. It was the wrong one, or maybe the right one carried out in the wrong way, but his intentions had been pure. Why couldn't they see he'd done it to protect the rest of us? I hated that he had done it, but at least I understood. As far as evil went, that one seemed so small.

I stopped walking dead in my tracks and shivered, hugging myself. *Murder, a small evil? What the hell is wrong with me? This is a slippery slope you're on, Ember. Be careful not to fall.*

Thunder growled, rolling through the sky above. I stared up into the black sky and watched lightning make shadows of the distant peaks. We'd reach them tomorrow, and be done with all this in a day or two. Then we could all go our separate ways. Life could get back to normal. Whatever post-Ash normal was.

I let out a slow breath through pursed lips, rolled my shoulders back, and continued to Ash's tent. The tent flaps were closed. I wondered if I should knock, but there wasn't much to knock on. "Hello? Ash?"

"Ember." His voice startled me from behind.

I spun around and almost staggered back a step from how close he stood. Ash had changed out of his traveling clothes and donned a black long-sleeved shirt with gold sunburst buttons and a stiff collar. His black cloak with the crimson dragon broach was pinned to his shoulder. It looked too formal for wandering around in the wilderness, like something he'd wear to meet royalty.

I swallowed and smiled awkwardly, looking down at my dirty riding pants and faded t-shirt under a leather jacket. "Now I feel under dressed."

"Never." He offered me a hand and gestured to another tent set up beside his own. "Shall we?"

I put my hand in his. "Lead the way."

As we stepped toward the tent, two of Ash's people lifted the flaps wide so that we could pass through. Inside, an intricately carved table and chairs waited, the table piled high with several beautiful dishes on fine china. There was a whole roasted duck on a bed of pomegranate seeds. Another plate was piled high with garlic potatoes. Yet another dish held saffron rice. There were stuffed mushrooms, fresh baked rolls, and even tiny lemon cakes. An unopened bottle of wine sat at the center of the table with two glasses.

I didn't know what to do or say. All sensible thought had vacated my mind, replaced by a strange sense that I had stepped out of reality and into another dream. I bit my tongue until I tasted copper, just to make sure I was awake.

"How?" I sputtered out. "We're miles from any city. Do we even have an oven?"

Ash chuckled. "You can achieve a lot with a little magic and a lot of ingenuity."

"Magic?" I gave him a questioning look.

"Not like you're thinking." He waved dismissively and went to pull out a chair for me.

I took the offered seat. "Then how?"

"You'll just have to trust me. Let the food speak for itself." He went around to his side of the table to sit in his chair. "I wish I could say I cooked it myself but…"

"You? Cook?" I laughed. "The idea of touching dead animals used to make you turn colors."

"I have always been useless in the kitchen." He took up a knife and carved a large slice of the duck, placing it gingerly on my plate. "Do you remember that time Old Jim decided we were going to have a proper Thanksgiving?"

"You mean when you found out how real gravy is made?" I laughed even harder. "I thought for sure you'd swear off meat forever and turn into a vegan after that."

"I didn't eat meat for a week." He smiled and served himself a slice of duck. "Thankfully, I got over it. I'm still a terrible cook, though. I have someone who does it full time for me now. He's a culinary genius. Magically gifted. I don't know what he does, or how he does it, but everything he makes is perfect every time. And in half the time it'd take a normal chef. Go on. Try the duck and tell me it's not the best roast duck you've ever had."

"Can't say I've ever had roast duck." I put a piece in my mouth. It almost melted, it was so tender and juicy. Whatever glaze he'd put on it was a flawless blend of tangy and sweet. I couldn't help but let out a small, contented sigh.

Ash leaned in, waiting excitedly for my review. "Good, right?"

"Good doesn't do it justice. This is an orgasm in meat form."

Ash laughed so loud I was sure they heard it all the way on the other side of camp. "I will let him know you said that! It'll be the highlight of his career."

We dug into our food. Everything on the table was just as good as the duck, except for maybe the wine. I like a good red as much as the next girl, but I would always be a beer girl at heart. Wine just wasn't me.

"We're making good time, despite having lost a few days," Ash said, pouring me a second glass. "We should be at the bottom of Black Mountain by sundown tomorrow. Then it's a day's hike up the mountain."

"About that." I picked up the wine glass and took a sip before continuing. "I spoke with Ike and Dex before coming here. They seemed concerned about morale. After what happened, aren't you the least bit worried they won't have your back? I mean, there are more of them than there are of you."

He shook his head. "I could take Ike and

Dex by myself. The dwarf is another matter. I think he's a berserker. It'd be a tough fight if they came at me all at once, but between me and Zia's vampires, I still think my side would win."

I put the glass down. "You're not listening to me. We're supposed to all be on the same team, right? If they suddenly decide this is too much trouble, and they turn around, you won't make it to the top of Black Mountain, Ash. You need to talk to them. Apologize."

"Apologize?" He huffed air through his nose. "What would I apologize for? I saved them from having to do it themselves. Kenny clearly wouldn't do it himself. It'd be cruel to ask Dex to kill his best friend and Ike... Ike had as much right as I did. If he or Foggy had made the killing blow, you'd all be mad at them instead of me. What I did was selfless. It was quick and painless for Kenny. If people hate me for making the right decision, then let them hate me. I will not bow to the demands of squabbling masses. Besides, when the dragon is slain and they're rolling in riches, they'll forget about the blood on my hands."

"That's naïve, to think you can buy their forgiveness."

His lip twitched as he considered his wine glass. "I do not want their forgiveness, Ember. Those men out there are a means to an end for me and nothing more. Men like Ike and Dex don't aspire to be anything greater than they are. That makes them tools for people like us."

"People like *us*? And what are we exactly?"

"Dreamers." His eyes sparkled with the promise of something dark. "Trailblazers. The future, Ember. For most people, it's just a word, something that happens to them. But not for us. We will make the future happen."

I pushed my plate away, my appetite suddenly vanishing. "And how will we do that?"

Ash lowered his glass and considered me carefully in silence.

I sighed and looked down at my hands in my lap. "Ash, we have too many secrets. I can't—"

"Wait!" He lifted a finger, silencing me. "Whatever you're going to say, please wait. There's something I want to show you first." He rose and offered me his hand again.

I frowned at it before looking up at him.

"Indulge me just a little longer, Ember. We were apart for five years. All I ask is an hour. Please."

Reluctantly, I rose and put my hand in his.

Ash led me out of the tent and into the night. There was a heaviness in the air, accompanied by the familiar stillness of night just before a storm. Laughter and a slightly jollier tune than before drifted out of the guild camp. I was glad they'd found something to be happy about after the long, hard days behind us.

We went away from their camp and to the edge of the clearing where the horses were kept. Ash's horse had already been prepped for a ride, though Scorch didn't have her saddle. Ash climbed up into the saddle and offered me his hand.

I looked at the sky. "Are you sure? It's going to storm soon."

He smiled warmly. "I've never been so sure of anything in my entire life."

I took his hand. He pulled me effortlessly up into the saddle behind him, and we took off.

With my arms wrapped around him, breathing in his familiar scent, and the electric quiet all around us, it was impossible not to get lost in what could have been. I often used to entertain myself—or torture myself, depending on my mood—imagining how my life might've been different with Ash in it. Even before that night at the rift, there had been something blossoming between us. Something more than childhood friendship. We were ripped apart so quickly that neither of us ever had time to tell the other, nor had we ever acted on it. It was just a feeling, and it had been as alive and beating as our hearts. I knew as sure as breathing that Ash and I would be together forever… until we weren't.

I built a fantasy world where he had never left, and in it, that attraction blossomed into love. We struggled together and built a life for the both of us, and maybe a kid or two. It was a modest life, spent in and out of guilds, but it was ours. I always thought we would be happy just being who we were.

But the Ash I had grown up with was long gone. That fantasy could never be, and I couldn't see a way to build a world where the two of us were happy together. It would never work. Not now, not ever. Not after the rift.

Yet as we rode through the mountain forest that night, with the storm threatening above us, it felt like I could make it happen. The Ash I knew was still in there, somewhere. He'd been away a long time, and come back to be influenced by the wrong people. With time, patience, and enough reminders about how good life could be, maybe things could go back to the way they were.

Then my fingers brushed against the crimson dragon broach at his shoulder, and the terrible truth came back to me. I still didn't know if he really *was* Ash or something monstrous sent through the rift.

In the back of my mind, a voice wondered if it really mattered. If we could be happy together, why did it matter so much whether he was real?

"Ash?"

He gave a small, thoughtful grunt in reply.

"I was just wondering. We've come all this way, and someone has died. More people might die. Why do you want the dragon's heart so badly? The truth."

"It will all make sense after," he said.

We crested a small hill overlooking a valley, and my breath caught in my throat. Below, a rift glowed in the night, casting eerie shadows out over the valley. Magicite crystals jutted out of the ground in strange formations. Pale, yellow mist floated over everything.

Ash dismounted, but I stayed where I was, ready to bolt. "Ash, don't you see the rift? We're too close! We need to go."

"It's all right. I promise, nothing bad is going to happen to either of us tonight." He gestured for me to come down off the horse.

I stayed in the saddle. "I've heard that one before. A lot of things can go wrong this close to a rift, Ash. Please, let's just go."

"Not until you see what I came out here to show you." He lifted his arms to help me off the horse.

Reluctantly, I dismounted.

Ash took my hands in his and squeezed them before bringing my knuckles to his lips. "Do you trust me?"

"I..."

"Yes, or no, Ember. Do you trust me?"

I stared at our intertwined fingers. "Yes. I trust you."

"Then don't let go." He turned toward the rift and started walking.

I wanted to pull away, to dig my feet into the ground and halt our progress. All I could think of was the moment I had lost him five years before. Here it was, replaying in real time, and there was nothing I could do to stop it.

We stopped halfway down the hill with the rift floating twenty or thirty yards ahead of us, maybe ten feet off the ground. The yellow mist flowed around our ankles. Wind howled like angry static.

Ash let go of my hand and I immediately panicked, turning to check that he was still with me. He took my face in his hands and leaned down to press his lips against mine. When he straightened, the green light of the rift danced in his slate-blue eyes. "I love you, Ember Dixon," he said and turned away.

I fumbled for words, to stay standing. My heart traveled into my throat and choked the air out of me. Stinging wind bit my cheeks. I wanted to cry, to scream, to tackle him to the ground and drag his stupid ass back to camp where we belonged. Instead, I stood there like a stunned idiot.

Ash raised a hand in tandem with another snarl of thunder. Shadowy tendrils shot out of his palm like lightning and wrapped around the rift, a cloud of obsidian black against ethereal green. He closed his eyes and lifted his chin. A deep breath, bared teeth. Magic swelled strong enough to buzz against my skin. Lightning flashed in the sky above.

He closed his fist.

The rift screamed like a living thing and shattered into a thousand viridian gems, scattering to the ground.

It was gone. Ash had done what the combined might of nations had once thought impossible. He had closed a rift.

He let out a pained cry and fell to his knees, holding his wrist.

"Ash!" I went to my knees beside him. "Are you okay? How did you...? When...?"

He gave me a tired smile. "Ever since I came back. The first was the rift I came out of. I did it without even thinking. Zia found me, saw what I could do, and swore herself to my side. She was also sworn to keep it a secret. If DEMO or The Institute found out, they'd dissect me, take me apart a piece at a time until they could replicate what I can do. Or worse, they'd send their own people through rifts, hoping to replicate it that way. I can't allow that."

"Why?" I shook my head. I couldn't believe what I was hearing. "Ash, do you know what this means? You can close rifts! This changes everything!"

"That power comes at a terrible price." He reached up and carefully unbuttoned his shirt. There, glowing with a dull indigo sheen in a diagonal line across his chest, was a thick line of magicite crystals.

Ash was infected, just like me.

Chapter Eighteen

I stood in the dark, magicite crystals glowing all around me, in front of me, in me.

Ash was infected.

Ash was infected! And he could close rifts.

That was too much to process. I hugged myself and turned away, squeezing my eyes closed. Fabric rustled behind me as he rose.

"Ember?" A hand closed on my shoulder.

I shrugged it off and spun around my throat tight and fists clenched. He staggered back seeing the look in my eyes. "It *was* murder, wasn't it?"

He looked like I had slapped him for a moment before making a full recovery. "No, no, no, Ember!" Ash placed his hands on my shoulders. "Kenny wouldn't have been like me. What happened to me, my ability, it's because I went through the rift. Don't you see? It's *changed* me."

I shrugged his hands away and took two steps back. "But you're infected just like Kenny was. You knew there was a chance, and you killed him anyway."

"Ember..."

"Don't deny it! That scar would've spread by now. The magicite would've eaten its way into your bones if you weren't doing something to stop it. You have a treatment, and you kept it a secret and now someone is dead because of it!"

Ash let out a small huff of breath and shook his head. "The treatment needs ingredients to synthesize. Expensive ingredients. The antigen is very costly and time consuming to make. Besides, it's not a cure. It achieves stasis at best." He waved a hand dismissively. "But that's why we have to find this dragon. There were writings in the Institute libraries, ancient alchemical texts in Elvish that claimed the heart of a dragon had healing properties. Don't you see, Ember? With one final potion, I can be cured."

"Maybe you can, but what about the rest of us?" I tugged up the lower hem of my shirt, revealing the scar across my stomach.

Ash's eyes widened. "Ember... You?"

"It happened the night you disappeared." I dropped my shirt and smoothed my hands over the fabric. "I've been taking antigen this whole time. That's why I'm not in a guild, Ash. It's why I work alone. Everything I've done since that day is because of this thing growing out of me. And now you're telling me that, not only is there a cure for the thing that's been ruining my life, but that you can close rifts? What else don't I know about you?"

He opened his mouth and snapped his jaw closed in thought before blurting, "We can find another elder dragon. There's one. There must be more, right? We'll kill this one, I'll take the cure, and then we'll hunt another one to cure you. Simple!"

"You'll take the cure?" I clenched my jaw.

His face twisted in disbelief. "Well, yes. It is *my* hunt, Ember. Besides, I'm the only one who can close rifts, aren't I? No offense, but that makes my survival take precedence over everyone else's."

"I don't believe what I'm hearing. I did not just hear you say your life is more important than anyone else's!" Tears fell when I blinked. I pushed them away. I wasn't crying because I was unhappy. Yes, his words hurt, but it was worse knowing who he had been. "And once you're cured, what will you do then? You'll close all the rifts? All over the world?"

He let out a bitter laugh. "Don't be ridiculous. The world is broken, and anything I can do would just be a Band-Aid on a fatal blow. The world has changed, Ember. We can never go back. We can never close the rifts, not really. We wouldn't know how to live without them. Imagine a world where magic was suddenly a finite resource, the wars that would be waged over the magicite that remained. Is that what you want? Besides, even if I were to close the rifts, the monsters would still be here."

"The only monster I see is you." I turned my back and started up the side of the hill.

Ash called after me, but I didn't turn around. I couldn't. I had defended him against Dex and Ike, but they were right. The Ash I knew was gone and dead. I wanted nothing to do with this thing he had become.

The air a few feet in front of me crackled and split open with a banshee scream, ghostly green light bleeding into the night. Wind roared in my ears. The grass at my feet curled into black tendrils and died. Rocky soil lifted off the ground and floated, suspended as if there were no gravity.

A rift.

A rift had just opened directly in front of me. It began as the size of a hand mirror and grew by the minute.

I turned around to escape the rift's pull and saw Ash lower his hand. Sweat had beaded on his forehead. Bright red veins bulged in his lower eyelids. His nostrils flared. "You should think twice before walking away from me."

I glanced back at the rift. "Did you…?"

Ash grabbed my wrist and yanked me roughly away from the rift. A cold chill passed over me as he pulled me to him. The spectral light of the rift twisted in his eyes as he looked down at me. "Nobody walks away from me."

I twisted in his grip, fighting to get away.

"I don't want anything to do with you. Not anymore. You're not the Ash I remembered."

"No," he said through his teeth. "I'm *better*."

He finally let me go and I fell to the ground in a heap.

Ash closed his eyes, inhaled deeply, and lifted both hands, slowly spreading them apart. As his hands moved, so did the rift. It opened wider, the black shadow of death it cast over the ground spreading to where Ash stood.

"I did not come back to this world to slave away and die making other men rich," he shouted into the rift. "And I didn't survive the impossible to die as some forgotten coward, afraid of spiders. Even then, I knew what had to be done. We talked about it, Ember. Building a more just world, a place where the strong protected the weak. A new nation under one god: me. And this journey to Black Mountain was to be my pilgrimage. They'd write songs about me, the orphan boy who slew a dragon, ate its heart, and united the twelve kingdoms under one banner."

He closed his hands into fists and the rift exploded with an ear-splitting shriek, just as the other one had. I put my hands over my ears.

Ash turned his back to the green crystals of magicite falling from the sky to extend a hand to me. "And you will be by my side, Ember."

I scooted away from his outstretched hand

and rose to my feet. "Not on your life. Not for all the antigen or cure in the world. I would rather die."

Slowly, he lowered his hand. "Unfortunately, I can't accept that answer. Now that I've found you, I can't just let you walk away. That would ruin everything." He took a step toward me.

I drew my sword, intending to use it to scare him off. But as soon as the blade was free, something bit into my palm and I swore I could feel roots growing under my skin. The sensation was so surprising that I hesitated and gave Ash all the time he needed to backhand me.

The world spun upside down. I was on my ass in dead grass, blinking away stinging tears. The coppery taste of fresh blood filled my mouth. I touched my lip with shaky hands and watched my fingers come away red.

Something in Ash's face changed. He recoiled. "God, Ember! I'm sorry. Please, I never meant..." Ash was closing in on where I had fallen, but the sword was still in my hand.

Do it, urged a throaty voice in my mind. *Cut him down now! While you still can.*

Of all the times for me to start hearing voices! I shifted my grip on the sword and waited for Ash to come closer. "You're *sorry*? You're just proving I'm right. Ash would never hurt me."

He halted. A dark shadow passed over his face. "You're not leaving me a choice, though, are you? There are *rules*." He reached down to grab a handful of hair, intending to yank me to my feet.

I jammed the pommel of my sword into his sternum, knocking all the hot air out of him.

Ash immediately doubled over and staggered backward, wheezing and gasping like a fish out of water.

I scrambled to my feet and ran for the horse, getting up into the saddle just as the rain started. Long before he recovered, I was galloping back toward camp. It'd take a while for him to catch up on foot, even if he could open and close rifts. Wouldn't help him much this time.

Just in case, I pushed the horse faster.

Back at camp, everything had died down. Dex, Ike, and the others had taken their drinking into the tents to avoid the rain, and there was no sign of Zia. A few of Ash's people rushed from the center of camp back to their tents, pulling their cloaks over their heads to shield them from the rain. None of them knew.

Or maybe they did. Zia and the other people who had come with Ash, did they know who he really was? Dex and Ike had tried to tell me and I hadn't listened.

I should warn them, I thought, dismounting. But there wasn't time. I needed to be gone before Ash made it back to camp.

Mud splashed around my ankles as I ran for my tent. I didn't care when I tracked it inside. I didn't have time to care. I just started grabbing everything I had and jamming it into a pack small enough to fit on my back. The tent and its trappings wouldn't fit, nor would most of the food, but I could hunt for what I needed and sleep on the ground.

My fingers curled around the tiny glass vial, my last dose of antigen. I lifted it and watched the dark liquid swirl inside. Without the money from this job, I didn't know how I'd get another dose, and I was already spreading them out as it was. How long before I was as insane as Ash?

As long as possible. I jammed the antigen into my pack and exited the tent.

I only took two steps before invisible claws raked through the air in front of me, opening a rift. It widened enough for Ash to step through it.

"Oh, you've got to be kidding me!" I turned and tried to run, but Ash's fingers latched onto my backpack.

He yanked me back and wrapped an arm around the front of me, pressing my back against his front. "And just where do you think you're going?"

"Away from you." I tried to elbow him, but he grabbed my arm and held it, fingers pressing in hard enough to leave bruises.

"Take one step outside of this camp without my permission and I will have the vampires hunt you down."

"Maybe I'd prefer that to spending another minute here."

"Maybe. But if you leave, I also can't guarantee the safety of your guild friends. They might make excellent dragon bait."

I spun around so angry that I was surprised the rain didn't boil. A minute ago, I'd been ready to leave them. After all, both Dex and Ike had lied to me. But that was when I thought the worst thing that could happen to them would be getting shorted on payment. If he set those vampires lose on the camp…

Scratching, clawing, pacing, waiting. Vampires are patient. They can see in complete darkness and smell blood a half mile away. Death by vampire is slow, painful, the worst way to go.

I squeezed my eyes closed and swallowed, pushing away the memory of that day in Macon. He knew I hated vampires, knew I wouldn't have let anyone die in a vampire's claws if I could help it. The bastard knew, and he'd exploited it.

Tents opened and several people stepped out, murmuring. It must've been a confusing sight, seeing me and Ash standing there in front of an open rift. A cry went up to retrieve a rope and tie it off to a tree.

"No need," Ash said, still locking eyes with me. He stretched a hand behind him and made a fist.

The crowd flinched as the rift exploded, showering the tents and wagons with tiny green crystals.

"I'll be an elf's uncle," Foggy grunted. "Did I just see what I thought I saw?"

"Ember?" Dex was closer, almost within arm's reach. "Is everything okay?"

"Everything's great." It was a lot of effort to say that believably.

Zia came out of her tent, her hair a mess, eyes bleary.

Ash let go of my arm. He adjusted his cloak and scanned the crowd of curious onlookers. "There's no reason to be alarmed. The danger has passed. You can all return to your tents."

"Not without an explanation. It looks like you just closed that rift. How the hell did you do that?" Ike crossed his arms and waited while others mumbled their agreement.

I swallowed and took two steps back. *The floor's all yours. Let's see how you spin this one.*

Ash put on his best sheepish smile. "I suppose there's no keeping it a secret now, is there? We all have our gifts, Commander Tolliver. You can turn rocks into golems. Ember can wield a blade expertly and I… I can close rifts."

Ike didn't seem satisfied. "And one just randomly opened in the center of camp so you could demonstrate that for us?"

Ash dismissed his doubt with a shrug. "Stranger things have happened. We all know how unstable rifts can be, and we are moving toward a large one, the largest one in the area. We must be on alert at all times, expecting trouble from every direction." He glanced quickly at me and then away.

I shivered under his gaze.

"We'll double the guard," Zia offered. "And you guild people will have to help with patrols."

"Aye, we'll patrol our side and you yours. Deal?" Foggy spat on the ground.

Zia shifted into a more aggressive stance. "Did I miss something? I thought we were all here for the same reason. There's a dragon that needs slaying and riches to be had for all, but only for those of you who can follow orders. Now, give me ten minutes to wake up and I'll be putting together a modified patrol schedule at the command tent. I expect both Ike and Dex to be in attendance. Ember, you too. Might as well put that sword to use." She combed her fingers through her wet hair and stormed back to her tent, mumbling about the weather.

Dex pressed in closer, but kept a friendly distance. "Ember, a word if you have a minute? That is, if it's okay with you, Ash."

Ash's smile was friendly, but venom pooled beneath the surface. "She's still a free woman last time I checked. Just remember what we talked about, Ember. The offer remains open. Your choice." He nodded to Dex, folded his hands behind his back and walked away.

Some choice, I thought.

"Are you okay, Ember? Really?"

I felt like flies were buzzing in my stomach. I would've traded a year's wages for a stiff drink and a long sleep, but I wasn't going to get either of those. And if I told Dex the truth, he'd want to confront Ash. That would just get him killed. Somehow, I had to make it through all of this, at least long enough to find time to slip away unnoticed. That meant distancing myself as much as possible from everyone, not just Ash.

I shook rain from my shoulders, though it was a pointless endeavor. The rain was still coming down full force. "I'm fine. Never better."

Dex wasn't convinced. He pointed to his chin. "What happened here?"

I touched my chin and pulled my fingers away, watching the rain rinse watery blood from my fingers. "I… fell. Slippery when the rain started, and dark. Couldn't see a thing."

"Right," he said, drawing out the vowel. "Well, if you're going to go anywhere near vampires, maybe you should get that cleaned up. I have some stuff over at our camp if you want. And a shelter from the rain."

"That's fine. I can…" I trailed off, realizing I had dropped my pack in the mud. Any bandages I had in there would be no good. I'd tracked mud through my tent too in my hurry to get out of camp. Half my stuff would be ruined. I sighed and let my shoulders slump. "Okay, yeah."

I followed Dex back to his camp with my head low except for when I glanced over my shoulder to see if Ash was watching. I didn't spot him, but I swore I could feel his eyes scraping against the back of my neck like steel wool.

I should've fought harder. Should've seen it sooner. A knot formed in my chest where my heart should've been. How could I have ever let him lay a hand on me? If it had been anyone else, they'd be in a body bag by now. But this was Ash, and Ash had caught me off guard. My memory of him had made me weak when I couldn't afford weakness. I couldn't let Dex, Ike, and Foggy pay for my mistake.

Dex led me to a small lean-to shelter open on two sides. A folding table had been set up along with two simple stools. He cleared a game of cards from the table and gestured for me to sit.

"I wanted to thank you for earlier," he said, bringing out a metal toolbox and placing it on the table. Dex removed his hat and put on the back of his chair.

"Me? For what?"

"For staying." He opened the toolbox. A tray spread out containing all the ingredients of a basic first aid kit. "At Kenny's funeral? You didn't know him and he was kind of an ass to you. I think, if you two had gotten to know each other, maybe you'd have liked him. You have a lot in common. Had. Shit, I'll never get used to that."

"I know what you mean. It's hard to think of people we cared about in the past tense." I touched my chin to see if it was still bleeding.

"Quit messing with it. Your fingers are caked in mud. Here." Dex pulled a rag down from where it hung on a string and held it out in the rain for a minute. When it was properly soaked, he sat down across from me and held out a hand.

I stared at it, not sure what he wanted.

"Your hands so I can clean them."

"Oh. I could do that myself," I said and gave him my right hand anyway.

"You could," he said, gently drawing the rag over my fingertips. "But you know, just because you can do everything yourself, you don't have to. Humans aren't solitary mammals. We're meant to be together."

"We are?" I raised an eyebrow.

He cleared his throat. "I mean people. In general. We're stronger together. That's why, even in the face of the end of the world, we fight it in groups. Might be a losing battle, killing all these monsters, but we try."

"Maybe not now that Ash is here. Imagine if we could close all the rifts."

"Yeah, imagine. Now, can I take a look at that chin?"

I lifted my chin for him to see better. "That's what I came here for."

"I know that, but it's still polite to ask a lady before you touch her."

"Says the half-elven son of a whore."

He smirked and dabbed at my chin with some gauze. "Is that really so bad? All my aunties taught me something men like Ash will never understand."

"Really? And what's that?"

"The sexiest thing a woman can ever say is yes."

"Just don't try to pay me when we're done, okay? Ow!" I winced and pulled away.

He frowned. "What'd you say happened?"

"Ran into a tree branch. In the dark."

"Must've been one hell of a tree branch to leave a bruise like a fist and split open your chin like that."

I stood. "You know what? On second thought, maybe it'll heal on its own."

"I saw my fair share of bad stuff at the brothel too," Dex said as I moved away. "Assholes who wanted to get rough with the girls. I know what that looks like when I see it, Ember."

I hesitated under the cover. The rain had picked up. "Look, I appreciate your concern, but I can handle it."

"I don't doubt that you can. You're a hell of a woman. Strong as hell. You punched me, remember? But you should know that you don't have to do it alone. I'm here. That's all I'm saying."

I turned back around, my throat tight. My cheeks felt like they were on fire. Was it shame that made my skin burn or the oppressive humidity, the stifling, rebreathed air under the lean-to?

Dex put his hat back on and tugged it down slightly. "You let me know when and how I can help. When you're ready. Until then…" He kicked out the stool across from him. "We can talk about pink fluffy bunnies or whatever you want, just so long as you let me put a little disinfectant on that wound."

"Pink fluffy bunnies?"

He shrugged. "Makeup? Swords? I don't know. Just don't ask me to braid your hair because I'm all thumbs with hair."

"I figured you'd say you were good with your hands."

"Oh, I am. It's the hair that's the problem. Never could do a thing with it." He grinned ear to pointy ear.

I laughed and went to sit back down. It felt good to laugh after everything that had just happened. Maybe there was something to what Dex was saying about humans not being solitary creatures. I'd been on my own so long, spent so much time dreaming about Ash coming back that I jumped headfirst into this hunt. I was tired of fighting alone, of being alone. Part of me had always hoped we'd get the chance to go back to the way things were. For a minute, when I saw he could seal the rifts, I thought maybe that could happen.

But Ash was right about one thing. The man I thought I knew was dead and gone.

At least there's the dragon's heart, I thought

as Dex carefully bandaged my chin. *If I can get it instead of Ash, maybe I won't have to die alone.* I curled my fingers on the table. *That's what I'll do then. I'll take the dragon's heart for myself.*

"There," he said, leaning back to admire his handiwork. "Damn, is there anything I can't do?"

"Maybe humility."

"What are you talking about? I'm the humblest half-elf you've ever met."

"You're the only half elf."

The temperature seemed to drop. I shivered and pulled the cloak closer until I remembered it belonged to Ash. I wanted to throw it off in disgust, but it was the only thing keeping me from freezing in the cold mountain rain.

"Do you still love him?"

I looked up from the cloak. All the smiles had faded from Dex's face, all the joy. He was more serious than I'd ever seen him. "Who? Ash?"

"You said before you thought you were in love with him once."

I shook my head. "I don't know how I feel about anything anymore. I just want to kill this stupid dragon and move on with my life, forget all this ever happened."

"I don't want to forget you," Dex said solemnly. "And I don't want you to forget me."

I shifted in my seat without looking at him, the air suddenly heavier. Silence stretched out, thinning into a dozen strands between us.

"Shit." Dex drew a hand over his face and slapped a palm on the table. "I've had too much to drink. I'm just spitting out everything, aren't I? I'm surprised my hands were steady enough to get the bandage on straight."

"Well, you'd better sober up. Zia said to meet her at the command tent in ten minutes. We're probably already late." I stood up.

"Yeah, probably." Dex stood with me and let out a relieved sigh. "I'll, uh, meet you there. All that beer, straight to the bladder. Stall for me, will you?"

I nodded and trudged off. Even though the rain was cold, and the night colder, I took off Ash's cloak and let it fall into the mud.

Chapter Nineteen

Ash placed a guard outside my tent to make sure I didn't leave. He didn't tell me that's what he was doing, but I noted the guard's presence all the same when I returned from the command tent. Much to my disappointment, I had drawn the short straw and pulled the sunrise shift, which meant I'd get a whopping three hours of sleep. Considering the limited time I had to enjoy said sleep, I decided it was best not to argue with the guard leisurely patrolling out in front of my tent.

I fell asleep to the sound of rain on the tent walls.

My dreams took me back to the ancient forest with its mossy floor and misty air, but the shadow warrior was not there. I turned a full circle in the chilling silence. My breath came out in small white clouds, almost indistinguishable in the fog.

"Where are you?"

The only answer was my echo, shouting

back at me.

"I know you're here. You brought me here for a reason, creature, so speak!"

Silence.

I clenched my fists. "Tell me what you want from me!"

"What *I* want does not matter." The voice that answered was a whisper and a scream at the same time, filling the air like thunder.

I turned, scanning the dark forest for any sign of movement, but all was still. "Then what does matter to you? What am I to you, creature?"

"A means to an end," it replied. "What end, I cannot say. That is for you to decide."

"Why me? What makes me so special?" I heard a sound behind me, so I turned again, but the air was empty except for more trees, more mist.

"Nothing. Everything. Like all life, you are a product of circumstance, the bastard child of chance and fate."

The voice seemed to be shifting, moving somewhere in the tree line, just beyond where I could see. I kept turning, trying to follow it, to pinpoint its location, but it was always a few steps ahead of me. "Anyone could have picked up that sword at the blacksmith shop."

"And yet *you* did. It was chance that you were even in Atlanta that day, chance that you damaged your weapon battling the troll, chance that the postal wagon convoy leader did not listen when you advised against that route. A thousand things had to happen, all of them beyond your control, to bring us together. And here we are, partners in this endeavor."

I gave up searching for the source of the voice. "Doesn't seem like a partnership. I have gotten nothing out of it, and I still don't know what you want. So far, it's all nightmares and weird voices in my head."

"Ash!" My voice echoed through the forest, though I had said nothing. Green specters materialized in the fog, outlines of Ash and I standing in the rift's light. I reached for him as he disappeared into it. "Ash, don't leave me!"

To my right, more green silhouettes appeared. I watched as Ash's outline struck my face.

I turned away from the scene. "Why are you showing me this?"

"You hear. I see," replied the shadow warrior. "Through your eyes, I know the world."

"Is that what you want? To control my body?"

"No." Fog swirled, materializing into a misty version of the creature's body. "I am without form by choice. Form is limiting. Being is limitless."

"Seems pretty limiting to me. You can't touch or be touched, can't interact with the real world. Without me, you're just a dead spirit in a forgotten sword." I folded my arms. "I don't have time for this. If you don't start making some sense, I'm going to wake up right now."

The shadow warrior dropped to all fours and let out a roar that shook the leaves from the trees. "You would not be so trite with me, girl, if you knew what was coming. I have seen the Black City at the broken edge of reality, and peered at what lies beyond it. I have seen the corruption its whispers bring, and there is no waking from that nightmare."

I unfolded my arms. "I don't understand. That's the third time I've heard about this Black City. What is it?"

"It is the home of the Ashen Throne. Once, it was the seat of the god Hastur, lord of shepherds. Now, the throne is empty. When heaven is empty of gods, the foolish seek to become them. But there are older things than elves, beings from before time. They feed."

I swallowed, my mouth suddenly dry. "On what?"

"Greed. Suffering. Nightmares. The Old Ones hunger for many unpleasant things. With their claws and their carapaces, they reach through holes in the Black City and into new worlds, new feeding grounds. They whisper without detection, patient cultivators, and grow misery like fields of dead corn stalks for their feasting. One by one, they make the worlds go dark."

The shadow warrior lifted a long claw and pointed skyward. The fog cleared, revealing a shadowy throne, sparkling like black ice in the moonlight. "We heard the whispers too late, and in our pride, sought a way into the Black City to slam closed the breaches that let their voices through. Yet the whispers corrupted even that. Those who looked upon the Ashen Throne wanted it for themselves. We fought. And when the wars nearly destroyed our people, desperation drove us."

"I know the elves opened the rifts," I said. "Your people destroyed my world."

The shadow warrior shook his head, antlers rattling. "It is not the flight of the Elves of which I speak. I speak of the last stand of my people. When it looked as if all was lost, the Felmor gathered. It was decided that one warrior from each clan would enter the Black City, not as a living creature, but as a formless monster. A weapon, capable of tearing down the throne of the gods and silencing the Old Ones forever. We believed those without form were immune to the whispers of the Old Ones."

I stared at the black throne, almost transfixed by the way it drank in the light. "You're one of those warriors?"

"I was sent forth at a great cost. Every man, woman, and child shed their blood to fuel the magic that would transform me. That is the cost of assaulting the Ashen Throne. Yet even at that price, we could not succeed." The shadow warrior curled his claws around the moon and pulled it down, plunging the whole forest into darkness. "The Black City shut its gates to us. My people died for nothing!"

I spun around in the pitch black, searching in a panic for any source of light and finding none. "That's not my fault!"

"Fool," it spat. "Listen, as I have. Do you hear the whispers as I do? I know they are lies, and the very sound of their voices makes me hate them. The whispers have come to your world now, girl, and your people are too fractured to even fight them."

Slowly, light returned to the sky, but it was a sickly yellow light hanging just below the tree line. The shadow warrior knelt in the grass before me. It raised its head slightly to look at me with red eyes. "You ask me what I am. I am a weapon that has grown dull. Sharpen me. Hone me. Use me. Whether you an instrument of the gods I once sought to subvert, or a champion against them, I care not. Both are better than the dull silence I have known these last years. Either way, it is an end." The shadow creature lowered his head. "I am yours to command."

I sat up in my tent, gasping for air. It was too hot, and everything smelled like mud and sweat. I started to move my hand, only to realize that I had drawn my sword in my sleep. Looking down at my palm, I noticed a strange green tendril growing out of the pommel. When I moved my hand, the other end of the tendril detached itself from the center of my palm and curled back into the sword like a dying root.

Shocked and disgusted, I recoiled and threw the sword away from me. *What the hell was that?* I lifted my palm. There was a bleeding hole in the center of it where the root had detached. Was that thing feeding on me? I shuddered at the thought. Maybe I shouldn't take information obtained in dreams at face value. For all I knew, the thing that had been speaking to me was one of those Old Ones whispering in my head. But then, why would it tell me about itself? Maybe because it wanted me to use the sword...

I rubbed my aching forehead. It was all very confusing. Better to focus on the problem at hand.

Ash. I felt sick to my stomach, just thinking about what had happened. How was I going to deal with him? More importantly, how would I ensure I got the dragon's heart and not him?

I donned a cloak and stepped out of my tent. The rain had stopped, but there were still puddles throughout the camp. There were also more people awake than I thought there would be. It was still dark out, probably about time for me to take my first shift on guard duty. Yet there were campfires still going, shadowy figures hunched over them. I frowned at the sight and reported to the command tent to sign in.

Zia was waiting. "There you are," she said.

She had dark circles under her eyes, but otherwise looked as flawless as ever.

I frowned, surprised to see her. "Where's Foggy? I thought he was supposed to be my watch partner."

"There's been a change in schedule. Ash's orders."

Of course he'd send her to keep an eye on me.

She flipped her hood up, and we started our first walk around the perimeter. "You look terrible."

"Must be all the sunshine," I grumbled.

She frowned at me, brows knitted in concern. "Sunshine didn't do that to your face."

I stopped walking and turned to her. "Just how well do you know Ash?"

Zia blinked. "Excuse me?"

"You knew we were headed straight for a rift, didn't you? Yet you never showed an ounce of concern. When you saw Ash close that rift in the center of camp and he made his announcement, you didn't look surprised, either. You knew, didn't you?"

She set her jaw and stood up straighter. "Ash's power can reshape the world. He can fix this. All of this. When I saw what he could do, I swore I would protect him. I'd die for him."

"But you don't know him. What he's capable of."

"I know he can close the rifts," she said and

started walking again. "That's all that matters. His survival is all that matters."

"Did you know he could open them too?"

She halted and gave me a wary glance.

"Ash has no intention of going around, closing rifts, Zia, and you know that."

She shrugged it off. "He just needs some time. The man was trapped in one for years. He lost everything. Once he adjusts, he'll come around."

"Do you really believe that?" I crossed my arms.

"I must." Her words were as sharp as a blade. "If I don't believe that we can fix this and heal the world, then what else is left? Am I just supposed to pretend like I'm okay with fighting through every day, watching people die? Watching the world shrink? If we can't fix this, then things are just going to get worse. No matter how we fight and claw to hold on to every shred of civilization and humanity, it will all fall apart. Maybe not in my lifetime, but one day it will happen. Without belief, there's only doom. I choose to believe in a world that can be saved." She marched away.

I grasped her arm, holding her back. "Ash is no savior."

She scowled at my hand on her wrist. I let her go.

Zia folded her hands behind her back and went back to patrolling. "You know, when he woke up, you were the first person he asked for. I used all my resources to track you down, but you didn't exist. No matter how many people I threatened or bribed, no one had ever heard of an Ember Dixon. But then I got a very interesting message from a courier who had been in contact with the postmaster general in Chattanooga. I moved heaven and Earth to put Ash in Atlanta at the right time."

I stepped in front of her, blocking her path. "You arranged that? How?"

She smirked. "Of course. You didn't think it was chance that brought you back together, did you? Please. The Institute doesn't believe in chance and neither do I. We make things happen through careful planning and contacts."

My mind reeled at the implications. Had an Institute spy and whispers from another world had manipulated me this entire time? How many choices had been my own since I'd come to Atlanta? How much had they influenced?

But all I could get out was a single, shaky word. "Why?"

Zia shrugged one shoulder. "Because I believed seeing you would change him, soften him to the cause. If anyone could convince that lovesick idiot to do the right thing, I figured it would be you."

"Your cause? Or the Institute's?"

"I am not the enemy here, Ember. We want

the same thing."

"Do we?" I shook my head and took a step back. "If you had seen how he really was..."

"Well maybe he wouldn't be that way if you weren't so selfish."

"Me?" My jaw fell open. "Selfish? You think I have this bruise on my face because I'm being selfish?"

She whirled around, eyes blazing, and closed on me, stopping when her nose was only inches from mine. "I sat at his bedside for months while we thought he was dying. Every day, it was the same. Every day, he would sweat and cry out for you to save him. You! I was there when he broke and wept because he thought you were dead. I held his hand while he mourned and held him back when he tried to throw himself back into the first rift he saw because he didn't want to be in this world without you."

I shrank back. "I... I had no idea."

"Why would you? You never asked. You never cared. When he saw you in Atlanta, he wouldn't stop talking about you all day. He almost forgot about the mission. I thought maybe he had changed, finally snapped out of that depressive mood that had gripped him. But then he went to your room and came back broken. Dejected. A shell of the man he'd been working so hard to become. Because you rejected him!"

"Nothing I did justifies his behavior."

"No?" she spat. "Then tell me why he went

into the rift in the first place?"

I opened my mouth, but no words would come out. She was right. Ash had pushed me out of the way. He had saved me, and in doing so doomed himself. It was my fault he'd gone into the rift in the first place, my fault whatever was in there had twisted him, my fault he'd even gotten the powers he had.

My fault.

"If he is broken, then it is you who broke him," Zia spat. "Ash is the only one who can do what must be done. It's my job to keep him alive, and your job to undo what's been done. I don't care what that takes. If he hits you, take it. And if he wants you, then you give yourself. Whatever it takes to fix the world, Ember."

I felt sick. My knees were weak and the air suddenly colder. I hugged myself and shook my head, fighting back tears. "How can you say that?"

"I didn't say it was right," Zia said, her tone softening slightly. "Or fair, or even good. But this isn't about good and evil. It's about survival, the future of the world. Ash was given a gift that cannot be denied, not even if he tries to. We weren't chosen. He was. That means he leads. We either bow or we break. There are no other options."

"Listen to what you're saying. Just because he has power, it doesn't mean we should submit to whatever he wants of us."

"When that power pertains to the survival

of our species, then that's exactly what it means." She sighed and shook her head. "The rifts are growing. More appear all over the world every day. Even with the guilds, DEMO, the Institute… Monsters and magic are gaining ground. How long before we must abandon the cities to huddle in caves, waiting to die like they do out west? How long before this experiment at rebuilding fails just like the Coalition and the United States before that? I would suffer a thousand tyrants if it meant I served the greater good."

"Then you're as insane as he is."

"There is a difference between pragmatism and insanity. Insanity is doing the same thing we've been doing as a species for years and expecting different results."

I shook my head and turned to march away. There was no reasoning with a fanatic, and that was exactly what Zia had become. Ash was dangerous, and I had to stop him myself because no one else was going to help me.

If you want something done right…

Chapter Twenty

In the morning, there were no songs, no speeches, no jokes. Fog clung to the valley where we had made camp and rain glistened on every surface. In hushed whispers, everyone packed their belongings in, looking more weary than rested.

Ash marched through the camp in all black embroidered with gold thread, two guards at his side at all times. His movements drew heated looks from everyone but the few he had brought with him. Something boiled beneath the surface of our group of dragon hunters, and the pressure built with every passing minute.

Just as I finished packing in my tent, two of Ash's guards arrived. One tugged back the side of his coat to reveal he had a gun, a rare weapon. Bullets were scarce. "You're to come with us."

I stood up straight and put my hands on my hips. "And if I refuse? Will you waste a bullet on me?"

"Our orders are not to harm you," said the

other guard, his hand moving toward the sword at his hip. "Everyone else in camp is expendable."

"You wouldn't want to make a scene, would you?" said the first guard.

I glanced over at where Dex had been working to load the wagon. He'd stopped, watching the scene unfold with sharp eyes. The tight coiled muscles, set jaw... He'd do something stupid soon if I stuck around much longer.

I lifted my chin and lowered my arms to my side. "Wouldn't want that," I said and went with the guards.

Ash and Zia waited at the front of the convoy, already on their horses. One of Ash's guards brought Scorch out for me.

"Good of you to join us," Zia said, a proud smirk on her lips.

"Sorry. Some of us have to tear down our own tents." I pulled myself up into the saddle.

"This will be the last time you do that," Ash said. "I've also removed you from the watch roster. There's no reason for you to be in the rotation. We have plenty of other able-bodied people for the work."

"Are you insinuating I'm not able-bodied?" Scorch shook her mane as I took up the reins.

He frowned down at the sword at my side.

I felt him looking at it as if something were clawing at my thigh and moved a protective hand over the hilt. "Problem?"

"No problem," he replied with a strained

smile. "You will ride at the front with us to the base camp."

"I suppose I don't have any choice in the matter?"

"No." He gestured in a circle and gave a whistle before we started off on our horses.

I rode for a few minutes, stewing in my anger. A part of me wanted to draw that sword and hit him with something other than the pommel. But Ash didn't deserve to die. I didn't know how else to stop him, though. With Zia egging him on, he was beyond reason.

At length, I asked, "So am I your prisoner? I assume this means I'm not getting paid for the job."

Ash chuckled darkly. "I don't allow my prisoners to ride with me at the front, armed to the teeth. I see no cage, no chains. If you turned your horse and rode off, there would be little I could do to stop you."

I turned my head toward him. "Except I can't, not if I don't want you hurting more people."

He kept his gaze forward. "Is that why you remain? Tell me what it is about that half-elf mongrel that makes you care?"

I didn't answer.

"I'm not blind, Ember. I see the way he looks at you, and you at him. Do you really think the half-breed son of a whore gives a damn about you? If your roles were reversed, he wouldn't hesitate to save himself. You're nothing to him, and he should be nothing to you."

"You don't know him," I snapped. "You don't know the first thing about anyone, and you don't care about anyone but yourself."

"I care about you. About us." His tone was cold, distant.

"There is no us. There never will be."

Ash laughed as if it were a joke. "We'll see how you feel about that after I have the dragon's heart."

After that, we rode in silence.

The sun never really rose. Light hung in the sky, out of reach, filtered through heavy gray clouds. Slowly, that light became less bright and more green. Our path curved around the bottom of a mountain where the trees were sparse. Jagged rock formations protruded from the walls. Moss and vines grew up over old telephone poles, breaking them down, feasting on the remains of the past.

As we went on, the vegetation thinned out and rocks became more prominent. The space between the people on horseback and the carriages increased enough that we had to slow our pace to prevent them from falling too far behind.

At mid-day, we crested the small peak and got our first glimpse of the valley where we would make camp, and of Black Mountain.

The valley was a rocky wasteland, barren of trees and bushes. At the far edges of the valley, large green crystal formations grew out of the rock and reached for the hole in the sky. Despite the hour, it felt like twilight. The green rift spun above, a halo on the mountain, bathing the battlements of an old fort in a sickly green light.

"It's almost beautiful," Zia whispered, watching the rift spin.

A high-pitched roar tore open the air and made my skin prickle. The horses spooked, some rearing to throw their riders. Others simply shifted and shook their heads, stamping their hooves, eager to be elsewhere. The air chilled and everyone in the convoy held their breaths as a massive black shadow passed over us.

I lifted my eyes to the sky.

The dragon of Black Mountain had a wingspan wide enough to block out the light of the rift. Onyx and ruby scales colored the beast's underside while the tougher outer scales were the color of an angry sea at midnight. Strange glowing green horns protruded from the tops of the dragon's head, its chin, and its back.

Magicite. The dragon had magicite crystals growing out of its skin, just like the heretics.

Curved talons raked at a peak on the other side of the valley, pulling down rocks. The dragon's talons were large enough to pick up a horse and rider with ease. The dragon's teeth must have been as large as me. Another roar shook the valley, and the dragon circled the rift before touching down and disappearing into a cave.

"The dragon's lair," Ash remarked. "What luck."

Zia shook her head. "There's no direct path that I can see from here."

Ash smiled and took up the reins he had dropped in awe of the beast. "Well then, we'll just have to find one."

We made camp in the rift's light. I should say everyone else was allowed to make camp. I was escorted from my horse straight to where they were erecting the command tent and told to sit in an uncomfortable wooden chair that looked suspiciously like a throne. Ash's people offered me water, wine, food, everything they thought I wanted. Everything except freedom. I declined it all. They kept me in the chair while the tent walls went up around me, while they set up the table and placed models of the terrain on it, while the day waned and night came.

By the time Ash made an appearance, it was dark enough that someone lit some lamps. The guards outside had made sure I stayed in the tent, but at least I could get up to pace, which was what I was doing when he walked in. I stopped mid-step to glare at him. "Am I expected to curtsey to my future lord and savior?"

"No," he answered matter-of-factly and went straight to the table to study the terrain.

I didn't want to look at him, and I couldn't pace without getting close to him, so I gave up and plopped down into the chair, arms crossed.

"This sullen child act is beneath you, Ember," he remarked, adjusting some items on the table.

"Apparently, a lot of things are suddenly beneath me. Why am I here?"

He finished making the adjustments to the terrain map and stepped back to admire his work. "That sword, where did you get it?"

"Does it matter?"

Ash finally looked away from the table to me. He looked me up and down, rolling his tongue over the inside of his cheek in thought. "I suppose not."

I swallowed and fought to sit up straighter under the intensity of his gaze. "You didn't answer my question. Why am I here?"

"There is to be a meeting shortly. The guild leaders and I will discuss our strategy for how we'll proceed. Before they arrive, we need to discuss this *thing* between you and Dex."

I turned my head away. "You're paranoid. There is no thing between me and Dex."

He slammed his fist down on the table so hard I jumped. The violent explosion of temper made several pieces fall over, and his hair fell out of place. He pushed it back, breathing deeply. "I am trying to make you see reason without losing my temper, but you are not making it easy! Nothing is easy with you, is it? Even before." He put his hands flat on the table, fingers slowly curling in.

For a moment, he looked like his old self, lost and afraid of being alone. Zia's words echoed through my mind. She was harsh and rude, but maybe she had a point. Maybe all Ash needed was a little compassion and guidance. Maybe he wasn't completely unreachable. I owed it to our friendship to try.

I rose out of the chair and went to his side. Slowly, I slid my hand over his.

He looked at our hands, together but apart. "I have loved you since we were children, Ember. Ever since that day at the fort where Old Jim took us in. And it was with such a fierceness that, it hurt. Loving you is like looking at the sun. You always knew the right thing to do, to say. You were always there to protect me."

I took his face in my hands and turned him to face me. "So let me protect you now. Let me protect you from yourself. I don't know what happened to you, but we can fix it together. Without all of this. No vampires. No institute. No power. Leave with me right now, Ash, and you can have me."

He closed his eyes and leaned into my hands. For a moment, I thought he would do it, but when he opened his eyes again, I knew. Ash would never come back to me.

He swallowed, lips parting to answer.

Before he could speak, Zia ducked into the tent. She saw us standing together and stopped dead in her tracks. "Oh. I'm sorry. I didn't realize you two were..."

"No, it's fine." Ash turned away and cleared his throat, folding his hands behind his back. "You have something to report?"

Zia's eyes flicked over to me standing behind him before continuing. "Some of the men are showing symptoms. I told you we should've camped on the other end of the valley."

"We're less visible prey for the dragon and other beasts here," Ash said.

I stepped up. "Wait a minute. Symptoms? Of what?"

"We're inside the rift's red zone," Zia explained. "Have been since the moment we came up over that rise."

"That means everyone's been exposed to magicite." I looked from Ash's face to Zia's and back again. "Ash, that can be fatal!"

"Only in high doses."

Zia shrugged. "Well, there must be enough of it in the air in vapor form to affect people. The stomach upset is spreading through the camp. We're already down two people to violent headaches. We'll have lesions and hemorrhagic fever by morning at this rate, Ash. We have to move camp."

"No," Ash said flatly.

Zia knitted her brows together and tilted her head. "Excuse me?"

"You heard me. I said no."

She looked at me as if I should change his mind, but Ash would not listen to me any better than he had her. “Ash, if we don’t move camp, people will die.”

Ash gestured vaguely to the camp beyond. “Why do you think we brought so many? Or did you really think it would take twenty good men to kill a dragon?”

“You can’t be serious.” I felt sick, and I was sure it showed on my face.

“People die on hunts all the time,” Ash continued. “I had to account for that. Understand that I did not intend for it to be like this, but I understood it was possible and make decisions based on every scenario. There’s no good way forward now. If we move camp back to the hilltop, we’re practically inviting a dragon attack. We would lose more people moving camp than we will to the sickness.”

“I understand,” Zia said. “But if there’s no help, then we could open the supplies up, ease their suffering.”

Ash grunted. “They’re dragon food or they’re dead weight. It would be a kindness to slit their throats and be done with it.”

“There is help,” I said, and moved between Zia and Ash. “That dragon’s heart could save everyone.”

Ash shook his head. “Impossible.”

“Is it?” I pressed in. “You saw how big that thing is. Surely, you don’t need the whole thing to cure yourself. You could share it with everyone you tricked into coming out here, me included. Nobody else has to die."

"You still think I want the dragon's heart to cure myself?"

I stared at him. "But you said..."

He laughed. "I said it *could* be used in a tonic. I never said I wanted it to cure me. I only presented that possibility."

"If you don't want it to make a treatment, then what do you want it for?"

"The elves did not just write about how they used dragon's hearts for curative tonics. The heart is the center of the beast's strength. Our dragon has been feeding on a steady diet of magicite-infused rock for years, meaning its blood is ripe with raw power. And the heart is the center of that power. The possibilities are limitless. It's too valuable a thing to grind into a paste and distribute among idiot hunters. I won't give it up, not for them."

"Of course not," I grumbled. I didn't know what I was expecting. He hadn't even offered it to me when I showed him my scar. As much as I didn't want to believe it, there wasn't an ounce of empathy left in him.

The tent doors opened, and a haggard looking Ike stepped in. He didn't look near as bad as Dex, who had paled two shades and had dark circles under his eyes. He looked as if he could barely stand.

Ash didn't even seem to notice. "Ah, there you are. Thank you for coming."

"Dex, are you okay?" I asked, drawing a warning look from Ash.

Dex forced a grin and a wink. "Never better."

"We'll all be better once this over," Ike said. "We came to talk strategy, so let's talk. How are we going at that thing?"

"We can't until we've done a few other things first, the least of which is scouting a path upward." Ash pointed to the map. "Our best chance to kill it is to strike while it sleeps. The dragon's lair is here. However, it's likely only one entrance of many. There could be a whole cave system up there, or old mines. We need both a map of the path up to the cave, and a rough map of the cave's layout."

Zia folded her hands behind her back. "My vampires will provide this map. However, because of the rift, my range of control is significantly less here. I will need to remain close to them during this process. I will need an armed contingent of men to escort me. While I'm controlling the vampires, I'll be unable to do anything else. You will watch my body and keep any threats at bay while I work."

"I don't see why Ash can't do that," Ike suggested. "Hasn't he always been your guard?"

"I will be busy closing the rift," Ash said. "But I won't be going alone. I will also need someone to accompany me."

"Then I volunteer," Ike said. "Foggy and I will be your forward guard."

Ash's smile reminded me of a snake's. "Actually, I was thinking Dex would be the better fit. How about it, Dex? Up for a little mountain climbing?"

"Just you and me, eh, Ash?" Dex leaned heavily on the table. He was clearly not in any condition to be going anywhere, but Ash didn't care.

"Just you and me," Ash repeated. "I don't expect trouble. We'll be well above the dragon's nest. Unless something drops out of the rift right onto our head, we'll have it closed before Zia finishes her scouting."

Dex shifted his hat and stood. "Why not? Maybe a little good, clean rift air is exactly what I need."

Ash nodded. "Ember, you and Foggy will accompany Zia. The two of you should be more than enough to deal with anything up there."

"If Foggy goes, I'm going." Ike crossed his arms.

"No," said Ash. "I need someone here at camp in case there's an attack here. Besides, sending too many people will just invite trouble by attracting attention. We want to do as little of that as possible for now."

Ike frowned. "So I'm just supposed to sit here and do nothing?"

"I can't leave the camp unguarded, can I? Someone with command experience must remain to respond in an emergency." Ash sighed. "If it'll make you happy, I'll put you in the vanguard push when we go to deal with the dragon. Will that suffice?"

Ike studied the faces around the table before he uncrossed his arms. "I suppose I can't argue with that logic."

"Good," said Ash, pushing away from the table. "I'll give everyone a half hour to get their things together, and then we'll set off."

Ike, Dex, and Zia nodded before moving slowly toward the door.

I stepped up to Ash. "Am I free to go, or am I still your prisoner here?"

"Thirty minutes," Ash said. "And my people will be watching you."

"Nice to know you trust me." I rushed out of the tent to catch up with Dex. It wasn't too difficult considering how slowly he was moving. "Dex!"

He paused, turning to me with a big smile. "Well, hey. Fancy seeing you here."

I glanced around, searching for whatever guards Ash had sent to follow me, and found them coming my way. "You know this is a trap, right?" I lowered my voice so the approaching guards wouldn't hear me. "Ash seems to think you're his rival. He's going to kill you, Dex."

Dex removed his hat and fanned his face.

"Well, he's gonna have to try pretty hard. I've survived worse men than him."

"Yes, but you haven't survived a rift. He has."

He stopped walking. "What do you mean?"

I looked back. The guards were almost on me. "I don't have time to explain, but be on your guard. Don't trust him, no matter what. Understand?" I tucked my head and kept walking before the guards could catch up with me.

Chapter Twenty-One

I downed the last of my antigen with nothing to cut the taste and grimaced. Then I went to mount Scorch. Zia waited on her horse, a blood bay mare. Her two vampires were with her, enchanted leads buckled around their torsos. Those leads attached to her saddle. The vampires squinted in the dim light, blinking as if it were too bright. White streaks of sunblock that hadn't quite been rubbed in all the way marked their naked backs.

Zia looked me over once, frowning, and then turned around in her saddle.

"Where's Foggy?" I asked.

"Right behind you, lass." The dwarf walked up and planted the pommel of his hammer in the dirt. "Ready when you are."

Zia nodded to Foggy. "Where's your horse?"

Foggy raised a bushy eyebrow. "Have you ever seen a dwarf on a horse? I've lost a lot over the years, but I've still got my self-respect. I'll walk."

Zia looked like she wanted to argue, but she swallowed it. "Suit yourself. Just make sure you keep up. I don't stop for stragglers."

I glanced over at where Dex and Ash had mounted their horses. Dex dabbed at his forehead with a handkerchief before nodding to me and tugging his hat down. I wondered if that would be the last time I'd ever see him. I hoped not.

We set off, carefully making our way up a narrow rocky slope. It was only wide enough for the horses to move in single file. After a half hour of careful climbing, I wondered if Foggy wasn't the smart one.

"Nothing but dead stone," Zia muttered.

"She may look dead, but even Black Mountain sings," Foggy replied. He shifted his grip on the hammer resting against his shoulder. "Look to the north and see where the crystals grow. And we're headed to the lair of a dragon. Even in the most inhospitable of places, life manages."

"Is it true your people eat rocks?" The way Zia said it, her question was clearly meant to be an insult, but Foggy took it in stride.

He gave a deep belly laugh. "I've eaten worse, that much is for sure."

"I don't know very much about dwarves," I said. "Your people came through the rifts like the elves?"

"Aye, we did. Generations ago, but our path

wasn't quite the same. The elves call their migration something fancy. The flight of the elves or some nonsense, like they flew in on bloody eagles. They've got fancy names and words for everything."

"There's no common dwarven tongue?" I watched one of Zia's vampires get distracted by a shining crystal. It tried to grab it before the horse pulled it out of reach.

"There was once," Foggy said. "But that was long before my father's father was a glint in his father's eye. We remember some words, though. Mostly curses and insults. And the names of some excellent ales."

"The Institute has scholars of the Dwarven diaspora," Zia said. "They say that, genetically, time is making your people even less dwarven. Exposure to Earth metals and toxins has altered your evolutionary path. With the population in decline due to interbreeding with humans, in several thousand generations, dwarves may be functionally extinct."

Foggy struck a fist twice against his chest. "Takes more than DNA to make a dwarf. And before you state the obvious, height's not the determining factor either. A dwarf's a dwarf because he is."

Zia frowned. "That makes no sense. A people must have a common heritage or homeland. Otherwise, there's nothing to unite them."

Foggy snorted, then spat. "Whatever

homeland we had is gone. If we sat around moaning about it, we'd be elves, not dwarves. That's not to say we don't have our fair share of culture and tradition. We dwarves are well known for our ballads." He lowered his hammer and tapped the brass pommel against the rocks, using it like a walking stick while singing a jaunty tune.

"There once was a dwarf named Thrasimus Shale
Who lived in the tavern called the Rusty Nail.
He drank his ale
From a garbage pail,
And kissed the stonemason's daughter.
When the mason heard the news,
The old man came and got her.
But he was no fighter,
So Thrass held her tighter
And they drank 'til the sun came up!"

"Quiet," Zia snapped. "Voices carry, and you'll attract monsters."

"Good." Foggy hefted his hammer back onto his shoulder. "I didn't bring this for nothing."

The light of the rift flickered to the north, and I wondered if Dex and Ash had reached it yet. If they had, Ash hadn't closed it. I tried not to think of what that flicker might mean for Dex.

The mountain suddenly rumbled. The horses balked, stamping and pulling back rather than pushing forward. To keep from getting thrown, both Zia and I dismounted. Tiny pebbles on the surface of the narrow path leapt and jumped into the air at our feet. A draconic scream shredded the air.

Foggy readied his hammer while we covered our ears. "It's awake!"

A moment later, the dragon emerged from a cave entrance roughly a hundred meters above us. A sheer cliff wall was the only thing standing between us and the dragon. It came to the edge, extended its wings and neck before letting out another ear-splitting roar. Foggy and I threw ourselves flat against the rocks while Zia scrambled to grab the leashes for her vampires. It was the only thing that kept us from falling off the narrow ledge when the dragon swooped down from its perch. Backdraft from its massive wings pulled the rocks from the ledge along with Zia's horse. The horse let out a terrified scream as it fell, but the sound was cut short as the dragon came back around and caught the horse in its talons.

With another roar, the dragon flapped its wings and rose higher into the sky, disappearing into the mountains.

Foggy stuck a pinky finger in his ear. "Well, looks like we're both walking now, m'lady necromancer."

Zia let out a loud breath.

One of her vampires wandered to the edge of the cliff, looking down. It cocked its head sideways and made a small chirping sound before Zia pulled it back to safety.

She made sure the vampires' headpieces were secure. "We should be close enough to scout, anyway."

I patted down Scorch and did my best to calm her, but didn't get back in the saddle. If the dragon came back around, I didn't want to get grabbed along with the horse.

Slowly, Zia removed the vampires' restraints. The vampires squatted in front of her as she pressed her back firmly against the rock wall. "The rest of this should be easy for you two. All you've got to do is make sure nothing happens to me while I scout out the cave. Think you can handle that?"

"Aye, we'll make sure you don't break a nail," Foggy said.

She shot him a warning glare before settling in, eyes closed in concentration.

A silver sheen passed over the vampires' eyes before their posture changed. In unison, they leapt onto the sheer cliff wall, finding invisible handholds, and they began to climb. In a matter of seconds, the vampires scaled the cliff and scampered into the opening the dragon had crawled out of, disappearing.

With my hand on my sword, I turned away from watching the cave opening and looked up at the rift still flickering in the sky.

"He'll be all right, lass," Foggy offered.

"There's more to Dex than a cocky smile. He's got raw talent of his own."

"I don't doubt he's capable when he's at full strength, but... I saw him. He's not well."

He frowned and put his hammer down, leaning on the long handle. "I suspected, but I didn't want to say anything. Not after what happened with Kenny. The magicite is in the air, isn't it? We've been breathing it in since we came to this cursed place."

I nodded.

"By my grandfather's beard, I knew it." He spat on the rocks. "We won't all die; you know that? Not at first. Some are more sensitive to it than others. People like Dex, they draw in the magic on instinct. That's the problem with his type of mage. A good many others will go, too. And there's not a bloody thing that can be done."

I glanced over at Zia to make sure she was still in her trance. Could she hear us? Did I even care? I kept my voice low, just in case. "There is, but..." I gestured to Zia.

Foggy followed my meaning and nodded. "You just tell me what needs smashing. That's what I'm here for. We can go over details later."

"Provided Ash doesn't just push Dex straight into the rift." I sighed and sat down. "How did I even get into this mess?"

He grunted. "Now you sound like Ike."

Zia made a sudden movement, her head jerking to the side. Sweat formed on her brow.

"Is that normal?" Foggy asked, gesturing to her.

I shrugged. "I don't know. I've only seen her do this once, and I wasn't really paying attention."

Above, the rift suddenly crackled and swelled, doubling in size. Thunder boomed through the valley, and the wind rose, pushing Foggy and me back against the cliff wall. Then, with a resounding boom, it exploded. Green hail rained down, shattering against the rocks.

Zia cried out and grabbed at her arm, wincing as if she'd just been injured. Her fingers twitched. The sweat on her forehead glistened.

There was an unfamiliar noise, a deep barking, sounded three times followed by an eerie chirp. Claws scratched against the rock. A moment later, a slick reptilian form, roughly the size of a large dog, came snaking its way down the mountain. It had stunted bat wings and cat like claws. Bright yellow eyes searched the darkness while a blood red tongue flickered out, tasting the air.

Another followed behind it, headed straight for us.

Scorch reared into the air and pulled away, trotting down the path to disappear behind an outcropping of rock.

"Dragonlings," Foggy spat and readied his hammer.

I drew my sword and tried to ignore the

strange pricking sensation of something growing from the sword into my palm.

The first dragonling reached our ledge and clicked its flint-like teeth together. Sparks lit shimmering air and the monster belched a narrow column of flame at us. Foggy evaded the fire and stepped in, swinging his massive hammer with a grunt. The dragonling ducked its reptilian head, avoiding the blow.

Another dropped onto the ledge behind me. I didn't give it the chance to spark fire. Gathering momentum from my turn, I brought the blade down in a perfect horizontal slice. The dragonling let out a primal screech as the sword bit into the side of its neck. A superficial slice and nothing more. The damn thing had moved away at the last second.

"Zia!" I shouted, and took another swing. "Hurry up!"

A less draconic screech sounded above us, near the cave entrance. A beat later, the pale white body of a vampire, streaked with blood, tumbled through the air. It fell, twisting like a cat, as if it could land safely on its feet. But it missed the ledge and smashed into the rocks below. Zia let out a desperate scream and gripped the silver band on her head. She clawed at it, ripping at skin and hair with blind eyes, her face locked in an expression of pure terror. Her fingers froze, curled into claws, and her head fell back, her entire body going rigid while she made choking sounds.

"What the hell is happening?" I brought my sword up, deflecting the claws of a dragonling.

Foggy kicked his foe back and smashed the pommel of his hammer into its throat. "Whiplash! She was in that thing's head when it died."

The dragonling reared, curved claws swiping through the air. I thrust the sword forward in a perfect strike, piercing a weak spot at the base of its neck, just above the ribcage. It flailed around a moment before making a misstep and sliding off the side of the cliff. With wings still too small to fly, it too fell to its death far below.

I turned to help Foggy with his dragon, but paused when I saw more of them pouring out of the den above us. There must have been a dozen or more dragonlings, some of them large enough that it wouldn't be an easy fight. They came clawing their way down the sheer rock face, tongues flicking and teeth clicking.

"Screw this," I spat, and reached down to lift Zia over my shoulder. She was heavy, but I'd lifted heavier. Carrying her limp body down the mountain, however, wasn't going to happen. I needed Scorch. "Foggy, quit playing around and let's go!"

The dwarf gave one last mighty swing of his hammer, smashing the dragonling's head to a bloody pulp against the cave wall. He turned and followed just as a larger dragonling dropped onto the ledge behind him.

"Foggy! Behind you!"

He turned too late. The dragonling opened its jaws, a ball of white-hot flame forming in its mouth.

A dark shadow dropped out of nowhere and landed between Foggy and the dragonling. In the dim light, I thought it might be another dragonling until Ash stood up. "Get behind me!" He thrust a hand forward, opening a rift in the air just big enough to swallow the dragon's fire.

The dragonling belched out the last of its flame. Ash pushed the rift bigger. Pebbles along the narrow path rose, suspended in mid-air by the magic. As the rift grew wider, the pull became stronger. First, it only swallowed the pebbles. Then, I felt it pulling on my clothes.

With a grunt, Ash pushed his arm forward, and with it the rift. The dragonlings turned to flee, but they weren't fast enough. In a matter of seconds, the swirling rift swallowed them all. Once they were inside the rift, he closed his fist and the world exploded in a shower of green light and flame. He teetered in place for a moment before falling to his knees.

I pushed Zia at Foggy and went to Ash to grip him by his cloak. "Where is Dex?"

He stared at me, wheezing. The left side of his face twitched into a sneer. "I just saved your life and the first thing you do is ask about him?" He shakily pushed to his feet.

I tried to help him, but he shoved me away. My back hit the cliff wall, and I held on, shaken. "Ash, where is he? What did you do? Answer me!"

Ash ran his fingers through his hair and adjusted his cloak. "It was a big rift. I told him to stay back, that he was just there to make sure I could finish the job uninterrupted. Even drew a line on the ground and told him not to cross. It's not my fault, Ember."

I stared at him, imagining it in my head. Had he pushed Dex over the line? Tripped him? Dex had been so weak, so sick. I shouldn't have let him go.

The guilt quickly spun into anger. My fingers curled against the smooth rock face. "You bastard!" I lunged at Ash.

He sidestepped and swung out a foot, knocking me off balance. My breath caught as I tipped over the cliff, but Ash grabbed me by my belt. Rather than pull me back, he let me dangle over the black abyss, a deadly drop of several hundred feet onto sharp stone.

"I wouldn't if I were you," he said to Foggy. "Hit me and I might lose my grip."

The dwarf's nostrils flared as he held his hammer at the ready. "If she dies, you die."

Ash ignored the dwarf and looked at me while I flailed my arms helplessly. "I could let you fall. I could kill you both and then tell any story I wanted."

I swallowed and tried to calm my panicked

breathing. The anger was still there, but it had pushed behind the fear of falling to my death.

Ash yanked me back onto solid ground. "But remember that I didn't."

I wanted to stand, but my legs wouldn't hold me.

Foggy backed slowly away from Ash and put a hand on my shoulder. "You okay, lass?"

I nodded shakily and slowly got back to my feet. Inside, I was a maelstrom of emotion. Anger, fear, grief, sadness… It swirled in a tight ball in the center of my chest. "I want to see where it happened."

Ash shook his head. "It was far up the mountain. Besides, there's nothing there. He's gone, Ember. Accept it."

"I'll accept nothing from you, you lying, traitorous ass!"

He heaved a heavy sigh. "Regardless, you're not going up that mountain."

Foggy put a hand on my shoulder, his expression grave. "I hate to say it, but he's right, lass. Zia's other vampire is still up there somewhere, and without her controlling it…" He trailed off. "And that's saying nothing of any other dragonlings or other creatures who will come to investigate what's happened here. The paths are narrow, and we don't have sufficient light to make the trip now."

"Come." Ash walked over, picked up my sword from where it lay on the rocks, and held it out to me. "The dragon will return from its hunt soon. It will feast and sleep with a fully belly. We'll come back up in the daylight and you can inspect whatever you like."

I jerked the sword away from him, trembling with rage. Knowing they were both right didn't make it any easier to believe. Dex was gone.

More people would die needlessly if I left Ash to succeed. The only way I was going to save anyone was if I stayed alive long enough to claim the dragon's heart from under him.

Chapter Twenty-Two

We found Scorch a short distance away and put Zia on her. Zia hadn't moved. She still wore the same blank, wide-eyed stare she'd had when she slumped over.

"Will she recover?" I asked Ash. I was still furious with him for what had happened with Dex. All the way down the path, the only thing I could think about was pushing him off the mountain. But if I killed Ash, I wouldn't be any better than he was. What was it Old Jim used to say? If you kill a killer, the number of killers in the world stays the same.

Ash took Scorch's reins and pulled. "You were supposed to protect her."

"We did." I took Scorch's reins away from him.

"As best we could," Foggy agreed. "No one could've known about the dragonlings."

Ash scowled and walked on, keeping both of us in front. "Dragonlings complicate things. It means our dragon is mated."

"Two dragons?" We had only seen one, but that didn't mean there wasn't another hiding somewhere else in the mountain range. There were more than enough peaks and cliffs for each dragon to have their own.

But Ash shook his head. "No. A dragon's territory is vast, and they don't overlap. Once they reach maturity, they either leave or become food for other dragons."

Foggy sighed. "Well, at least that's gone right. One dragon, we can kill. Two? Even I know fighting two is stupid."

"Our dragon must be a female, which means there is a male somewhere out here," Ash continued. "Those were older dragonlings, close to outgrowing the nest. How old, I can't say. It's possible, however, the dragon's had time to mate again. She could have an egg in there."

"And you'll find no fiercer mother than a dragon." Foggy ran his fingers through her beard. "This is a fight that will be hard fought."

"Dammit, Zia," Ash muttered, lowering his head. "Why now? If anyone would've known about the mating habits of dragons, it would've been her. All that valuable Institute knowledge wasted. And we didn't even get a map of the cavern system." He pinched the bridge of his nose. "Oh well. It can't be helped. The Institute won't be happy about losing one of their own."

My fist closed tighter around Scorch's reins. "Zia's not dead."

"She might as well be. She's useless to me as a catatonic. I told her not to take any risks with those vampires. Now what do I do with what's left of her?"

I stopped and spun around, blocking Ash's path forward. "You're getting a healer to look at her."

Ash glared down his nose at me. "We didn't bring a healer."

"Then after. You take her wherever you have to, and you make sure she's taken care of, Ash. Like she did for you. I may not like Zia, but she doesn't deserve to be discarded because she's no longer useful. She's a person, not a broken toy you can just throw away."

"We'll talk about what happens after later. For now, walk." He grabbed my arm and forced me to go forward.

Foggy shifted his grip on his hammer and squinted at Ash. Ash sneered back at the dwarf, but released my arm so I could walk on my own. Foggy relaxed.

As we neared camp, the clamor of shouting voices greeted us. A handful of the non-affiliated fighters we'd brought with us had gathered in the middle of camp, surrounding Ike, and they didn't look happy.

"I told you already the wagons belong to the expedition," Ike shouted. "And so do the supplies."

"How do you expect us to make it back

then?" a man in the crowd shouted back. "Half of us are already too sick to walk. No telling how many we'll lose if we have to walk the whole way."

Someone drew a knife. "Then we take it by force."

"Don't make me fight you." Ike lifted his hammer from his belt, but they outnumbered him. He looked past the crowd and spotted Ash. A relieved expression crossed his face. "There. You want to take it up with someone? He's the one who brought us here." He pointed at Ash.

Faces turned to us, scowling. More hands found weapons.

"Desperation," Foggy whispered. "Nothing more dangerous in a group of armed men."

"He's brought us here to kill us all," someone shouted. "That way he doesn't have to pay us."

"We're dragon bait," someone else added.

Ash stepped away from me, Zia, and Foggy. "There's no need for violence."

"Easy for you to say," said the man with the knife. "You're not sick. Why are you immune? Why are any of you immune?" His knife shifted from being pointed at Ash to pointing at me and then Foggy. "Eddie's gone blind. Torrin's got a fever and rash. Good men, both of 'em and they'll die here for you. And for what? What will you do for them? Didn't even build a pyre for the last one you killed. You left him where he fell."

Ash lifted his chin. "I explained the danger back at the tavern. You signed a waiver."

"Paper," spat the man. "Means nothing out here. You said so yourself. If we kill you, who'll we answer to?"

Ash lifted one hand, and the man flinched. "Think carefully before you let your cowardice in the face of death guide you. You've seen what I can do. With one stroke of my blade, I decapitated the last man who challenged me. I have magic at my disposal and armed guards posted around the camp."

I scanned the camp perimeter. Since we'd arrived, several guards had stepped forward, their hands on their weapons.

"Do you really want to attack *me*?" Ash's words dripped with unearned confidence.

The man licked his lips and looked around, counting the guards. He shifted his weight from one foot to the other. "Whatever's killing people, it's a slow and painful death. Maybe this way is faster."

Ash shrugged. "And maybe you won't get sick at all. Maybe they're weak and you're strong. Maybe you'd be better off surviving to bury your friends."

There was a pregnant pause in the camp. With the rift gone, the night was so quiet we could hear one another breathing.

It came out of the shadows at the edge of camp, a blur of pale flesh and fangs. One minute the man with the knife was standing in front of us, weighing his options, and the next he was on the ground gurgling while the vampire ripped a chunk of flesh out of his throat.

The vampire lifted its head, blood dripping down its chin, and let out a wet snarl.

Someone shouted, "Vampire!"

There was the sound of several swords unsheathing at once before the camp erupted into chaos.

The vampire leapt into the crowd, tearing into whoever was unlucky enough to come face to face with it. Those close to the victim tried to pull the vampire off, but it turned on them instead. Vampire claws raked across faces, tearing them to the bone. Teeth tore open bodies like ripe melons. Powerful legs kicked out, knocking down more victims. The crowd scattered, stampeding over one another to get away.

Ash's guards had brandished pistols out of nowhere and had them pointed at the crowd, waiting for his order to shoot, an order he was prepared to give without hesitation.

I grabbed Ash's arm. "You'll hit your own people!"

"There's no way to tell who's infected now and who isn't. Better to kill them all." He shook free of my grip and turned his back to me.

Do it, said the shadow warrior's voice in my head. *Use me!*

And then the sword was in my hand. I

didn't remember drawing it, but I didn't fight whatever had driven me to do it. Inside, I was numb. I was tired of watching people I cared about die, tired of not doing anything to stop it. Ash was my responsibility.

My fault.

I lifted the sword, ready to strike.

A gun went off to my right, the sound a deafening boom. I felt the impact of something wet on my side. It hit me hard enough to make me stumble. Stunned, I lowered the sword and touched my side, only to have my hand come away bloody.

Ash had turned around by the time I looked up, and he looked at me with a horrified expression.

I tried to say something, but my chest was sinking into my toes. The world tilted sideways, and I fell.

With a frustrated growl, Ash turned on the guard who'd shot me and stabbed him. Before he could jerk his blade free, the vampire vaulted out of the crowd and leapt onto Ash's back.

It all happened so fast, yet I swore I was watching it in slow motion with sound pulsing in and out of existence in time with my heartbeat.

"Lass!" Foggy was on the ground with me. He had blood in his beard.

There was blood on my fingers. Was that my blood in his beard or someone else's?

He lifted his head and looked around as if he were searching for someone, but the camp was chaos. I couldn't even see Ash anymore.

"I'll be back," Foggy promised.

"No! Don't..." I tried to grab onto him, but he was already gone. I let my arm fall limply into the blood-soaked ground. "Don't leave me."

It was cold on the ground, and my side burned like it was on fire. Everyone was screaming, but the shouts were getting quieter, further away. The ground felt like it was far away, too. If I didn't know any better, I could've sworn I was flying.

Open your eyes. The shadow warrior was talking again.

So pushy. Didn't that thing ever shut up?

Open your eyes!

I sucked in a gasp and forced my eyes open, only to find myself staring into a pile of rocks. I was no longer on the ground, but the ground was beneath me, moving. No, I was moving, and the rocks were carrying me.

"What's happening?" I tried to twist free in a panic, but white-hot pain shot through my side.

"Try not to move. You've lost a lot of blood." Ike's voice.

The whole thing suddenly made sense. This was his golem. *I must've lost consciousness at some point. Ike made another golem, and it's taking me... somewhere.* "Where are we going? What about Ash and the rest of the hunting party?" I turned my head so I could see Ike walking alongside the golem.

Ike shook his head. "Dead. Everyone's dead except for that bastard, and a few of his crew. I knew this wouldn't end well."

"At least we got you out, Lass." Foggy's tone was grim.

I swallowed. My mouth was so dry. "Ash will notice I'm gone. He'll come looking."

Ike nodded. "He'll go after the dragon first, giving us all the time we need to slip away. That's always been his priority."

I stared up at the sky. It was a red dawn, as if the sky itself was bleeding. "Dex..."

"I know. I wanted him to pay for it. For everything. I could have. He was right there." Ike made a fist and then released it, letting his shoulders slump. "But I had to make a choice. Saving who I could was more important."

"The *right* choice," Foggy reminded him.

The golem halted. With a gesture from Ike, it lowered me to the ground. I winced when its arms struck the dirt.

Ike knelt next to me and lifted the dressing someone had hastily applied over my clothes to stop the worst of the bleeding. "I'll do what I can, but I'm not a healer. I have... I have people who do that for me in the guild. We should have brought Fiona. Dammit!"

Foggy patted Ike on the back. "Ash

would've never let you bring both of us."

"It doesn't matter. Healing magic doesn't work on me." I winced and lifted my shirt, revealing the magicite scar running across my stomach.

Foggy's eyes widened. "Stones, when did that happen?"

"Five years ago. About the same time a rift swallowed Ash." I lowered my shirt. "And then he came back. I didn't think it was him at first, but there he was. Except he's not like he was before, and it's my fault."

Ike touched my forehead, frowning. "No fever. She could be delirious from blood loss or shock."

The dwarf shook his head and pressed the cloth back to my bleeding wound. "I don't think she's delirious. Think about it. DEMO doesn't get interested in people for no reason. We both saw Ash close that rift, and we suspected he might've also opened it too. That power, it could be because he's been exposed to the rift more than anyone. He could've gone and come back."

"Nobody comes back," Ike insisted. "Everybody knows that."

"Ash did." I put my hand over the compress on the wound and winced. "I thought it was a second chance. Maybe the universe was on my side for a change. But I was wrong. Ash is infected with magicite too, and now all those people are dead."

Ike sighed. “Ember, if that’s true… God. No wonder DEMO wanted us to watch him. We can’t tell them the truth, Foggy. They’ll use him, and not for good either. If you think he’s dangerous now, wait until DEMO gets control of him.”

“We’ll worry about the boulders when we’ve dealt with the mountain,” Foggy said and lifted the bandage. He poked and prodded at my wound, drawing a hiss of pain. “Entry and exit wounds. Lucky there, but you’ve got a right hole in you. We need to stop the bleeding and close it up. Lacking needle and thread, fire’s the best option.”

“What about the magicite infection? It will kill her.”

“I’m right here,” I reminded them, and swallowed dry air. “I’ve stayed alive this long with the antigen. And so has Ash.”

Foggy stood. “I’ll get a small fire going.”

Ike eased me from the golem's arms to the ground and ordered the golem to keep watch. It turned around and stood still as a statue.

“You know, you didn’t have to tell us about the magicite infection, or the truth about Ash. Especially after we kept the truth from you,” Ike said.

I looked up at the sky. A golden band had crept up above the horizon. “I should’ve said something sooner. Then Kenny would be alive and Dex might…” I choked on the words, my throat suddenly too thick to speak. “I’m sorry.

This is all because of me. Because I wanted to believe Ash was back, that he was alive, and we could be happy. That was stupid."

"No, Ember. Wanting to be happy doesn't make you stupid." He put a hand on my shoulder. "And neither does seeing the best in people, though maybe you could've warned the rest of us a little sooner what we were dealing with."

"I'm sorry," I repeated.

"So am I." He patted my shoulder gently. "We could all be better than we were on this hunt."

Foggy returned with a small pile of sticks. He built up a small fire with dry kindling and an old lighter, while Ike did his best to clean my wound with a canteen of water. Foggy drew a knife, cleaned it with the last of the water and held it in the flame.

"What happens now?" I asked, watching the metal change colors.

Ike sighed again, his shoulders heaving with the effort. "Now we go back to Atlanta. We come up with a story to tell DEMO."

"And you just leave Ash out there?" I shook my head and regretted it because it left me slightly dizzy. "After everything he's done, you just let him win?"

"The man can open and close rifts at will, Ember," Ike said. "Even with our limited power, there's nothing we can do that would stop him from just opening one under our feet the minute he saw us coming. We'd never be able to get close enough. I'm sorry, but this is going to have to fall to someone else."

"Besides," added Foggy, turning the knife over, "we don't even know where he is. We barely know where we are."

"But we know where he's going. And I can get close." I propped myself up on my elbows and whimpered at the sudden pain.

Ike helped me lay flat again. "You're injured, and I'd be a terrible person if I let you walk back there, knowing you're going to your death. If they survived the vampire attack, he'll still have armed guards loyal to his cause."

"And the dragon. Don't forget about the dragon," Foggy added. He lifted the knife, studied it, and grunted. "Best give her something to bite down on. This'll be a real kick to the ovaries for you, lass."

Ike looked around and eventually picked up a stick. He turned it over in his hand, shrugged, and offered it to me.

"Are you two idiots really going to make her put that in her mouth?" said a voice in the darkness.

Ike dropped the stick and rose to his feet, hammer in hand.

Foggy joined him, gripping the red-hot knife. He held the blade out to the darkness. "Show yourself!"

Dex slowly limped out of the darkness,

gripping his side. His hat was misshapen, his clothes bloodied and torn, but it was him. I could scarcely believe my own eyes! If I'd been able to get up without bleeding everywhere and falling right back over, I would've jumped up and run to hug him.

"Dex!" Ike stammered. "I thought..."

"Ash said..." I still couldn't finish the thought.

"What? That I was dead? Takes more than a little tumble off a cliff to kill me." He limped closer to the fire and offered Foggy a toothy grin. "Man, you should see your face! You look like you swallowed a whole boulder! Now give me that before you poke your eye out." He pried the dagger out of Foggy's hand and limped over to me.

"Ash threw you off a cliff?" Ike shifted to make room.

"Well, no. He threw my hat off the cliff. Bastard stabbed me in the gut and left me to bleed out. Lucky for me I know how to cauterize a wound, no fancy knife tricks required." He tossed the knife in the air and caught it before offering it back to Foggy. "Course, I had to go get my hat. Otherwise, I'd have been here sooner. Sorry I'm late." He tugged on the torn brim of his hat.

"Show off," Ike muttered.

Dex ignored him and knelt in front of me. He clicked his tongue once and shook his head. "I leave you alone with Ash for a couple hours and come back to find you with some fresh injury. I'm starting to think he's a little bad for you, Ember."

"You think?"

"Hmm." He cracked his knuckles. "Well, I lost my fancy gloves, but there's plenty of magicite in the air. I think I can manage a little fire spell."

Ike halted Dex by grabbing his shoulder. "Dex, she's infected. You hit her with magic, and it'll spread like crazy."

Dex's face fell. "Oh. Since when?"

"Since five years ago. Ash is apparently infected too," Foggy said.

"What? How?"

I rolled my eyes. "Hello? Bleeding here. Can we please not do this song and dance?"

"Well then, here." Dex removed his belt, dusted a little dirt from it and offered it to me to bite down on. "You know, somehow, knowing Ash is infected makes a strange amount of sense."

They cleaned the knife again and heated it back up. This time, the responsibility of cauterizing fell to Dex, since he was the only one with any actual healing experience. That amounted to a first aid course once a year, but it was better than either Foggy or Ike had.

The cauterizing hurt almost as bad as taking a bullet did, but at least it stopped the bleeding.

Dex whistled when I gave him the belt

back and held it up. The leather was sporting a brand-new permanent bite mark. "This'll make for interesting bar chatter," he said, putting it back on. He stopped halfway through to lift his shirt with a big grin. "Hey, look! We have matching burn scars!"

Foggy smacked him in the back of the head. "Flirt later, elf boy."

"Half. I'm only half a pompous elf. The good half, too," Dex muttered and finished putting on his belt.

I sat up. Ike objected, but I wouldn't have it. Pain or no, I wouldn't lie on the ground while the rest of them sat around worrying about me. I let him help me up, though.

I took a few shaky breaths, working through the pain. "Okay, now that I'm not bleeding everywhere, we need a plan."

Foggy crossed his arms firmly over his chest. "We told you the plan, lass. Get out of here and back to safety before Ash decides to hunt us instead of the dragon."

I shook my head. "If you think running back to Atlanta will somehow save you, then you don't know Ash. If he thinks you're a threat, he'll hunt you down no matter where you go, and probably take out half the city to do it."

"I'm a dead man walking thanks to that bastard, and so are half the people back at camp," Dex said, his voice serious for once.

"There likely isn't anyone back there." Ike

stared blankly into the fire.

"Vampire attack," I whispered. "Ash ordered his people to kill everyone that might be infected and if I know Ash..."

"Shit." Dex removed his hat.

"Yeah."

There was a long silence until Dex clicked his tongue and put his hat back on. "Well, I know this sickness is fatal, but I don't have to let it kill me. I'd rather go out taking that bastard with me, and I've been saving a spell for just such an occasion." He rose.

I grabbed his arm. "Before you go turning yourself into a walking bomb, Dex, there's something you should know."

He straightened his hat without looking at me. "If you're about to confess your undying love and offer me a night of passion, then I accept."

"What? No!" I kicked him in the shin. "I was going to tell you why Ash wants the dragon's heart!"

"Oh." He plopped back down, winced, and rubbed his side. "Why?"

"Ash is on some insane quest to unite all twelve kingdoms. He believes eating the dragon's heart will give him some sort of power that will help him achieve a godlike status."

Ike and Foggy exchanged a look.

Dex made a face. "And I thought I had bad eating habits."

"Ash also told me there were ancient elvish writings at the Institute that detailed how to make an alchemical healing concoction, one that would heal any ailment. Including yours, Dex."

His face lit up. "If we got the dragon's heart instead of Ash, we could take it back to Leseran, maybe convince him to help us."

Foggy leaned in to whisper to Ike. "Who's Leseran?"

Ike shrugged.

Dex's face fell. "But what about you, Ember? If it will cure anything, won't it cure your magicite infection?"

"Don't worry about me. I've survived this long."

"But Ember, that infection is fatal."

"So is yours, and what you have will kill you a lot faster than this will kill me." I patted the scar through my shirt. "Who knows? Maybe we can make more than one potion out of it. That's what I was trying to convince Ash to do instead, to help all the sick people at camp, but he didn't want to waste it on *lesser people*."

"Sick bastard." Foggy spat into the fire.

"You're forgetting something important," Ike pointed out. "To get that heart, we'd have to slay the dragon ourselves, and we'd have to do it before Ash. It might already be too late."

I shook my head. "Ash's plan was to wait until mid-day, after the dragon had fed and bedded down. We're not that far from Black Mountain. With a little help from your golems, and some luck, we might make it before he does."

Ike frowned and looked around the small circle. I could see the wheels turning in his head, calculating the odds of success. "Maybe..."

"Maybe?" Foggy coughed and stood, gripping his hammer with both hands. "Lad, we've seen less favorable odds. Do you remember the reverse centaurs?"

Ike shuddered. "How could I forget? I hate fusion magic."

"Then why are we standing around here clutching our gems? Let's go slay us a dragon!"

Chapter Twenty-Three

Black Mountain was quiet. There was no sign of Ash or anyone else. Our path up the mountain didn't give us a prime view of the camp—or whatever might've been left of it—but I imagined there wasn't much left of that either. I had seen firsthand the sort of destruction a vampire could cause. The survivors would pick through the rubble, searching and cataloging their provisions. That would give us an hour head start, maybe two. We'd need every minute we could get.

Our plan was reckless. We all knew it, and yet no one dared voice it. Dex and I were injured; Ike and Foggy hadn't slept in days. It showed in their sluggish movements, the dark circles under their eyes. Determination and desperation would have to make up the difference.

Without a map of the caverns, we didn't know what we were walking into. The dragon could be just a few yards in, or sleeping miles deep in the mountain. The one thing we knew was that she wasn't alone. Her dragonlings were in there with her, and we would have to fight our way through them to get to her.

After a long hike, we found the ledge below the dragon's cave where Zia, Foggy, and I had been attacked by the dragonlings the night before. The cave entrance was just a few hundred yards above us, straight up a sheer cliff. While the dragonlings and vampires had climbed up and down the space using their sharp claws, the four of us didn't have that advantage.

I frowned up at the yawning black hole in the mountain's side. "How are we getting up there?"

"You might want to step back." Ike brandished his hammer.

The rest of us moved away as he approached the side of the mountain. Eyes closed, Ike lifted his hammer and touched two fingers to the hammer. A brilliant blue glyph appeared on the flat surface of the hammer. When he touched those fingers to the stone again, the glyph copied from the hammer to the rock face, bathing us all in electric blue. In one quick downward motion, Ike struck the hammer to the side of the mountain with a loud metallic *tink*.

The stone rumbled, but bowed to Ike's will. Cracks formed in the stone all the way to the ledge above us, and then the space exploded in a shower of fine pebbles, revealing a carved stone staircase.

"Now who's the show off?" Dex grumbled and limped up the stairs.

Foggy patted Ike's back. "Well done."

I glanced back the way we'd come. "That was loud. Do you think they heard?"

"Probably," Ike said. "But if you wanted this to be a clandestine operation, you should've said so. You could've sent the elf to braid some ropes, maybe."

"Half elf," Dex called back. He paused at the top of the stairs. "Though it might've been faster considering how long it's taking you to get up here, old man. Hurry up."

We trudged up the stairs.

"I won't be so useful once we get inside the dragon's lair," Ike said. "My expertise is rock, and my spells take careful time and consideration. I could craft a few golems before we go in, but we may be walking through narrow spaces. They're more likely to get stuck than provide any cover if that's the case."

I nodded. "You and your hammer will hang back. If all else fails, I'm relying on you to bring the rock down and seal off the cave. Ash can't get the dragon's heart, Ike. Even if it means sealing us inside."

"Buried alive with a dragon. I could think of worse ways to go." Foggy shook his head.

We reached the top of the stairs and paused.

"If the dragonlings are anything to judge

by, that thing probably breathes fire," I said.

Dex held up his right hand. "Good. I've got both fire and ice covered."

"Do you think you can redirect dragon fire?"

He shrugged. "Never tried, but fire's fire, right?"

I hope so, I thought. "You'll provide cover fire so Foggy and I can get close. Hit it hard, hit it fast. Use ice to freeze its feet in place if you can. The last thing we want is for it to get airborne. And if it spits fire at us, you do what you can to keep it off us." I turned to Foggy. "Foggy, your job is to get me close."

"You ever kill a dragon before?" the dwarf asked, shifting his grip on his large hammer.

I shook my head. "But I imagine it's the same as almost any other big beast. Destroy the brain, or bleed it out, and it's dead. If it's anything like the dragonlings, the scales will be thinner on the underbelly."

"Getting that close means being close to claws and fangs, lass."

"Can you do it?"

The dwarf nodded. "Aye, I can."

Dex smirked and flexed his fingers. "I bet Leseran's never killed a dragon. Imagine his face..." He conjured a small flame between his thumb and first two fingers, holding it up to illuminate the entrance to the cave. "Hey, Ike. You know what the entrance to this cave looks like?"

"Grow up." Ike shook his head and gave Dex a light shove.

In another life, the two of them could've been brothers.

We entered the cave, our footsteps going before us in echoes. Pebbles and larger rocks had been cleared from the entrance, though a few clung to the sides. The cave floor sloped upward at first, smooth as polished marble. Broken stalagmites and stalactites of magicite divided the passage in two. It was just wide enough for a dragon to slip through. Ike's golems might've fit, but not without breaking some of the magicite. They wouldn't have had the dragon's grace.

Ike frowned and leaned in to study a thick sparkling vein in the rock. "This is… What is this? I've seen nothing like it."

Dex ran a hand over the sparkling black vein. It responded to his touch, turning viridian green and then a lighter, more yellowish shade. "It's almost as if the rift has changed the structure of the rock, but rather than infecting it and changing it into magicite, it's become something new. I can feel the magic coming off it. It feels like standing under the rift."

I reached out to touch the rock, but a sudden sharp pain in my stomach made me cry out and double over in pain. Ike and Dex both reached to help me, but I shoved them away. "I think I'm okay."

"That didn't sound okay," Ike said with a

frown.

I carefully lifted my shirt to look at the magicite scar running across my stomach. The indigo scar was glowing.

"It's responding to whatever's in the rock," Ike said. "I wonder what that means?"

"It means I don't want to stay in here any longer than I have to," I said, dropping my shirt and clutching the scar.

"Does it hurt?" Ike asked.

I shook my head. "No, not now. Initially it did. But now?"

"It's like a dull, painless gnawing," Dex said, watching the lights dance across the cave wall. "A hunger you didn't know you had. I feel it too. I don't like it."

"*Eldarghrott,*" Foggy said, frowning. "Thirst stone. My people have stories about it. The old songs say that when magic bleeds into a place, it taints it. The ground becomes cursed and all who walk on it bear that mark."

Dex retracted his hand. "What mark?"

Foggy shook his head. "Don't know. Stories are unclear on that. But those stories aren't tales of heroes, lad. Those are tales of gods and older things, of a time before counting. Could be just an old legend."

"Legends are often based in truth. We shouldn't linger." Ike gestured for us to go forward.

Dex moved away from the cavern walls,

careful to keep his distance from the shining magic rock.

Deeper in the cave, we found the first signs of dragons nesting. Thick brown pellets full of bone and other discarded material sat in piles. Dragon dung. It was laced with magicite, confirming our suspicions that the dragon had been eating it.

Just beyond the dung chamber was a huge cavern. It was as large as a stadium. A small hole in the cavern wall let in enough sunlight to allow a single tree to grow. At the rear of the cave, a waterfall poured in, creating a narrow river through the center. The tree stood on a pile of rocks, leaning over the river as if it were reaching for that single ray of sunshine.

The sight would've been breathtaking if it wasn't for the enormous dragon sleeping on the other side of the river. She was curled up with her head over top her tail, protecting any straightforward path to her underside. A host of dragonlings huddled around her, sleeping restlessly.

I pointed to the tree. It would provide a perfect vantage point for Dex to cast his spells. Dex nodded and crept toward it as silently as possible.

Ike motioned he would hold position at the cavern entrance as our rear guard. Foggy and I traced out the path we would take with gestures.

We would get one surprise attack. After

that, the dragon would wake, and we'd be knee deep in the fight. I wanted to make it count, get as close as possible before that happened, but there was no way to get to the dragon without wading through dragonlings.

Once we agreed on a path, we moved carefully and quietly to the edge of the stream. The noise of the waterfall masked most of our sound, but we hadn't accounted for scent. One dragonling must've caught it. It rolled over and shook its head, waking up. Foggy and I froze in place, midway through the stream. Icy water lapped at my ankles and numbed my feet through my boots. Red gold eyes focused on us. I held my breath.

The dragonling let out a high-pitched warning shriek. Its brothers and sisters stirred. The dragon's eyes snapped open.

So much for our surprise attack.

Foggy let out a guttural war cry and raised his hammer high. Crimson light poured from his tattoos, his eyes, and his hammer as he charged forward, swinging. A dragonling lunged. He smashed the hammer into the side of its chest, caving it in with a single blow. Another snapped its jaws at me. I batted it away with my sword and kicked it back.

The elder dragon rose, shaking sleep from her body. The cavern floor trembled with her movements. She shifted, moving to face us. Her massive, magicite lined jaws opened, and I felt heat against the side of my face.

My blade slid along the tough, scaly exterior of an older dragonling's foreleg, producing sparks. Claws raked at my face, forcing me back. "Dex!"

Searing fire exploded out of the elder dragon's mouth in a wide column aimed straight at me. Just moments before it burned me alive, the column of fire turned and made a half circle around the edge of the cave. Moss caught fire, burning to a blackened crisp. I turned around to see Dex stagger. He caught himself on the tree trunk, pushed back up, and lifted his left hand in a fist. The river rose, solidifying into a wall of icy spikes. He kept his left hand raised and made a cutting gesture with his right. A lance of orange flame sliced the ice wall in half. With a loud grunt, Dex directed the sharpened stakes of ice toward the dragon, impaling several dragonlings in one move.

Foggy rushed forward and smashed his way through two more, creating an opening.

The dragon roared, the vibration of sound shattering all the ice into a fine mist of snow. Razor-sharp claws sliced through the air, pulling down rock. She readied another mouthful of fire, but this one was different, green instead of fiery red. Dex tried to redirect it, but this strange green fire didn't obey. The dragon breathed it over the cave, unhindered. I dove behind a large stalagmite and hugged myself tightly to keep from getting caught in the blast.

When it passed, I emerged to find everything burning with a strange green fire the color of the rifts. *Rift fire,* I thought. I could feel the same energy pulling at me, tugging on the scar. Dex had abandoned the tree, which was also on fire. He emerged from the shallow stream he'd jumped into and patted the fire out of his hat.

Foggy pinched a flame from his beard and kicked back another dragonling with a yell. "Sooner's better than later, lass! It's a bit warm in here!"

That was an understatement. The ambient temperature had to be over a hundred and rising quickly. With eerie green smoke billowing toward the cave's ceiling, we'd soon be choking *and* burning. The dragons didn't seem to mind the sudden heat. They were still fighting as fiercely as ever.

The elder dragon spread her leathery wings and let out a roar that shook the mountain. If she took off, we were done for. We'd never get another chance to finish this.

"Dex, keep her on the ground!" I shouted and stabbed my sword through the side of a nearby dragonling. It shrieked and tried to pull away, but I'd found a weak spot just behind its front limbs. My sword came away bloody. The dragonling thrashed and fell over, dying.

The elder dragon flapped her wings, creating a whirlwind that threatened to push us all back to the mouth of the cave. I leaned into it, fighting for every step forward.

A moment later, the waterfall solidified into a block of ice. Dex drew the ice out into a platform and pulled it up, wrapping it around the dragon's legs. She snapped at the growing ice around her feet and spat fire at it, melting it almost as fast as Dex could build it. A glance back at Dex told me he was straining to keep up. I needed to buy him time, distract the dragon so he could finish. But how?

I looked around for something, anything, that would help and found a fist-sized chunk of magicite at my feet. I picked it up and threw it at the dragon, hitting her in the face. She snarled, and her head snapped up, eyes searching.

"Hey! Over here!" I jumped up and waved my arms. "That's right. I threw it! What are you going to do about it?"

She made a clicking sound in her throat and more flame erupted, but this time aimed at me. I dodged behind the stalagmite again. Her claws lashed out and broke the rock. Heat lashed at my back, but it wasn't the dragon fire. I'd gotten lucky and only been grazed by a claw. I rolled out of the way and came up with two dragonlings on me. One snapped its jaws at me, and I jammed the blade of my sword into its mouth. It backed away, spitting blood.

Rock rose out of the ground like a spear, impaling the other. I looked behind me. Ike nodded and mouthed, "Go."

Dex had built up enough ice around the dragon's rear legs she was frozen in place, though the ice was melting fast. Foggy was off to my left. He'd attracted most of the dragons and was nearly overwhelmed by them. Blood dripped from several gashes on his face and arms, but still he swung his hammer, laughing as he smashed it against their wings, heads, and limbs.

This is the best chance I'll get. I took off running, sword in hand.

My movement caught the dragon's eye. She turned all her attention to me and opened her mouth. Green fire lit in the back of her throat. Even if I turned and ran, I would never make it out of the way in time.

"Ember!" Dex twisted his fingers, and the water jumped out of the stream bed, forming a slippery, frozen platform. The platform grew, spreading through the cave like a road. I jumped on it and ran along it, narrowly avoiding the blast of magic fire. The ice crumbled beneath my feet, even as I raced along it. I had no choice but to jump while I still had something solid enough to allow it.

I leapt off the ice platform and threw myself at the dragon, sword out. The blade went home, landing wedged between two scales just in front of her left foreleg. I hadn't penetrated deep enough to reach anything vital, but she definitely felt it. Blood seeped from the wound. The dragon reared and roared. I gripped the sword and held on as she tried to throw me off. Twice I thought I should have lost my grip, but the strange root that secured my hand to the grip kept me attached.

Her flailing threw me back against her neck, and I fought to grip another scale. Foggy, having dealt with the dragonlings, was at her feet. He drove his hammer into the joint of one of her forelegs, drawing the dragon's attention back to him instead of me.

She screeched and batted him aside. Foggy smashed against the cave wall and fell still.

I yanked my sword free and gripped her scales to keep from being flung off. *I'm in the wrong position! I was supposed to go to her underbelly. How am I supposed to kill her from up here?*

The dragon's scales were thick and overlapping, growing thicker closer to the spine. But there was one place that wasn't so protected. I never would have seen it if I hadn't climbed onto her back. There, at the base of her skull, where the scale pattern changed, allowing the magicite horns to grow out of her skin, was a small patch of exposed gray skin. All I had to do was make it there. "Dex, Ike, keep her busy!"

They looked at each other and nodded once. Dex moved as if he were pulling back a bow string, and an arrow of ice materialized out of the air. He fired it at the dragon, striking her just below the eye. Ike brought his hammer down on the rock and a sharp lance of stone jutted from the ground just in front of her, nearly stabbing her.

The dragon snarled and broke the rock with her claws. Her roar shattered the ice at her feet and a blast of flame helped melt what little was left. She spread her wings and flapped, the force of her wings knocking Ike and Dex onto their backs.

I fought to climb her scales like a ladder. When she lifted off the ground, the sudden upward movement tipped me to one side. I stayed on her by stabbing her in the side of the neck. The sword went in shallow, blocked by a second layer of scales, but it was enough to keep me from falling off.

The dragon rose into the air of the cavern. Choking smoke stung my eyes. She banked to one side, a wing smashing protruding rock. The rocks scraped against the side of my face as they fell, and still I held on. With a grunt, I hauled myself back onto her neck and pulled myself forward. Inch by hard-won inch, I moved while she rampaged around the cavern, spitting fire and smashing rocks.

She'll pull the whole cavern down on top of us if we don't burn to death! I pulled myself forward. The small, vulnerable spot was just out of reach. One more inch and I would be on top of it.

The dragon banked hard to one side and grabbed more rock with her talons. She held onto it this time until we came around and dropped it directly on Dex and Ike. They scattered to keep from getting hit.

I finally made it into position. With a shout, I lifted my sword and drove the point down into the small opening. Skin gave way. I felt the snap of tendon, the resistance of bone, and pushed through. The dragon roared and jerked its head to the right. The movement was enough to sever the spine.

She dropped like a leaf, drifting first in one direction and then the other. When we hit the ground, it shook free the rocks of the cavern ceiling. Half the cavern caved in immediately, with the other half threatening.

I pulled my blade free, my body trembling. Beneath me, the dragon snorted and snarled, but its body no longer responded. Carefully, I slid down the side and stood on shaky legs. All I needed to do was deliver the killing blow, and the heart was mine.

I moved carefully into position and lifted my sword, but looked into the dragon's eyes. I expected to see vicious anger, the face of a monster lashing out in pain. There was pain in her eyes, but nothing about her seemed violent now. I glanced around, my heart in my throat. The bodies of her children lay smashed and slaughtered at my feet, her lair burned and broken.

She suddenly seemed less a monster and more a mother.

The dragon let out a wounded bray and closed her eyes, resigning herself to her fate.

"I'm sorry, but your death will save someone I care about." I put a hand on the dragon's head, a comforting gesture.

There was a sudden flash of light and I found myself transported from the broken cavern to the forest where I had met the shadow warrior. Before me knelt a woman wearing a crown of magicite thorns. The magicite grew into her skin like barbed wire, looping in and out of her body at the joints. She held a still child in her arms.

Stunned, I staggered back a step and looked around, panicked. "What's happening?"

"She hurts." The shadow warrior was suddenly beside me, looking at her. "And now you can see her pain."

"Why?" I looked back at her and swallowed, watching as she held her child and wept.

A strange woman's voice echoed through the forest. "Where am I? What is this place? Why does it hurt? I want to go home! Home! But the way is blocked. I cannot go home, and it hurts to be here."

The shadow warrior tilted his horned head to one side, watching with me. "She was dying before, and so were her children. The magic stone ate away at who they were, what they were, twisting them to its purpose, as it does with all things. You have ended their pain, but she still grieves. She wants to join them."

"I don't understand. Why am I seeing any of this?"

He stepped between me and the dragon. "I am a tool, a slave to your will. I see only what you show me, feel only what you feel. My last master… Hot rage, glowing like the end of a blade fresh from the forge. It seared all it touched. They were the enemy. They must die." He stepped aside and put a hand on the woman's shoulder. "But you are deep and sad, a broken well in a desert overgrown and forgotten. You see a different way. It should hurt more to kill than to die."

I looked down at my hands. They were stained red. "I think I understand."

"Release me," the dragon in her human form whispered. "Please, I just want to go home."

"I'm sorry about your children." It didn't feel like enough to apologize, but what else could I say?

"You freed them." She clutched the still child to her chest. "This world is wrong, not ours. It… hurts to be here. Can't think. Can't breathe. The rocks cry out, but they are not ours. We want to be free of their song."

"You want me to kill you?" I dropped my bloodstained hands to my sides.

"Yes," whispered the dragon mother. "I want to end what I have become. What we have become. We aren't right. This is not our home. We can't grow here, can't *be* here. Everything is wrong; everything is pain and fire." Her head suddenly shot up. She looked to one side, wide eyed.

The vision faded, and I was back in the cavern. I pulled my hand away from the dragon and gasped for breath, as if I had been under water.

There wasn't time to understand what had just happened. Movement at the cavern entrance caught my attention. I turned away from the dragon in time to see Ash and a handful of his guards march in.

Dex launched an ice arrow at him.

Ash lifted a hand, opened a rift, and let it swallow the arrow. He dismissed the rift with a flick of his hand. "There you are. I wondered where you'd run off to. I suppose I should thank you for slaying the dragon for me. You've saved me the trouble. Now, step away, Ember. While you still can."

Chapter Twenty-Four

I looked over at the dragon. She was still breathing, still in pain. I wanted to help. Ash wouldn't be so kind. He wanted the heart, yes, but he didn't care if she was hurting. He wouldn't respect the beast he had to kill.

And he certainly didn't deserve its heart.

"I won't ask twice." There was a dark warning in Ash's words.

"Get your own dragon," Dex spat and readied another arrow.

Ash lifted two fingers. "Careful, half-breed. I can open a rift inside your chest cavity far faster than you can fire that magic arrow."

"Stand down." I lowered my sword and stepped away from the dragon.

An expression I couldn't quite read crossed Dex's face. He looked from me to Ash and back again without canceling his spelled arrow. *He's thinking about how he's dead either way. What does he have to lose? Maybe letting a madman use his magic to rip his heart out of his chest would be faster, cleaner. And maybe he could take that madman with him.*

I gave a subtle shake of my head and mouthed, "Trust me."

Dex let the arrow evaporate. He lowered his head and lifted his hands in surrender. I dropped my sword to the ground, and Ike did the same with his hammer.

Ash sent people around to collect our weapons—including the unconscious Foggy's hammer—and to tie Dex's hands behind his back.

Once Dex was bound, Ash stepped up to him, his hand on the hilt of his sword. "You should've died on that ledge," he said and punched Dex in the gut.

Dex groaned and doubled over, but before Ash could walk away, he spat through gritted teeth, "You're not worthy."

"Of what?" Ash grabbed him by the chin and lifted his head.

"Of her. Of the dragon's heart. Of anything."

Ash smirked. "Is that so? And what makes you think you are? I've beaten you. All of you. What do I care what you think I'm worth? This time tomorrow, you'll be dead and I'll be a god well on my way to conquering the continent. No one will remember you ever existed."

Dex lunged at Ash, only to get a knee to the stomach and an elbow in the back. He fell face first to the rocky floor of the cavern, but even that didn't keep him down. He clawed at the ground and tried to rise.

Ash slammed a foot into his back.

"Enough!" I shouted. "What sort of god beats a dying man? You came for the dragon. Take it."

Ash glowered at the man beneath his heel for a moment before lifting his foot. "You're right. He's beneath me. Let him die there." He trudged up to the dragon and placed a hand on its scaly back. "What an ugly creature. Makes you wonder why nature makes such ugly beasts." He smiled at me as if it were a joke.

"Maybe the only way you can appreciate something beautiful is to see something so incomprehensibly ugly that you never forget," I said.

"Suppose it doesn't matter now." He unsheathed his sword.

The dragon let out one last cry of pain before it fell silent.

I turned away. I couldn't watch him butcher her.

Dex had struggled to his knees. There were guards all around him and Ike, but none were paying any attention. They were all leaning forward, eager to watch their leader dig through the dragon's guts. Ike made a small motion with his head, gesturing to his hammer. It was hooked on one of the guard's belts, just within reach. My sword rested on a flattened rock right next to Dex, the blade still bare. Dex gave it a sideways glance.

I shook my head once. *Don't do it, you idiots. He'll kill you both.*

There was the sound of a blade slicing through stubborn meat, of wet insides pouring out.

"Finally," Ash said in a breathy voice. "The heart."

Ike lunged for the hammer.

Two guards turned to stop him, but he punched one in the jaw, laying him out flat. The other missed his initial grab. Ike yanked the hammer from the third guard's belt and kicked the guard away, all before Ash knew what was happening.

Ash looked up from his prize just as Dex set fire to the rope binding his hands. Dex grabbed my sword and tossed it to me.

I caught it by the hilt and quickly turned the blade on Ash, holding it against his throat.

Dex rubbed the singe marks from his wrists. "You should've used iron. Never use flammable restraints on a fire mage, idiot."

Ash ignored him, sneering at me. "You won't kill me, Ember. You *love* me."

"Love you?" I stepped in, pressing the blade in enough to draw a small trickle of blood. "I don't even know you."

"She doesn't have to kill you." Dex unleashed a weak blast of flame from his fingertips before grunting and falling to his knees, exhausted.

Ash easily dodged the fire by moving his head to one side. "Pathetic. All that and you didn't even hit me!"

Dex chuckled. "I wasn't trying to hit you, asshole. I was buying Ike time."

"Ember!" Ike shouted. "Move!" He brought his hammer down on the cavern floor with a loud smash and a flash of blue light.

Rock rumbled above and giant boulders came smashing down from the cavern ceiling.

I pulled my sword back and stabbed it into Ash's stomach while rocks came down all around us.

Ash's eyes widened. He dropped the dragon's heart as if it meant nothing and stared down at my sword sticking out of his gut. "Ember, you… You've killed me."

"You died five years ago when you stepped into that rift, Ash. I just didn't know it."

"Ember, watch out!" Dex tackled me out of the way of a massive falling rock.

We fell to the cave floor, my back scraping against a thousand tiny sharp pebbles. More rocks fell all around us and on top of us. Dex let out a pained grunt, but stayed where he was, shielding me from the collapse. For one stunned moment, I couldn't breathe. I couldn't think. There was no way out of the cave-in. He was going to die, and it was going to be my fault.

"I... always wanted to die... on top of a beautiful woman," Dex managed.

I could've punched him if I wasn't so sure we'd both be dead in the next thirty seconds. Instead, I closed my eyes tight and held onto him as best I could.

The rocks suddenly stopped falling and a dustier version of Ike appeared with Foggy slung over one shoulder. In his other hand, he held an umbrella shaped rock. Smaller rocks bounced off of it and tumbled to the ground. "Will you two quit messing around? The entire mountain is coming down on us! We need to go!"

I pushed Dex away. "Guess you don't get to cross that one off the bucket list just yet."

"Damn. So close." He pulled me to my feet.

The ground shook, and I almost fell over. The place where Ash had been standing only moments ago was a pile of rubble, but all the falling rocks had somehow missed the dragon's heart he had dropped. I lunged to grab it.

Ike grabbed me by the belt just as my hands closed around it and practically dragged me away.

With the dragon's heart pressed against my chest, we fled the cave, dodging rocks as they came down.

"It's blocked ahead. Look!" Dex pointed.

"Hold him." Ike shoved the dwarf at Dex. He struck the cave in with his hammer and the rocks curled, reshaping themselves to create a tunnel just big enough for us to walk through. Ike came back to collect the dwarf.

"You're more useful than I thought," Dex said.

Ike's answer was an annoyed grunt.

We ran as fast as we could through the last part of the cave and found daylight waiting for us on the other side. The mid-day sun never looked so beautiful. But we weren't clear yet. The stairs Ike had fashioned earlier were crumbling. We raced down them.

At the bottom, Dex collapsed.

I ran back to him, but I couldn't carry the dragon's heart and Dex, so I shoved the heart at him. "Here! You carry that and I'll carry you."

"Carry me? You can't—Whoa, hey!"

I slung him over my shoulder with a grunt.

"Huh," he said. "Maybe you can."

"Shut up and think lightweight thoughts," I ground out through my teeth.

We half walked, half slid down the narrow mountain path, dodging rocks and boulders as they rolled our way. It wasn't until we were halfway out of the desolate no-man's zone the rift had created that I turned around to look.

Ike wasn't kidding when he said the mountain was coming down. One whole side looked like a giant had reached down to scoop up the rock in its palm.

There was no way Ash had survived. The

realization left me weak. I had to put Dex down. As I did, I noted the lack of resistance. He hadn't said anything in a while, either. I lowered him as gently as I could. His eyes were closed, and the heart was tucked in his shirt, secured there.

"Hey!" I slapped his face.

No response.

"Ike! Help!"

Ike rushed to my side. "What happened?"

I shook my head. "I don't know. He collapsed at the bottom of the staircase, but he was still cracking jokes, so I thought..."

Ike pulled the dragon's heart free, tossed it to the ground, and pressed his ear to Dex's chest.

Please, please don't be dead!

"He's breathing," Ike announced, "but he's feverish and non-responsive. Could be a coma, Ember. I don't know if he'll make it back to Atlanta." He looked at me, apologetic.

"No, no, no! There must be something we can do." I shook my head and thought as hard as I could. We didn't go through all of that just to let Dex die. There had to be something, anything... "The elves! We can take Dex to the elves."

"Do you even know where they are or how to contact them?"

"Not exactly. Only a general idea, but we have to try."

Foggy groaned. He was coming around finally. The dwarf put a hand to his forehead. "Stones, did anyone get the name of the broad that hit me? I think I'm in love."

"That would be a dragon, my friend." Ike went to Foggy's side and offered him his canteen.

The dwarf twisted off the cap, drank some, and spat it back out. "Water? Might as well force feed me piss, why don't you?" He turned to me, wiping his beard. "What's the problem, lass? I see you have the heart. Does that mean we won?"

"Not if we don't use it." I picked up the heart and stepped away, trying to think. Even if I could get back to where the elves were—which I wasn't sure I could do without a map—I'd have to convince the Telmara to help him. They didn't seem very interested in him before, but maybe they would listen to me. But how would we get there? Ike could make golems, but they'd move too slow. I couldn't carry Dex, and I'd get lost on my own.

Something nearby snorted. I looked up on the grassy ridge at the edge of the rift zone where Scorch lazily stomped on some grass, as if it had offended her. Wide-eyed, I turned back to Ike. "Ike…"

He nodded. "I'll help you get him on the saddle."

Ike picked up Dex while I went to get Scorch. She gave me an irritated glance and shook out her mane as if to say, "What took you so long?"

I took her reins and patted her nose. "I know. Thank you for waiting."

Ike grunted and placed Dex on the back of the horse. "Ride south until the sun is about here." He pointed to a place in the sky. "Then if you go west another few miles, you should find the clearing we made camp that night. I hope you can orient yourself from there."

I nodded. "I can. What about you? Will you and Foggy be all right?"

He smiled. "I expect so. I also expect to see you when you bring this idiot back to Atlanta, alive and well. I owe you a drink and an apology."

I threw my arms around him and squeezed. "You don't owe me anything, but I'll take that drink just the same."

Ike stiffened a moment before he patted my back. "Here," he said, stepping back. He shed his jacket and stripped off his shirt, which he wrapped around the dragon's heart, using the sleeves to tie it to the saddle. "Don't lose it on the way."

"I won't." I climbed up into the saddle. "Ike, in case something happens..."

"Something always happens," he said with a tired smile. "And when it does, you'll come and tell me about it. You and that stupid half-elf both. See you when I see you?"

I nodded and took up Scorch's reins. It didn't feel like a goodbye, leaving them behind at the edge of no-man's-land. I knew they'd be okay. Whatever happened to Ike and Foggy, they'd make it back to Atlanta one way or another.

Chapter Twenty-Five

I rode in the direction Ike pointed out to me, pushing Scorch as fast as I dared. The forest was thick with vines, bushes, and fallen trees. She leapt over moss-covered trunks and dodged hanging vines as if it were second nature.

Hold on, Dex. Just hold on.

The journey to the old campsite felt like it took hours, though the sun had barely moved in the sky. True to Ike's words, I knew it as soon as I stumbled on it. The ashes of old fires slept in their pits and indentations on the ground marked where we had pitched our tents. A dark stain lay on the ground where Kenny had died.

I circled the camp once to get my bearings and then went west.

The abandoned ruins where the heretics had kept us were empty, dead and silent. I pulled Scorch to a stop among them. "Leseran!"

My voice bounced off the decaying stone.

"Someone! Anyone, please!"

My heart sank as time stretched on without answer. I knew the elven encampment was somewhere nearby, but I didn't know in which direction or how far. Were they even close enough to hear my frantic shouts? Even if they could hear me, they might not care. Dex wasn't one of their own, and I was an outsider, a stranger. They had no reason to help either of us.

It's no use. I lowered my head and curled my fingers around Dex's shirt. Through it, I could feel his ragged, shallow breathing. Dammit, he didn't deserve to go this way. Killed by the very thing that had let him save me. If I hadn't demanded so much, if he hadn't drawn in so much magic, he might've made it back to Atlanta.

My shoulders shook. Hot tears stained my cheeks. "I'm so sorry. It's all my fault!"

"Awfully selfish of you," Dex suddenly said, his voice strained, "taking all the blame. Seems to me there's plenty to go around."

"Dex!" Hope made my heart jump into my throat. I dismounted and quickly pulled him down from the horse, gently laying him out on the ground where he'd be more comfortable. When I saw him, that hope quickly faded. His color was off. Not just pale, but a shade of gray. "Don't you die on me. I won't let you."

"Pretty sure you don't get a say." He wheezed and coughed. "It's okay."

I shook my head and pushed away more tears. "No. No, it's not! Don't you dare say it is!"

"Just… do me one… favor?" His clammy

fingers brushed against the side of my face. “Don’t forget me, huh?”

I grabbed his hand and squeezed. “Never.”

“Good.” He smiled and closed his eyes.

A wave of white magic rolled over his body, and he froze in place.

“Dex?” I reached down to shake him, but he didn’t respond.

“He won’t be able to answer,” said a voice from behind me.

I rose and spun, drawing my sword as I did, only to find Leseran and two other elves behind me. The elves on either side of him had their bows drawn, arrows trained on me.

I ignored them, gripping my sword tightly. “What did you do to him?”

“A stasis spell. Nothing more. It will keep his condition from progressing, but only for a short time. May I?” He gestured to Dex.

I lowered the sword and stepped aside. The elves lowered their bows.

Leseran knelt beside Dex and sniffed the air. “Magicite poisoning. I was worried something like this would happen. Your people can only channel so much of it through your bodies before it does damage.”

“Dex isn’t human.”

He rolled his eyes at me. “Why do you think I’m here?”

“I thought you hated your brother.”

Leseran sighed and stood. He gave me a

bored glance. “I hate that his continued existence is a point of shame for a respected elder in my community. Blood is still blood, however, and I am bound by oath and honor to respect that.”

“In other words, no one kills your brother but you.”

He shrugged. “If you like, although there is little even our greatest healers can do for his condition.”

I untied the heart from the saddle and held it out to Leseran. “What about with this?”

Leseran’s eyes widened as he took the package and unwrapped it. He turned to the other elves and said something quick and sharp in his native tongue. They nodded and came forward to lift Dex’s body between them. “How did you come by this?” Leseran asked me.

“Not easily.”

The shadow of a smile touched his thin lips. “I imagine. You do not know the power such an item has.”

I stood up straighter and licked my lips, watching them handle Dex carefully. “I was told it could cure any ailment.”

“Almost any,” Leseran agreed. “But there are… side effects. And to prepare one treatment, we’ll have to use the entire thing. It’s unfortunate. An ingredient like this could do so much more.”

“Can your healers use it to save him or not?”

Leseran wrapped the heart back up and nodded once. "I believe they can. Come. You will follow us back to camp. The Telmara will want to meet the one who killed the *drekhmal*."

***

Hours passed. I spent them pacing outside the medical hut, separated from it by a ring of sacred stones. The elves had taken both Dex and the heart inside, but forbid me to enter under penalty of death. I didn't care, so long as he came back out. Smoke poured from the hole in the roof, gray, white, then black. Lights flashed inside, illuminating strange silhouettes.

I hugged myself and paced, waiting, watching. Hoping for the best.

At dusk, the healers were still at work. Leseran approached me. "The Telmara have summoned you."

"I can't. What if something happens while I'm gone?"

Leseran frowned in the direction of the healer's hut. "He is in good hands. Trust that he will be healed, and he will. Belief is a power all its own. The Telmara won't be denied. We must go."

Reluctantly, I left my post and followed Leseran to the Telmara's tent. They had already gathered and sat, waiting in their chairs, their faces hidden behind strange veils. Leseran presented me with a bow and backed away. For a long, heavy moment, no one spoke.

"We have been informed that you killed

the beast of Black Mountain," said one off to my right.

"Then you heard wrong," I replied. "I defeated the dragon, but I didn't strike the killing blow. I meant to, but we were interrupted by someone else."

Another of the Telmara leaned forward, tenting their fingers. "And the rift? Closing it was your doing?"

"I wish I could say it was, but no. Not entirely."

The Telmara exchanged quick glances.

"Then what exactly was your part in all this?"

I looked around, weighing my words. If I said the wrong thing, it might cost Dex his life. "The one who interrupted us. I knew him in another life. We were friends, maybe something more. I saw him going down a dark path and believed I could save him. But he didn't want to be saved. All he wanted was more."

"More what, child?" pressed the Telmara.

"Of whatever he could get. Ash was hungry. And nothing in this world will ever be enough to fill him up. Not me, not all the power in the world, and not that dragon's heart. But he doesn't know that yet. He would've taken it, used it to make himself more powerful. I couldn't let him. I brought it here so your healers could save Dex."

"You gave no thought to taking the heart

for yourself?" one questioned.

"Why? What would I want with it?"

"Power," said another.

The second Telmara added, "You have your own illness, do you not? Do not fidget. I can sense the crystals within you. This expedition has made them grow. You are dying in slow motion."

I put a hand over the dull ache in my stomach and swallowed the dryness in my mouth. "Maybe, but I can always find another dragon or another way. I'd rather use it to help someone else. I only wish I could've used it to save more people."

"But you will suffer," said the elf. "Why would you choose to suffer so needlessly? For one you barely know?"

"Because it's the right thing to do. Because Dex is a good man who doesn't deserve to die. Because he's my friend. I've already watched one friend die today. I won't lose another."

They exchanged glances from behind their veils. After a moment of silent contemplation, the elf who had been questioning me rose and slowly lifted his veil. The other Telmara and guards in the room diverted their eyes to keep from seeing his face.

He was older, with a thin face and a stripe of a white beard. The elf elder's pale blue eyes seemed more gentle than harsh, the complete opposite of his voice. "I cannot speak as one of the Telmara when I say this. Our code of honor forbids it. I, however, cannot be silent. I owe you a debt for saving my son."

"*You're* Dex's father?"

He didn't answer. He didn't have to.

I clenched my fists. "No offense, but words are cheap. I don't want your thanks. I want nothing from you and never did. But Dex is a different story. All he ever wanted was for you to give a damn."

Dex's father sighed and winced as if he were in pain. "My position…"

"Screw your position, sir. He's your son. If you want to thank me, you'll stop treating him like such an outsider. You'll give him a place here if ever he wants it. You'll offer him the family he grew up wishing he had."

Dex's father lowered his head and let the veil fall back into place. He took a step back and sat in his seat. "This clan owes you a debt. Now that the dragon is dead, and the rift sealed, we can expand our hunting grounds and feed our people. We will have more resources for our children, and space to grow and explore further from human influence. For your assistance in this matter, the Telmara names you *Galahedron*, friend of the people. As is our custom, you are entitled to a single boon."

I fidgeted with my fingers. "What about Dex? Does saving him count?"

"No," said another of the Telmara. "He is of the blood, however impure that blood may be.

That bloodline must be protected for the good of the people."

"If you really mean that, then make him one of you. Officially. He will always be welcome here. You'll let him come and go as he pleases and stop treating him like an outsider. You will recognize him as the natural born child of one of your leaders and all that entails."

A long moment of silent tension passed.

Then Dex's father stood and tapped his staff against the ground. A wave of red magic swept through the tent, almost pushing me back a step. "Let it be known that henceforth that Dexter Cavalieres shall be known among the people as Dalondir. We greet and embrace him as one of the people."

"Dalondir," said another of the Telmara, rising and clapping their hands.

"Dalondir!"

One by one, they all rose and made the same motion.

"Tonight," continued Dex's father, "we celebrate the extension of our clan to both Dalondir and Galahedron! Let us prepare!"

"Dalondir," Leseran mused as he walked me out of the tent. "It's fitting."

"What does it mean?"

"Elf thorn," he replied. "A permanent reminder that his acceptance did not come easily. It could've been worse, I suppose. He could've been Gylfdin."

"And what does that mean?" I pressed.

"Goat rectum."

I nodded in agreement. "Guess he lucked out there."

Leseran brought me to another hut and paused outside. "They will have moved him here by now, I suspect. I'm told he's recovering remarkably well, considering." He turned to me. "Before you go in, you should know something."

I sucked in a breath. "Is it about those side effects you warned me about?"

He nodded. "The procedure he's been through, it is... You don't have an equivalent word, but I suppose you would call it a major sort of magic. It can change people, affect them in unusual ways that aren't obvious at first. Or the effects may be minor. It is not unlike being exposed to large amounts of dangerous radiation, except that its use is healing, not hurting."

"Like chemotherapy or something."

He thought for a moment. "Maybe. The point is, he may not be as you saw him last. I don't know his condition other than that his body is healing."

I nodded. "Thank you."

"You shouldn't thank me. And you may regret your decision to demand his naturalization. It will complicate him to live in both worlds. The Telmara will expect more than he will want to give." He opened the door to the hut. "But that's for tomorrow. *Sirim dereth amaderin cur'than,*

Galahedron."

"And that means?"

He smiled. "It means today we are friends, but tomorrow we may be enemies. Enjoy your evening."

I fought not to shudder at the grim warning. Whatever Leseran meant, I could worry about it later, after I made sure Dex was okay.

I stepped into the dimly lit hut.

Dex was lying on the bed under a thin blanket, his upper body bare. He had strange red marks, like paint on his face. "I'm dead," he groaned. "I'm dead and this is hell."

I pinched his arm.

"Ouch! What the hell?" He rubbed the red spot.

"Pretty sure the dead don't feel pain." I sat down on the bed beside him. "How are you?"

"Well, now my arm hurts." He sighed and put a hand over his face. "My head is throbbing. The rest of me feels like I got tossed into a wood pulper and then hung out to dry for good measure. Everything hurts, and I really do mean everything. You ever felt pain in your spleen? I didn't even know where my spleen was until now."

"But other than that, you feel fine?"

"Mostly, yeah. Not dying anymore is great."

I frowned. "Leseran said the treatment might change you."

Dex's eyes widened. He lifted the blanket and looked down before letting out a relieved sigh. "No change there. Good."

"Seriously?" I made a sour face.

"Hey, you can't blame a guy for checking." He checked himself over quickly. "Nothing seems different. You know, I should thank you. They told me you gave up something that could've saved your life, used it for me instead. I owe you."

I shrugged. "It was the right thing to do. Besides, we can always find another dragon."

He frowned. "Another dragon?"

"I know. After everything that happened with Ash, you'd think I'd be a little less than enthusiastic to go hunt down another dragon, but I might not have another choice."

"Ash?" Dex made a face I couldn't quite read.

I nodded. "I'm pretty sure he's dead. No one could've survived that cave in. At least Ike and Foggy are okay."

He blinked, frowning.

"Dex? Is everything okay?" I asked.

He rubbed the back of his head. "Look, you're nice and all, and it's sort of embarrassing to admit this, but I have no idea who you are or what you're talking about."

"You don't remember? What about Kenny?"

He shook his head again and suddenly I knew the price he had paid to stay alive. The potion that had saved his life had stolen some of his memories.

Epilogue

Broken stone dug into Ash's side. They were old friends, Ash and the stone. Judging by his cracked and bleeding lips and fading consciousness, however, the dehydration would kill him before the rock did.

There was just enough space in his tiny prison to move his left hand. Another boulder had pinned his right. His fingers ached as he moved them up his stomach to touch the open wound. The blood had long ago stopped pooling on his skin, but he was still bleeding internally. Though he couldn't feel the bleeding, his abdomen was bloated, and there was an unfamiliar soreness working its way through his muscles.

In the time he had spent pinned beneath the rocks, he'd called out for help. Then, he gave up and tried to move the rocks himself, even resorting to opening rifts to swallow them. A bad idea. Removing the wrong rock had made more come down on top of him. He was lucky one hadn't crushed his head. When he knew he couldn't move the rocks on his own, and that no one was left to come for him, Ash resigned himself to the slow and painful death that waited. It wasn't the end he would've chosen, but at least it was an end.

The thing inside of him, however, had other ideas. How it had screamed and fought when he told it the truth! It felt like a victory, dying with that thing trapped inside him. A small one, but still. In the end, at least he would have that.

The thing had taken everything else away, had hurt Ember, the only woman he'd ever truly loved. Now she hated him. Despised him. She had run him through and left him to die, as she should've.

Ash fought not to close his eyes. Sleep was the enemy. Sleep was death, and he wanted the thing to suffer as long as possible for taking his life away from him.

Even as Ash's body shut down, the thing that had taken his mind still whispered to him. It didn't speak in words, not comprehensible ones, anyway, but there were whispers just the same. Ever since he had stepped foot inside that cursed Black City, it had been there, in the back of his mind, tormenting him, the whisper of a voice just out of hearing.

At least I escaped from the Institute. They won't toy with my body after death now. The thing had done him a favor, killing those Institute soldiers. But it was his idea to convince Zia to help. Ash had hoped she would see through him, see how hard he was fighting against the thing. With her magic, maybe she could help.

But Zia was as blind as the rest of them, and now she was dead too, or something like it.

Ash's eyes snapped open. How long had he been asleep? What was that sound? He listened intently to a light scraping noise, close to where he lay. There… Was that a grunt? A voice?

Ash licked his lips and bit down on his tongue. The thing wanted him to cry out, to be found, but that would ruin everything. It would make him hurt more people. Death was his only escape.

He bit down until his tongue bled and filled his mouth with copper enough that he gagged on it.

The rock near his head moved enough to let in light. Ash squinted and prayed. *No, no, no! Put it back!*

"Over here!" The silhouette of a man leaned over the opening. "He's over here!"

"Let… me… die," he whispered. "Let *it* die!"

If the man heard him, he gave no sign.

A second ticked by, and the moment of clarity faded. He fought it, gnashing his teeth and cursing inwardly. But the thing was too strong, too eager.

Zia's face appeared above him through the opening, while others worked to clear the rubble.

She gestured frantically for them to free his arm. The moment the boulder over his arm came up, the agony returned. He hissed through his teeth and fought the urge to curl into a ball.

Zia ignored his twisted features, his bloody and broken appearance. So kind, so loyal, Zia. We should reward her. He would have to think of something worthy of her. “My king.” She went to one knee.

Ash fought to the front, just long enough to utter a single word. “Em… ber?”

Zia almost flinched, but she restrained her jealousy. “Gone, my king. She took the dragon’s heart. I’ve sent scouts to track them, but lost their trail about a day’s ride from here. We have, however, located the artificer and the dwarf. I have people standing by, ready to kill them on your order.”

Yes, said the thing. *Kill them now, before they can be more trouble.* But Ash held his tongue until he could say, “No.”

Zia frowned. “No? But they robbed you of your glory. They helped her escape, not to mention they left you like this. Surely you want them dead?”

“Small men,” Ash managed. “They mean nothing.”

The thing inside was satisfied with that answer, but it was done being quiet. Ash was out of energy to fight it and let it do what it wanted. He had saved Ike and Foggy’s life, at least, and found out Ember was alive. As long as they all lived, there was hope.

The men with Zia finished clearing the last of the rubble. Ash studied their faces, noting the crystalline growths on their chins, their ears, the tops of their heads. The sour taste of bile filled his throat. Heretics.

We can use them, said the thing. And it worked to form a plan.

While the thing worked, Ash floated in an existence of black nothingness, a prison in his own mind. Sometimes, it let him do small things. He could eat, piss, or read his books. Otherwise, it took charge, transforming him into a puppet that had to bend to its will.

"We'll get you the best healers," Zia promised, and directed the heretics to lift him onto a prepared stretcher. "In the meantime, what are your orders, sir? Where do we go now?"

Ash let out a wheezing breath. "The Kingdom of Atlanta must submit."

"We will need an army. Atlanta's defenses are strong."

He turned his head, looking at the surrounding heretics. "We have the beginnings of an army here. All we need to do is get word to the rest of them."

"The rest of them? But there are dozens of pockets all around the country. You'd have to unite them all under one banner against a common cause to even have a chance."

"Then that is what we do. Spread the word. Every man, woman, and child infected by the plague of magic on this world is welcome. They will be my citizens, my army. My *people*. And I will be their prophet. I have seen the Ashen throne and heard the whispers of the dead gods. I have walked through the rifts and returned, something no other man has done. I cannot die, Zia. Not until my mission is complete."

Inside, Ash was screaming, full of contempt and rage. If he had not been so weak, he would've pushed the thing out. But he was, and he was so very tired of fighting. Maybe it would be best if he just slept in the black void, giving himself over completely to the thing.

But Ember... He couldn't let it hurt Ember.

Zia was still talking, irritated. She worried about his body, but there was no reason. The thing wouldn't let him die. He should've seen that before.

"There are logistical issues. The heretics aren't alone in the forest," Zia continued.

"The elves torment us," the heretic said.

Zia nodded. "If you want Atlanta, you'll have to go through the elves. It won't be easy."

The thing licked his bloody lips. "Not if we point their attention elsewhere. Let them fight each other and we will be there to put their world back together."

The heretic bowed his head. "The faithful are yours to command. How may I honor you,

Rift Walker?"

Ash made a fist. "Bring me the ears of every elf you find between here and Atlanta."

THANK YOU FOR READING RIFT WALKER!

Please leave a review on Amazon or Goodreads! They really help!

Book two is coming soon! Visit www.eacopen.com to subscribe to my newsletter and be notified when it's available!

From the Author

One of the most common questions I get from readers is, "Where do you get your ideas from?"

The answer to that question is... It varies. Sometimes, all it takes is a song and BAM, I've got a whole world made up and ready to go. Ember and Ash's world took a lot more.

I knew I wanted to develop a big world with multiple series back in 2018, and I started to develop a few different ideas. At first, it was just supposed to be an IP (intellectual property) that I was going to develop and sell to someone else. I certainly didn't have the time to write it, not with another series taking off like wildfire.

I spent a month writing a guide to Rift World that was well over a hundred pages. It included maps, sketches, and a history for the world going back to 1986. Once I had that complete, I pitched the idea to the publisher I had been working with, but they passed on it without any explanation.

Slowly, over the next six months, I added more to the document, developing the world further. My intent shifted to turning Rift World into a multi-author venture, bringing in other authors I knew to write in the world I developed. I was still fully invested in other projects at the time. I knew Rift World was a good idea, and I really hated to see it not coming to life.

And then Covid-19 hit. Life got turned upside down. The people I had been working with backed out to work on other things, understandably. I was also facing burn out and needed some time off to work on some other ideas.

During 2020, I pitched the idea to a major editor with one of the top traditional publishing houses in the world. She liked the idea, but had to pass. Traditional publishing wasn't doing urban fantasy.

Of course, Rift World isn't really urban fantasy. I just didn't know it at the time. My plan had always been to build up an urban fantasy world with the focus being on multiple different characters, each in their own guild or city.

Over time, I found myself losing my passion for writing urban fantasy. My horror books weren't selling either. I really wanted to write something that other people would enjoy. I still knew Rift World was a good idea, but I was so burnt out with urban fantasy that I couldn't work on it.

And so it sat.

I fell into a deep depression that nothing could pull me out of. Everything started to slip away, and it felt like there was never going to be any hope of getting back the love for writing that I had lost. My prior experiences working with other people had left me with a bitter taste in my mouth, and I felt I could no longer enjoy writing. I almost gave up my dream of being an author.

But all it takes is a spark to remind you why you love something.

In April and the first part of May, I took time off to dig back into my old hobbies. I had abandoned watching TV, playing games, and reading for the joy of it. I binged my way through *Shadow and Bone*, all four seasons of *Castlevania*, and read a sizeable chunk of the *Shannara Chronicles* by Terry Brooks. I also revisited one of my favorite book series, the Kate Daniels series by Ilona Andrews and played through Dragon Age: Inquisition.

After that, everything sort of clicked. I realized Rift Walker and the subsequent stories in Rift World just didn't work as urban fantasy. They were contemporary fantasy, post-apocalyptic fantasy… Whatever you want to call them. Once I chucked the labels out of the way, I focused more on creating characters and crafting their relationships than the plot-heavy story I had initially wanted to tell.

Yes, the book needed plot, but I decided to let that sort of take a back seat to focus on what

I liked so much in my favorite shows, games, and books: the character relationship dynamics. The reason all the above stories work so well isn't because of a well-crafted plot, an interesting world, or any other mechanic. It's because whoever wrote those books, games, and shows created deeply flawed, relatable characters.

My biggest worry while writing this book was that the plot wouldn't be strong enough, or that I didn't have a particularly obvious antagonist. But I didn't set out to write that sort of story. Ember and Ash is a story about people. They make decisions, and those decisions have consequences. It's also a story about hope in the face of destruction, and—as corny as it sounds—the power of friendship and love to overcome the impossible.

I set out to tell a story where every character, no matter how minor, could have their own story told, even it takes a dozen installments to get there. Whether I've been successful at that... Well, I leave that up to you.

As for where I get my ideas from, the simple answer is I get them from other people and the works of art they create. No work is done in a vacuum. As a writer, the greatest compliment that anyone could ever give me would be to tell I've created something to help make their day a little brighter. I hope I've been able to make you smile a little today.

If this book made you smile, please consider recommending it to a friend, or posting a review on Amazon or Goodreads.

Thank you for reading!

~E.A. Copen

To see all my books, please visit www.eacopen.com

Made in the USA
Las Vegas, NV
31 January 2022

42689204R00236